**"M**att, can you believe it?" Meg said fervently. "We're really here!"

We really are, he was thinking. Back in Craigie. All those people to face who hated him. And the wall. . . the lousy wall. The Maitlands' gate was coming up on the left. In five more minutes he would be committed to this summer as irrevocably as if he were on a roller coaster ride. No way to get off except at the other end. . . .

Knock it off, McKendrick! he told himself, dealing ruthlessly with the nervous flutters before they became a raging panic. You made the choice, you can live with it. He grinned at Meg. "Just remember, old buddy, it's your fault we're here. I never would have come without you."

"Hedging your bets?" she asked impudently. "Okay, Big Bro . . . I'll take the blame if it's a disaster, but I get all the credit if it's as terrific as I think it's going to be."

"It's a deal," he agreed.

# CUTTING LOOSE

**Frances A. Miller**

FAWCETT JUNIPER • NEW YORK

Library of Congress Catalog Card Number: 91-91839

ISBN 0-449-70384-3

Manufactured in the United States of America

First Edition: July 1991

For
Matt, Meg, Will,
the people who love them,
and the people they love.

# 1

*M*att gave the Schuylers' doorbell his special treatment—three shorts and a long—but did not follow it up by opening the door and yelling "Hey, anybody home?" the way he'd been doing for the past two years. Now that the Schuylers' father and newly acquired stepmother were back in residence, he thought such casual informality might not be welcome.

The door swung open. Will ushered him inside with an imitation fanfare and a sweeping bow, but destroyed the illusion of pomp and ceremony by shouting, "Hey, Meg! Matt's here, but he didn't bring his trophy. Shall I send him home?"

"I tried, you guys, I really tried," Matt said. "It's four feet high and weighs a ton. Solid gold. Smashed the wheelbarrow flat when I rolled it in."

"Hah!" Meg snorted as she came up the hall. "I bet it's a little bitty plastic thing you can't even use for a paperweight."

The three of them stood in the front hall, trying to preserve the friendly atmosphere of skepticism and so-what-else-is-new? nonchalance a little longer. But Matt was riding so high on last night's fantastic finish to his high-school running career that he couldn't keep his face straight for more than thirty seconds at a time. The grin he had worn nonstop since the moment he'd known that the agony of wishing and worrying was over broke loose again. It had all worked out the way both he and his running rival, Duke Grieve, had wanted it to. His grin was instantly mirrored on the faces of his two closest friends.

"You really wanted him to win, didn't you?" Meg said, as if finally convinced that he meant what he had been telling them for the past six weeks. "Well, I don't care. If they hadn't given that award to both of you, I wouldn't be feeling like Christmas and the Fourth of July and everyone's birthdays all crammed into one super celebration!"

"Me neither," Will said, his effort to stifle his grin and project stern disapproval making him look slightly demented.

"Okay, okay, you guys," Matt said, laughing at Will's expression. "But you have to admit that the Duke needed that scholarship more than I did. Both of us being Runners of the Year makes it perfect, but if they'd given the scholarship and the award just to him, I still would have been a lot happier about it than if they'd given them both to me."

Following the two of them into the family room, Matt sprawled on the floor beside Meg while Will stretched out on the sofa. "It was so obvious what they were planning, now that I think about it," he went on. "They never would have asked both of us to the Sports Awards banquet if only one of us was going to win. When I think of all the hours I put in, worrying about who was going to get it and what I'd do if they gave it to me, I feel like such a jerk."

"Which is exactly what you are," Meg said. "For the past two weeks you've been absolutely impossible. Nobody could get anything out of you but scowls and incoherent mumblings and a lot of heavy breathing. Good thing it's all decided, or you might have ended up living on banana milkshakes like Will."

"How is 'Cousin It' coming along?" Matt asked. The ulcer that Will had developed through too much worrying of his own had been named for a classic TV character to make it easier for people to ask how "It" and Will were doing.

Will shrugged. "Okay, I guess. As long as I eat right and keep cool and calm, I've got everything under control."

His words were light, but he wasn't smiling. With a flicker of alarm Matt realized that keeping everything under control might not be as simple as it sounded. "How's everything going these days?" he said casually. "Anything your Big Bro can do to make himself useful?"

"Well, now that you've asked," said Meg, "how about lending us your brawn for the morning?"

"It's all yours. What's up?"

"Moving Day," Will said tersely.

"Dad and Gwen are home for good," Meg explained, "and Gwen wants to move the rest of her things into the house this afternoon. That's where she and Dad are now—loading all her stuff into a rented truck. We have to clear the old stuff out of the living room for them."

The old stuff? Their mother's stuff is what she meant. "Where are you putting it?" Matt asked. He was thinking how typical it was of their good-natured but insensitive father's inability to put himself in their place and appreciate their feelings that he could have asked his children to get rid of their dead mother's belongings in order to make room for their stepmother's things.

"Most of it into our rooms," said Will. "Dad was hoping he could quietly give it all to the Salvation Army without anyone noticing it was gone, but there was no way he could quietly shove it all out in a heap on the driveway, which is where they want it left, so he very generously said we could keep what we wanted if we moved the rest of it for him ourselves."

The silence that followed Will's comment lengthened noticeably as Matt and Meg digested the bitterness of his remark. Will had been looking forward to his father's marriage for a long time—had seen it as the answer to problems that had grown pressing over the last year. Something had obviously happened to change that.

Matt wondered guiltily how long Will had been keeping this new problem to himself. "How's it going otherwise?" he said, knowing better than to pin Will down with a direct question.

"Lousy!"

Will's explosive reaction almost drowned out Meg's calmer, "It's too soon to tell." She gave Will a look that Matt recognized as her this-has-gone-far-enough expression but did not challenge him either . . . yet. "It *is* too soon, Will," she insisted. "They've only been home for three weeks, and with both of them working until seven or eight every night, we haven't seen enough of them to know whether it's going to make any difference or not."

"I have," Will said, walking straight into the trap she had set for him.

Meg pounced. "All right, Will, what's eating you? You know you're not supposed to keep things bottled up inside anymore if you want that ulcer to heal. Come on, spit it out."

Will studied the ceiling, avoiding their eyes and wondering why silent pressure was so much harder to resist than a lot of noisy demands and threats.

"We're waiting," Meg said ominously.

Will sighed. Once Meg was on the trail of something, she would never quit. Hating to spoil Matt's high-flying mood, but secretly glad to get it out in the open and talked about, he gave in.

# 2

"It started the first weekend they were home," Will began slowly. "Sunday, after breakfast. I was clearing the mess off the table, and Gwen was in the living room reading the paper. Carey came in and saw her and . . . well, you know how Carey is." They knew. Carey, at thirteen, was the most sensitive of the four Schuylers to other people and the one most deeply hurt by ridicule or rejection. "I could see her trying to talk herself into taking the big step, and she finally did—sitting down on the sofa next to Gwen. And you know what Gwen did?"

"Moved away," Meg said tonelessly.

"You got it. Just a little twitch, but enough to make it obvious. And that wasn't the worst of it. Carey blushed and stammered a lot, but she got a conversation going, which is a miracle in itself. Ms. Gwen Wilder, brilliant attorney-at-law, may be hot stuff in the courtroom, but she's a dead loss when it comes to conversation with anyone under twenty-one."

"Come on, Will," Meg protested. "You're not being fair."

"Oh, I'm being fair, all right," Will said. "Never fairer. Just wait for the denouement, my friends—the coup de grace! About ten minutes later Dad came in and started talking to Gwen, interrupting her conversation with Carey as if it couldn't possibly be as important as what he had to say. Gwen obviously agreed with him, because they got into one of those fascinating legal debates they're so good at and cut Carey out of it completely. She could have been an old doll somebody had left there on the sofa. And then Dad and Gwen went off together. Without so much as a 'Good-bye, Carey' or a 'See you later.' ''

''What did Carey do . . . as if I couldn't guess.''

''Headed for her room, in tears. I felt like slamming a few doors myself, but somehow the swinging door into the kitchen doesn't do much for you in that department.'' He could laugh at himself now, remembering how he had turned and watched the door swinging wildly but silently back and forth, feeling stupid and furious and let down all at the same time. But he could also remember the surge of rage he had needed to release when he slammed that door behind him. It was no laughing matter for his stomach when he let feelings like that get out of control, and since his father and Gwen had come home he was finding it increasingly difficult to stay calm. Instead of making life easier for all of them, the way he had expected it to, his father's marriage was only making things worse.

''What about the housekeeping?'' Matt said, looking for some ray of hope in all this gloom. Since the accidental death of their mother more than two years ago, Meg—with the increasingly able assistance of Will, Carey, and ten-year-old Lew—had taken care of the shopping, cooking, cleaning, and chauffeuring for the four of them, and for their father when he was home, which wasn't often.

Jim Schuyler had taken a long time to recover from his first wife's death, and it was his job as a lawyer and not his family that he had turned to for distraction and support. He enjoyed his children and was enormously proud of the way they managed on their own—frequently telling them so—but his attitude toward them seemed like that of a divorced parent with visitation rights. He gave them pizza dinners or a day at the beach, but not the

~ interest in who they were and what they were doing that they really needed. The most important thing in his life was his work.

Gwen, a fellow lawyer in his firm, had gradually come to mean more to him than just another working partner. They had put off taking the final step until a month ago because, as Mr. Schuyler had explained to his family with his usual lack of tact, Gwen had chosen law over motherhood as a career twenty years ago and was not planning on changing directions now. This remark had killed Will's hopes that she would be able to fill in some of the gaps created by the loss of their mother for Carey and Lew, but he and Meg had assumed that the care of the house at least would no longer be their sole responsibility.

"That's the other thing that bugs me," Will admitted finally. "There's no end in sight. They've been back for three weeks, and whenever we bring up the subject of housekeepers, they tell us they'll do something about it as soon as they have time. I'm beginning to think they don't realize there's any work for a housekeeper to do."

"That's what I think," Meg agreed, and now it was her turn to sound bitter. "As long as you and I are around, Will, still doing everything as usual, it's never going to occur to them that the house, at least, is their responsibility. The thing that really gets me, though—"

She stopped abruptly. What she had been about to say sounded too much like begging for sympathy. After their mother died, someone had to take care of things. As the oldest, she had been elected. That was all there was to it. In two years of managing—of being tough and organized and keeping things going—she had done a good job of convincing her family that she could handle it all. Not even Will, as sensitive as he was to other people's moods and feelings—not even Matt, as much a part of their family now as if he really were their brother—had ever guessed how many times she had wanted to scream "It's not fair!" at them. Or how many times she had stayed awake all night, talking herself into hanging on for one more day.

She longed for relief from being the adult in the family—the one who took care of everyone else, making decisions and getting things done; the one was needed and who therefore could never let them see how much she needed someone herself. Not someone to take care of her, but to care about her. There was a difference.

But she had survived somehow. With the end in sight she was not going to break down and start whining about it now. Glancing up, she met Matt's eye. He grinned suddenly, giving her one of those rare, all-out smiles that always made her feel as if he had hung a medal around her neck. After last night's triumph a current of high-voltage happiness was humming through him. Before she could think of some way to turn the conversation back to his victory, he headed her off with a command of his own.

"Come on, old buddy. Spit it out."

Disarmed and distracted by his grin, she did. "It's just . . . well, I don't mind doing things for the four of us. Everyone helps, and besides, nobody should have to slave for us either. But having to run errands for the two of them, keep the house clean and all that, when they're not doing anything for us in return—it makes me mad. When I decided to stay home and go to UCLA, I didn't know it was going to be like this. I thought when Dad got married it would get better, not worse.

"Sometimes I feel like a character in one of those gothic novels—the ugly, meek-spirited eldest daughter who devotes her life to taking care of the rest of the family and ends up in a cage in somebody's attic—a loony old spinster!"

Far from being sympathetic, the other two found this idea hilarious. "My dear," Matt drawled, borrowing heavily from Will's famous-film-director impersonation, "you don't know how it pains me to tell you this, but you cannot play the ugly spinster daughter in my next production. You simply do not look the part.''

''That meek-spirited bit doesn't fit either,'' Will added with a laugh. ''Cheer up, old buddy. If you ever want to go on strike, I'm with you all the way. And if that doesn't work, you can always get a job and move into that apartment with your three soul mates.''

''And leave you and Carey to do all the work?''

''Not me,'' Will said emphatically. ''I don't look the part either. And they don't know Carey well enough to know how efficiently she could manage if she had to. When they think about her at all, they've got her labeled and pigeonholed under 'thirteen-year-old female adolescent.' Speak of the devil. . . .'' he added as the front door opened and closed. They heard Lew and Carey talking to each other in the front hall.

Meg raised her voice. ''Hey, you two, you ready to work? We've been waiting for you to come home so we could get started.''

''I guess so,'' Carey said unenthusiastically, looking in the door on her way down to her room with her sleeping bag and overnight case. ''Oh hi, Matt. Umm . . .'' She hesitated, then vanished, her voice drifting back up the hall. ''I'll be there in a second.''

''Hey, Big Bro,'' said Lew. He launched himself through the door as if propelled by a giant boot from the rear, making quite a production out of tripping over Matt's outstretched legs and crashing to the floor. With the patch over the eye that wasn't ''lazy,'' the ragged cutoffs, and his scabbed, scarred knees, he had the rakish appearance of a pirate's cabin boy and none of Carey's shyness about saying the wrong thing. ''Did you win?''

''Yeah,'' Matt said, ''and I've got a trophy to prove it. You can see it when you come down tomorrow for the big celebration. Oh—that reminds me. Sally said to tell you, anytime from four o'clock on, and wear your bathing suits.''

'' 'Big' is too puny a word for this celebration,'' Meg

said. "Runner of the Year, graduation . . . for you and
me, anyway—"

"Wait till next year," Will cut in. "Then you'll find
out what a *real* celebration is."

"And your father's marriage," Matt reminded her.

"Right. They're coming too, for once. It's going to be
the most fabulous celebration we've ever had, and we've
had some beauties, haven't we?"

"We sure have," Matt agreed, thinking about some of
the occasions they had celebrated in the two years since
he had first come to Los Angeles and met the Schuylers:
birthdays; key races he had won; his adoption by the
Ryders; the clearing up of the Palace Theater murder,
and the end to the accusations and attacks that for those
same two years had made every appearance in public and
every meeting with strangers absolute hell.

But that was behind him now. Ancient history. Today
was where he was living, and the way he was feeling he
wouldn't trade places with anyone else in the world.

Yesterday the awards banquet was still ahead of him,
his dread of the outcome increasing like a tsunami wave
of immense proportions, building and building until—if
they gave the award and the scholarship to the wrong
guy—it was going to break and smash him and the Duke,
and the Duke's future to bits.

Today the banquet was safely and successfully behind
him. With tonight's graduation ceremonies, tomorrow's
fabulous celebration, and one last gloriously irresponsible summer ahead, which his good buddy Gary Maitland
would be coming down from Matt's hometown in Idaho
to share with them—he felt as breathless and exhilarated
as if he had caught that giant wave and were riding its
crest, hurtling along at tremendous speeds with nothing
to stop him or get in the way. "Whoo-ee!" he whooped
suddenly. "Let's get this show on the road!"

Everyone leaped to attention, saluted him smartly, and
got down to work. Because they had decided in a late-
afternoon conference yesterday which of their mother's

things each of them would keep and which they were going to give away, the job was accomplished fairly efficiently. There was one awkward moment when the sofa appeared to be permanently wedged half in and half out of the front door, but eventually the treasured items were safely relocated in their bedrooms, the garage was full of things too large or not special enough to be worth saving, and the living room was completely bare.

"There," said Meg, dusting off her hands with exaggerated emphasis. "It's all theirs."

"They can have it," Lew said gruffly, disguising his panic under an elaborate show of not caring. The trouble was, he did care. Desperately. He had sworn to himself that he would never come into this room again.

As long as the house had stayed exactly the same, nothing in it changed from the way it had always been, it had not been impossible for him to pretend that his mother was off somewhere on a long trip. He had even convinced himself that no one else had wanted to change anything for the same reason—that they were hoping as much as he was that she would be coming back. But with the leftover stuff piled in the garage and the bare living room echoing unpleasantly like an empty wooden box, that hope was dead. Like she was. Pretending wasn't going to work anymore.

All afternoon he had distracted himself from thinking about his mother by rushing around entertaining the others with his favorite puns and one-liners. Now that the job was finished—now that he knew for certain that he would never open the door after school and find her home, waiting to hear how his day had gone, ready to listen and laugh with him about things and let him know she cared—he felt as lonely and shaken as if he had just helped kill her himself. Bolting out the front door, he grabbed his skateboard and took off, determined that today he was going to make it all the way down Verde Canyon Road to the bottom without falling off, if it killed him.

"I hope the family room isn't next in line for an attack of redecorating," Will was saying as the door slammed behind Lew.

Carey turned on him fiercely. "Don't be so mean, Will. It's not Gwen's fault." The unexpectedness of the remark made the other three stop wandering around the room and stare at her. "It's not! I wouldn't want to live in a house full of someone else's stuff either. Too much like being a guest or something . . . not really belonging there. Well, it *would*," she told Will defiantly. His raised eyebrows and slack jaw were eloquently expressing the astonishment they all felt.

What she had said was true, although they had not thought of it themselves—had not put themselves in Gwen's place until now. The amazing thing was that it was Carey who had seen it first when, by Will's account, she should have been the last person to be feeling any sympathy for Gwen.

Will shut his mouth with a click. "You know what, Care? You're a nice kid. A little weird, but nice."

She grinned at him uncertainly, the other two laughed—and suddenly they were freed from the peculiar reluctance to admit the job was finished that had kept them lingering in the living room. Someone mentioned food, and jostling and shoving, they raced each other to the refrigerator.

"What's next on the agenda?" Matt asked after lunch. He was full of restless energy and excitement and could not see himself lying around the house for the rest of the afternoon, waiting for tonight's ceremonies. "How about going up to the stable?"

"Great idea!" Meg agreed. "Come on, you two. If you stay here, you'll have to help move Gwen's things into the living room."

"I'm coming, I'm coming," Will said hastily, but Carey refused the invitation. They left her waiting for their father and Gwen and drove to the stable where Meg put Cricket, her half-Arabian gelding, over the jumps, and Matt exercised a couple of stir-crazy mares for Mr. Santini, the stable's owner. Will, as usual, could not be persuaded to mount even the most docile plodder in the barn and spent the afternoon with a couple of Mr. Santini's yard dogs for company, sunning himself on top of the hay bales and storing up strength for the coming confrontation with his father over the morning's events.

**3**

*L*ate in the afternoon, when Will and Meg breezed into the house, they met up with their stepmother for the first time that day. Gwen was obviously worn-out and irritated with them for running out on her and their father. Knowing he could not make a convincing job of saying he was sorry, Will left the apologizing to Meg, but by the time his father got home from returning the rented truck, Meg was on her way to the high school with Matt. Will was left to face his father alone.

Called up to the newly redecorated living room and accused of being thoughtless and inconsiderate, Will jammed his fists into the pockets of his jeans and leaned insolently against the door jamb, making no attempt to conceal the contempt he felt for their own thoughtlessness. Never in a million years would it occur to his father or Gwen that clearing away memories of their mother would have been hard enough on all of them without having to replace her things immediately with Gwen's stuff. Refusing to apologize, he made instead a deliberately offensive remark about not realizing his father considered them his personal slaves, and got a sharp reaction from Gwen.

"Do you always speak to your father in that tone of voice, Will?"

"No," he said, acknowledging her presence for the first time. "As a matter of fact, I don't speak to my father very often at all."

His father stood abruptly, reaching for Gwen as if she needed his protection. "Leave us, Will," he said curtly.

Will left. Scooping a tennis ball off the hall table and tossing and catching it in one hand, he maintained his pretense of being unmoved by what had happened until he reached his room. Closing the door quietly behind him, he hurled the ball furiously into a corner, from which it rebounded and knocked over two small tennis trophies and an orange-juice can full of pens and pencils before disappearing, probably forever, behind his desk.

Apologize? No way! he raged silently. I'm not the one who needs to apologize. I'm not the one who's falling down on the job. You are. You just can't see it, can you?

How could he have thought that having Gwen around was going to solve anything? How could he have looked forward to his father's remarriage for the last six months as if the ceremony itself were going to magically transform the two of them into parents—something they had never been before? How come there was no way to test out a choice ahead of time, before it was made and you were stuck with the results? And how come he had so many lousy questions and not a single lousy answer . . . ?

After that scene Will would have preferred to stay home when the rest of the family went to graduation, but since Matt and Meg were expecting him to be there, he swallowed his pride and went. As soon as they arrived at Lowell High he told his father he was going to sit with friends and invited Carey and Lew to come along.

Carey said no, she wanted to sit with their dad and Gwen. She also managed to tell Will privately that he was being rude and she wished he'd stop. Since he thought their parents were being much ruder, especially to Carey herself, and since he could not explain this to her without hurting her feelings again, Will shrugged and left, glad that Lew, at least, had chosen to tag along with him.

The graduation exercises were being held out-of-doors on the football field, and they wandered along in front of the crowded stands, looking for familiar faces among the hundreds of family groups. Suddenly Lew gave a shout. "Hey, Will, there's the Ryders! Let's go sit with them, okay?"

"Okay," Will agreed. If graduation was meant to be a family affair, Matt's adoptive family would be his first choice to attend it with. But he was still picking his way over people's feet and past people's knees and muttering "Excuse me" and "Sorry" long after Lew had crawled under the stands, shinnied up the supporting framework, and popped out under the Ryders' feet with a cheerful grin, wedging himself in next to Matt's seven-year-old brother, Michael.

When Will finally did arrive, he discovered to his embarrassment that there was not really room for him on the crowded seat. Before he could say hello and move on, Lieutenant Ryder had lifted five-year-old Jenny onto his lap and was inviting Will to join them. Les Ryder, a detective with the Homicide Division of the Los Angeles Police Department, was not the kind of man whose time you wasted by arguing over something for the sake of politeness. Will thanked him and sat, thinking—not for the first time—that he would never want to be accused of the murder of a little girl and have to face this formidable man across a table in an interrogation room, the way Matt had done in the first terrible days after his arrival in L.A. more than two years ago.

Matt had run away from his hometown in Idaho with

his small deaf sister, Katie, and come to L.A. to prevent her from being sent away to a school for the deaf. While he was hunting desperately for a job he had left her alone in the abandoned theater where she was murdered. It was his fault she was dead—he never denied that. But he was not the one who killed her.

If it had been me, Will was thinking, I don't think I would have made it. But Matt had a stubborn streak—an essential strength and toughness that rivaled Lieutenant Ryder's. In spite of the ugly accusations, the pressures put on him by police and public alike, and the agony of losing Katie so soon after both of his parents had died in a car accident, Matt had refused to give up his struggle to make them believe him. In the end, against the odds, he had won.

After a beginning like that one—about as lousy an introduction as you could ask for—it was funny how great everything had turned out between Lieutenant Ryder and Matt. They were really close, tuned in to each other. Father and son.

And Dad and I . . .? Will thought. We met each other in the hospital about half an hour after I was born. Never hated each other. Never even fought about anything until this afternoon. And what have we got to show for sixteen and a half years? Nothing. We're practically strangers. . . .

As if she had been listening to his thoughts, Sally Ryder suddenly leaned around her husband and asked Will where the rest of his family was.

"Over there somewhere." Will gestured vaguely. "We got here late and there wasn't room for all of us."

"Don't let them get away too soon after the ceremonies," Sally said. "I'd like to say hello to Gwen and make sure there's no problem about their coming tomorrow."

"All right," Will promised, glad to be spared further conversation about his father and stepmother by the appearance of the senior class filing into their seats on the field below. Wishing he were down there with Matt and Meg, instead of up in the stands with one more year to go, he settled back to watch his sister and his best friend put the finishing touches on one era in their lives before starting on the next.

Matt had been mentioned during the listing of honors as having last night received Runner of the Year, an annual award sponsored by the Los Angeles newspapers. In spite of the prohibition against applause for individual graduates, he was given a wild ovation as he came off the stage with his diploma. Hesitating for a second, he glanced at his applauding classmates and strode rapidly back to his seat, his gown flapping agitatedly around his long legs. He was smiling slightly, but Will could see how uncomfortable he was. In the past year he had taken a lot of abuse from crowds at the meets where he and Duke Grieve had been racing each other to their record-breaking finale, and he was not accustomed to this other kind of response. He did not trust it.

Grin and bear it, old buddy, Will was thinking as he and Lew and the Ryders added foot stamping, clapping, whistles, and cheers to the general uproar. After what Matt had been through—not only to win that award, but to survive the accusations and attacks that a hostile, misinformed public thought he deserved until that night last March when a dying wino finally confessed to having accidentally killed Matt's sister in the Palace Theater— he was overdue for cheers and congratulations. Until this moment his fans had been starved for opportunities to show their admiration and support.

Grin and bear it, Big Bro, Will told him again. You're long overdue.

When the ceremonies finally ended, the Ryders and Schuylers got together for a picture-taking session in which every possible combination of both families was photographed by Will's father and Sally Ryder. Meg finally rescued everyone by handing Will the keys to the Schuyler station wagon and hustling Matt off to join their

friends and thousands of other high-school graduates
from all over the country on an all-night celebration in
Disneyland.

Lew did not need any persuading to join Will for the
ride home, but Carey chose to stay with their father and
Gwen. When she turned up a short time later, Will knew
her scarlet face and trembling chin were not the result of
her race to catch up with them.

"What happened?" he said. She would not tell him,
but it didn't take a genius to guess that the two adults had
made it clear they no longer wanted her company.

Later that night, when he heard his father and Gwen
laughing softly at some shared joke as they passed his
closed door on the way to their bedroom, anger surged
through him before he could prevent it.

He wanted to jerk open the door and yell, "What's
wrong with you two? You're supposed to be so
brilliant—have such great legal minds. How come you're
so blind and stupid when it comes to us . . . ?

In the darkness of his bedroom he promised Carey that
her father and stepmother would not stay blind forever.
Not if he could help it. After tomorrow's celebration was
safely out of the way, he would step up his campaign to
open their eyes.

# 4

*M*eg, Will, Carey, and Lew all left for the Ryders' on the dot of four the next afternoon and were strolling up the drive when Matt drove in with Don Turner, a classmate of Matt's and Meg's and a good buddy from the stables. Ten minutes later the six of them were in the pool with Michael and Jenny, getting the celebration off to a flying start.

After an hour of life-threatening water games, Meg was ready to sit out for a while with Sally Ryder. Matt's adoptive mother was the only person to whom she had ever been able to admit her doubts and fears, and Meg looked forward to these family get-togethers as a chance to unwind in Sally's relaxing company.

As soon as Meg's father and stepmother arrived, however, Sally and Gwen settled down together in the lounge chairs. An hour later they were still talking. From time to time Meg glanced over and found the two of them looking toward the group in the pool. Talking about us, she thought, and decided to forget her own conversation with Sally. Gwen might be picking up a few useful hints on being a mother. Scrambling out of the pool, she offered her services to the Ryders' grandmotherly housekeeper, Mrs. B, instead.

As always, a fabulous feast followed the activity in the pool—a feast spiced, as always, with background music from the stereo and friendly, laughing conversation that went on long after the last plate had been cleared away.

But similar as it was in many ways to other celebrations, there was something different about this one.

For a moment in their lives it felt as though everything had been accomplished, all the loose ends tied. Behind them were days of worry and hope, of struggling to make things work out the way they should, of disasters and triumphs. Ahead of them . . . ? Anybody's guess. But for now they were explorers recovering from a wild journey through white water, drifting together on a broad calm stretch, sharing a sense of accomplishment and pride.

No one wanted the celebration to end. No one wanted to be the first to leave and break it up. What finally got people moving was the fact that Meg and Matt had been on the go for the last thirty-six hours. Eventually even the four younger Schuylers left, and Matt drove Don back to the veterinary hospital and kennels where he lived and worked. When Matt came in again and went down to his room for the first time since that morning, he found several notes on his pillow from Mrs. B.

*Call Gary,* the first one said. *Call Gary!* said the second. The third one left no room for argument. *Call Gary. No matter what time you come in. He said he would wait up all night!*

Call Gary? At twenty-three minutes past one, Craigie, Idaho, time? What if he woke up Aunt Belle or Uncle Frank? But Gary sounded as if he meant it. Riding high on the crest of his great wave, Matt took a chance and dialed.

After two and a half rings the phone was lifted. A sleepy voice grunted a barely recognizable, ''Matt?''

''This is the National Television Survey Company,'' Matt said in a falsetto. ''We'd like to ask you a—''

''Oh lord, spare me,'' Gary groaned. ''There must be a law against making stupid cracks this late at night.''

''You were asleep? At this hour? Man, you must be losing your grip. Whatever happened to the playboy of the western world?''

"Matt . . ." Gary said warningly, sounding more like his normal self. "Quit fooling around and listen. I called you because something's come up. It's a wild idea, but a great one when you think about it. Only you have to let them know right away. Next two days max!"

"Let who know what? What are you talking about? And speaking of letting people know—when are you going to tell us when you're coming down here? We've been waiting all month to hear so we could make some pl—"

"Matt, for cripes sake, you're as bad as my mom! Shut up a minute and listen, will you?" Absolute silence followed this request. "You still there?"

"I'm listening, you freak. I know the teachers at school never got it through your thick skull, but when you're listening, you keep your mouth shut."

Gary stifled a snort. "All right, all right. Don't get cranked up again. Listen, I called you because this summer's all screwed up."

"What?"

"Wait a minute. It's better than you think. Much better. It's going to work out great, in fact. I can't come down to L.A. after all because I blew too many courses sophomore year—thanks to you—to graduate. I need to go to summer school just to get out of their stupid high school, for crying out loud."

"You aren't coming?" Matt repeated blankly.

"No. But here's the proposition. Promise me you'll think about it before you make up your mind."

"Okay, okay. Quit stalling around and get to the point."

"Okay, this is it. This family in Craigie is opening up their ranch this summer as a guest ranch, and they need guys like you and Will to work—and girls, too. You can bring Meg."

"Come back to Craigie? Me? No way, Gare!"

"Matt, come on—you promised you'd give it a chance before you made up your mind. I know what you're thinking—about Katie, and the whole town hating you because of what happened. But they don't, Matt. I swear. It's . . . it's . . .'' Gary stumbled over his choice of words, then got it out in a rush. ''They think you got a raw deal and a lot of it was their fault, and they'd be glad of the chance to tell you they wish . . . they're sorry.''

''No.'' Flat and final. No arguments. For two years he had struggled to survive the accusations and the sometimes violent hatred of strangers who thought he had killed Katie. During that time the knowledge that most of the people in Craigie—people who had known him all his life—thought he had killed her too, had not made the ordeal any easier to live through. To hell with their feelings. He had feelings too. He was not going back.

''Matt, listen,'' Gary said into the silence. ''The guy can't get any kids from around here because they're all either working on their own families' ranches, or they're doing the tourist season jobs for the chamber of commerce and the local hot spots. There's no one left. If you three come up, you can practically write your own ticket. You can do trail rides, work with the horses, teach some kids how to ride—''

''Will ride? Are you crazy? I couldn't get him near a horse.''

''He could be general handyman, then. Dig postholes, build the bunkhouse, meet the guests in Boise . . . all that. They really need you, Matt.''

''How do you know so much about what they need?''

Gary hesitated. Hiding something, Matt thought instantly.

''They've been over here a lot, talking to Mom and Dad,'' Gary said quickly, ''trying to rope me into it too. But I won't have time—only afternoons, and there's work for me to do on our ranch. We told them about you guys, and they're desperate enough to like the sound of you.''

''Thanks a lot,'' Matt said automatically as his mind slowly began working its way through a thicket of objections toward some faint but positive reaction he couldn't put his finger on.

"It's two brothers," Gary continued without missing a beat. "One of them is a real rancher, and the other's in construction in Los Angeles. He's loaded, and he's got a lot of L.A. contacts all lined up to come spend a week playing gentlemen ranchers on his brother's place. Only they can't get the help they were counting on. It's good pay," Gary added, having saved the best for last. He was running out of arguments.

"How much?"

"Three hundred a week plus room and board. Room, that is, if they can get the bunkhouse built. The L.A brother only gets up on weekends, and he's doing all the work himself, so it doesn't go very fast."

"That's probably why Craigie isn't too enthusiastic about helping him out. If he's not sharing the work with anyone local, I don't blame them. Who is this guy?"

"No one you know. Anyway, Matt," Gary rushed on, "you can stay with us until they finish the bunkhouse and—"

Matt cut him off in mid-sentence. "Wait a second, Gare. Who are these guys I don't know, when I know every family for five miles around Craigie? Whose ranch is it?"

The silence lengthened. Matt knew the answer before Gary could bring himself to get it out. "It's your family's ranch, Matt. Oh, hell!" Gary knew the battle was lost.

"You weren't going to tell me until I got up there?"

"Not if I didn't have to."

"You're a real friend, you know that?"

"Matt, look—it's not so bad if you—"

"It stinks," Matt said flatly. "Forget it, Maitland. I've thought about it, and the answer is no."

"Hell," Gary said, wanting to say a lot more and knowing it would just make things worse if he got mad himself, or begged or cried—all things he felt like doing. He wanted Matt back for one last summer so badly that

he had been rehearsing this conversation in his mind for
days so he wouldn't blow it, and feeling almost sick to
his stomach at the possibility that he might. "Well, if
that's the way it is. . . ." He was hoping Matt would say
something, anything, that would give him an excuse to
keep trying. Matt remained obstinately silent and out of
reach. "Oh, hey," Gary said after a while, trying to
sound as if it mattered. "What happened at the awards
banquet?"

"We both got Runner of the Year, and Grieve got the
scholarship."

"It's what you wanted."

"Yeah."

"Well, hey, that's great. Matt . . . please?"

"No."

Gary took a deep breath. "Hell," he said so softly that
Matt heard it as a sigh. "Well, I guess that's it then. So
long, old buddy. I sure wish we could have worked
things out, but I guess you know what's—oh *hell*!"

Matt heard that one all right, loud and clear, before the
phone slammed down on its hook and all that was left of
their conversation was a monotonous humming in his
ear. He hung up himself, feeling wrung out and bone
weary. The wave he had been riding had hit land hard,
throwing him off and leaving him beached and gasping.
Back in his room a moment later, he shed his clothes and
fell heavily into bed.

Go back to Craigie after what happened to Katie? Face
all those people who would think it was his fault she was
dead, even if they knew he hadn't killed her himself?
Gary could swear all he wanted to, but he couldn't
change the facts. No matter what they said out loud,
underneath they would hate him for running away with
her and letting her get killed. Why shouldn't they? Whenever he thought about it, which he spent enormous
amounts of energy trying not to do, he hated himself. If
only he hadn't left her there alo—

*Don't!* Savagely he stopped himself from completing

the treacherous thought. *Don't say it!* It was true, but it was no good torturing himself with it. It wouldn't change anything.

Breathing hard, forcing himself to concentrate on the pale bars of moonlight reflected on his ceiling, he shoved his remorse down where, most of the time, he was able to keep it hidden from himself and the rest of the world. But he knew it was there. It would be there as long as he lived—a banked fire ready to blaze up inside him at any moment and sear him all over again with the agony of losing her.

In spite of his exhaustion he couldn't sleep. No matter what he did to distract it, his mind kept working its way back to Gary's proposal. Finally he gave in and took up the argument where he had left off.

As if being in Craigie wouldn't be bad enough, Gary was actually expecting him to work on his own ranch— to be someone else's hired hand on the land where he had spent nearly sixteen years of his life. If he went back there, he would be walking into a holocaust of memories he didn't want and couldn't handle.

The only way he was able to live with the loss of his mom and dad and Katie was not to think about them alive, not to remember anything about them. To cut himself off from his first sixteen years as if a wall had come between them and his life in Los Angeles. He could not break through that wall—go into the past and remember them alive—without paying the price each time.

For, from the other side, the wall was not a blank, impersonal barrier. It was the stark fact of their deaths. He could not come back from his memories without facing it—without seeing again their bruised and battered bodies in three dark drawers. Two years had gone by, and he still had not learned how to deal with the pain.

Even here in L.A. he was not safe from the past. When he was asleep and his defenses were down, or when a voice, a familiar smell, or someone using sign language caught him unawares, he would find himself remembering—fighting his way out of a nightmare or clenching his teeth until the ache in his throat subsided again. Going back to Craigie, to the ranch itself, he would be living every day on the other side of the wall.

The ranch as he had last seen it rose unwanted into his mind. Empty . . . lifeless. No horses in the corrals, no chickens or rabbits in the coops and hutches, no barking dogs. No sounds of motors to tell him where his father was and what he was doing. No cooking smells to start his stomach rumbling. And, hardest of all to face, no people. His mom and dad and Katie not there. Not anywhere. Dead . . . like the ranch itself.

If it were anyone else's ranch but theirs . . . The idea finally broke through the storm clouds of his resistance and presented itself like a small ray of sunlight. If it were any other ranch, he could almost see going. He and Meg riding horses all summer? Will out of his parents' house and kidding around again, keeping cool and calm? And Gary—crazy Gare, with his freckles and his wild enthusiasm for trying anything once?

A summer like that had definite possibilities. But not, he knew, on his own ranch. No way. Gary must have been crazier than usual to think he'd go for it.

# 5

*Matt* slept restlessly, dreaming about home and Katie until he woke himself up shouting unintelligible warnings. Dropping back to sleep, he woke later in a sweat, tormented by the nightmare vision of his old house abandoned, decaying, windows smashed and blinded, doors hanging crookedly on broken hinges. When he dragged himself out of bed the next morning, it was already 10:30.

After a quick breakfast, he headed for the Schuylers'. He needed Meg's tough-minded talent for zeroing in on the real issues and Will's lighthearted approach to seemingly mountainous problems to help him settle this impossible question of going to Craigie, and to squelch a nagging feeling he had not been able to shake off that it might not be so impossible after all.

Meg answered the door, took one look at him, and hustled him into the family room, where Will was thumbing idly through the morning paper. "For a famous runner who hit an all-time high in his career three days ago," she said tartly, "and a successful parolee from the local educational institution—you don't look so hot this morning. What's up?"

"Gary's not coming," Matt said bitterly.

"Oh hey . . . why not?"

"He has to go to summer school. He has this crazy idea that I should come up there instead, and bring you guys with me." If he had expected Meg and Will to agree with him that the whole idea was too crazy to even consider, he was in for a shock.

"When?" said Meg, as if she were already packed.

"For how long?" Will asked, like a drowning man grabbing an unexpected lifeline.

"All summer. To work." *What are you doing, McKendrick? Go ahead. Tell them we aren't going . . . and why.* But he couldn't tell them. Not about his fears, his private agony.

"Work?" Meg repeated. "You mean work that gets paid for, or work for the so-called fun of it?"

"For pay. Three hundred a week, plus room and board."

"Matt, are you serious?" Meg said incredulously. "Doing what?"

"Wrangling horses on a guest ranch and—"

"That lets me out," Will said. "A thousand bucks a week wouldn't tempt me to maim, torture, and probably kill myself riding horses."

"There are other jobs besides the horses," Matt heard himself saying, as if he were actually trying to persuade them to go. "The guy who needs the help is building stuff he needs for the guests. You could help him. I think Gary said the bunkhouse still has to be built."

"I know even less about building bunkhouses than I do about horses," Will said. Stretching out on the floor, he closed his eyes to indicate that he was no longer interested in the conversation.

"But, Matt . . . !" Meg was breathless with excitement. "You mean somebody really wants to pay us three hundred dollars a week to ride horses? How soon can we leave?"

Matt looked at her—at her glowing eyes, at her incredulous half smile, at her slight body tensed and leaning forward as if she were already on the back of a restless horse, reining him in until Matt gave the word and they could gallop away down a dusty road. *As long as we stay here*, he could hear her dispirited voice saying, *they're going to expect us to go on keeping house for them forever.*

Oh lord, it *was* a great idea—he and Meg riding all summer and getting paid; Meg shaking free from her two-year enslavement as family cook and housekeeper. If it weren't his ranch, he would not have hesitated. But it was his ranch. There was no way—

Suddenly, furiously, he swore at himself. *McKendrick, you lousy creep. . . ! So what if it is your ranch? It's that or nothing. You can't say no for yourself if it's going to mean no for her too. It won't kill you to go back. It will hurt like hell, but it won't kill you. And you owe them—Meg and Will both—for all the times they've come through for you.*

With the two of them there, and Gare as well, there would be plenty of distractions. He would survive. If he had to spend the summer watching Meg and Will fight their way wearily through day after day of housework and parent hassles, he would end up feeling a lot worse. "We can go anytime," he said quickly, before the wall threw its shadow over him again, and he lost his nerve. "Gary said we had two days to make up our minds, and I guess they'll take us whenever they can get us. He says they're desperate."

"What did Sally and Lieutenant Ryder say?"

"I haven't told them yet. I wanted to see how you two felt about it first. I won't go without you."

"You'll have to go without me," Will said from the floor, hoping he was successfully disguising the panic sweeping over him at the prospect of a lonely summer spent trying to bring Carey and Lew and their parents together without Meg and Matt's company to balance the load. "I can't think of a single thing I can do that would be worth even fifty bucks a week to anyone else."

"You could do lots of things, Will," Meg insisted. "You're good with your hands . . . and reasonably intelligent," she added, hoping to get a rise out of him. "You could learn basic carpentry skills easily."

"I'd rather stay here. Lying around all day in the hammock, sipping banana milkshakes, waited on by the younger generation—that's the life! Who needs work?"

Meg eyed him doubtfully, not convinced. Then another idea hit her, and she was off again. "Matt, do you think they'd let me bring Cricket? We could trailer him up behind the station wagon. Mr. Santini has that old double trailer no one ever uses, and I bet he'd let me rent it for practically nothing. Would they?"

"I don't know. I don't see why not. When I call Gary back, I'll ask him. But we can't abandon Will and leave him without wheels too." Matt had caught Will's muffled protest at the mention of the station wagon's going with them, and wished Will would quit lying there like a dying gladiator and take an interest in the planning. He and Meg were committed to going now. It was unthinkable that Will would not be coming too.

But having made up his mind that it wasn't for him, Will was determined to keep the momentum going for the other two. "Take the wheels!" he exclaimed dramatically. "If I don't have the wheels, I can't do the errands or the shopping either, can I? Make no mistake about it, this summer is shaping up very nicely."

Abandoning the argument temporarily, Matt and Meg made up a list of questions they needed answers to, and went off to the Ryders' together to make the phone call to Gary. They came back later in the afternoon—Matt complaining that his ears were still ringing from Gary's ecstatic reception of their news—to try to persuade Will to come up to the stable with them and to tell him the plan. If Mr. Santini was willing to rent them the trailer, they were going to leave early Thursday morning and hope to be in Craigie by Saturday afternoon or Sunday at the latest.

They begged Will to come. They demanded he come. They threatened him with kidnapping and bodily harm if he refused to come. Vigorously resisting, he made them leave him alone at last by making noises about wanting the car himself that afternoon. As they drove away, talking excitedly, he had his first bleak vision of what it would be like when they left him behind for good.

It was not entirely because of the horses that he had refused to go. It was as much a sense that someone was needed to stay at home and run interference between his brother and sister and their parents. Somebody had to keep trying to shake or shock his father and Gwen out of their preoccupation with each other and make them see they were needed. Make them understand that, as Meg had put it, they had to give their family something in return.

There were going to be two obstacles to his success at this job, one of them Gwen herself. She was smaller than he was, thin and athletic with black hair that curled loosely around her face, but she had extraordinary eyes that he could not look into for long without feeling himself shrinking under their laserlike intensity. It was probably the same look she used in the courtroom to terrify hostile witnesses and get the truth out of them, and she was going to make a formidable opponent.

The other problem was the stupid ulcer he had given himself by worrying too much over Carey's loneliness, Lew's lazy eye, and Matt's near-fatal rivalry with Duke Grieve. Cousin It did not take kindly to spasms of righteous wrath and reminded him spitefully at such times of its sharp-toothed existence.

Making himself an early supper, he armed himself with some crackers and a small carton of milk and went off to the movies with Don Turner. Like it or not, his job this summer was to bully Gwen and their father into noticing for themselves the small important ways they were essential to their kids. He and Meg did not need or want the listening ear and the adult support anymore— too late for us, he told himself with a slightly bitter laugh—but Lew and Carey did, and he was going to make sure they got it.

# 6

**W**hile Will was strengthening his fortifications for the coming campaign, Matt and Meg were looking for the right moment to tell the rest of their families about their plans. Matt's chance came during dinner. He had hoped to wait until Michael and Jenny had gone to bed, but Sally unexpectedly precipitated the discussion by asking if he'd heard anything from Gary about the summer.

"Yes," Matt said. "I called him last night. The plans have changed."

"Oh? When is he coming?"

"He's not."

"Oh Matt." Sally sounded genuinely disappointed. "What happened?"

"He has to go to summer school." Matt hesitated, not sure how the Ryders were going to react to his news. "He wants Meg and Will and me to come up there instead—to work on a guest ranch wrangling horses and building stuff." Glancing up, he caught Sally and Ryder looking at each other. "I said we would," he went on slowly, trying unsuccessfully to read the meaning of their silent exchange. "Meg and I are leaving Thursday, taking the Schuyler station wagon and trailering Cricket up. . . ."

Something was definitely wrong, but before he could ask them what it was, Jenny began bombarding him with questions. Where was he going? How long would he stay there? What could he do there that was better than what he could do at home? Why couldn't she go too? Who would ride bikes with her and take her to the beach and the zoo? "You promised!" she roared, punching him in the arm and calling him a rude name before Sally could intervene and hustle her off to her room for a talk and a calming chapter from *The Wizard of Oz.*

As silence descended again Ryder caught Matt's eye. "My feelings exactly," he said.

Matt thought he was kidding, but with Ryder it was hard to tell. He had a face that didn't reveal much about his feelings; the stronger his emotions, the deeper they were buried. It was a trick Matt was trying to learn. "You want me to stay here?"

Before Ryder could answer, Michael interrupted. "I want you to stay too, Matt. Please don't go. Please. . . ."

"It's only for the summer, Michael. Just a couple of months. I'll be back before you've noticed I'm gone. I promise."

Michael's eyes filled with tears. He slid off his chair. "Your promises are no good," he shouted, heading for the safety of his own room. "You never keep them!"

Ryder surveyed the vacated chairs and grinned. "Remind me not to invite you to our next dinner party," he said.

Matt's answering smile slowly faded. "I didn't expect all this. Maybe it's not such a good idea?"

As soon as he made the statement into a question he knew what Ryder's answer would be.

"You won't know unless you try it."

"But you and Sally don't—"

"Sally and I are old enough to know how quickly two

months go by. We were . . . surprised, that's all. If that's what you want to do, Matt, go for it. We won't yell about promises.''

"You're sure? It's not like I'm leaving for good, or anything.''

Ryder hesitated an instant too long, giving Matt a sudden understanding.

"Is that it? You think once I'm back in Craigie I'll want to stay?''

"You don't think that's. . . ?''

"No way!'' Matt said forcefully. "There's nothing there for me anymore. I'm going because it's a chance to get Meg out of the housekeeping rut she's been in at home for the last two years. That's all. This is where I belong. Isn't it?'' he challenged Ryder. "Isn't that what it says in those adoption papers? You're stuck with me for the rest of my life?''

"My god, is that what it says?'' Ryder exclaimed. "I knew I shouldn't have signed them without reading the fine print.'' They laughed at each other, the tension gone.

"Well, now we've got that straightened out,'' Matt said, "I guess I better go talk to Michael. If that's all he's worried about, I'll make him a promise he *can* believe in.''

Meg's announcement of her plans for the summer brought a different reaction from her father and Gwen. They were enjoying a late predinner drink in the living room when she interrupted them with a cheerful, "Hi, Dad . . . Gwen. Can you spare a minute?''

"Of course,'' her father said, without raising his eyes from *The Wall Street Journal*. "What's the problem?''

"No problem. I just want you to know about my summer plans.''

"Summer plans?'' Her father lowered the paper. "I thought you were planning to stay home this summer and—''

"No, I've got a job. A fabulous job, working with

horses! It pays three hundred dollars a week, plus room and board, and I can take Cricket with me. Matt and I are driving up. We're leaving early Thursday morning, and we'll be there by Saturday afternoon if—''

"Matt and you? Where are you going?"

"To Idaho. Craigie, Idaho. It's Matt's hometown.''

"This weekend? You and Matt driving to Idaho? No, Meg. I'm sorry, but it's not possible.''

Meg's mouth opened and closed several times. She was as astonished by her father's refusal as if a stranger had stopped her on the street and told her she couldn't go. Her reaction was not lost on Gwen.

When Meg finally spoke, she kept her voice soft, almost gentle, trying not to hurt her father's feelings. "Dad . . . I'm sorry, but I don't think you understand. I'm not asking for permission. I'm just telling you what my plans are so you'll know where I am.''

"You may be the one who doesn't understand, Meg.'' Her father sounded as if he resented having to point out the obvious. "We need you here this summer to help run things, keep the routines going while Gwen's getting settled in. It would be damned inconvenient if you went away and left us all at loose ends.''

"I'm sorry about the inconvenience to you, Dad''— the two red spots flaming across her cheekbones were the only signs of Meg's rising resentment—"but it's an inconvenience to me to stay. This is your house,'' she added, glancing pointedly around the redecorated living room, "and you don't need me to take care of it. You need a housekeeper. I'm not it, or her, or whatever. I've resigned. I'm going to Craigie with Matt so I can earn some money for next winter when I'll be housekeeping for myself. You knew you'd have to hire another housekeeper sooner or later. It's just sooner, that's all.''

Jim Schuyler seemed to be studying the backs of his hands with careful concentration. Taking his silence to mean acceptance, willing or not, of her proposal, Meg left the room. When he looked up and found her gone, Jim glanced at Gwen.

"Defense rests," Gwen told him, knowing he had been jolted by his daughter's uncompromising attitude and hoping to lighten the impact of Meg's words, "and Defense has done a damned good job."

Jim laughed ruefully. "When I said my children could manage beautifully on their own, I had no idea how beautifully, did I?"

"She's not a child, Jim. She's a capable, independent young woman, and obviously used to making her own decisions." And why not? Gwen was thinking. How many times had Jim been asked—or wanted to be asked—about anything in the last two years? Will's comment about not speaking to his father very often came back to her suddenly. Not many, apparently.

"We can't have it both ways," Gwen added. "Either we let them be responsible for themselves—and that includes making plans that don't include us—or we take on the job, the whole job, of running their lives for them." Which was not a job she was equipped to take on. She was a lawyer by choice and training, not the domestic, milk-and-warm-cookies type. She had no intention of being sucked into the morass of time-consuming, emotionally draining details and obligations that came with running a house and mothering a family. Sally Ryder had given her some valuable insights into the personalities of Jim's family, and they were beginning to emerge as separate and distinct individuals. On that basis, as she got to know them better, she was prepared to enjoy them. But as a mother—no.

This determination was strongly reinforced later that night when Will returned home while Gwen and his father were finishing a quiet, candle-lit dinner. He dropped uninvited into an empty chair with a request almost identical to Meg's for a minute or two of their time. "Lew's last Little League game is Wednesday night, Dad," he said without preamble. "It's the tiebreaker for the championship. Can you get home in time to see it?''

''I'm sorry, Will. I'm leaving for Washington at six o'clock Wednesday night.''

''Can't you go on Thursday? You haven't made a game of his all season.''

''I have to be in Washington for meetings at eight-thirty in the morning. I'm leaving too late as it is.''

Will drummed thin fingers on the table. ''What about you?'' he said abruptly, looking at Gwen. ''It starts at four-thirty.''

She had a court appearance on Wednesday. It was possible that it might be over by then, but she could never be sure. ''Probably not,'' she said. ''Is there another game on the weekend?''

''No, this is it. The last one until next year. He'd like it, Dad.''

''Will, I'm sorry. I'd like to come, but I can't.''

''What about Carey's piano recital, then—Saturday afternoon?''

''I won't be home until the following Thursday.''

Gwen remained silent. She refused to be pressured or bullied by anyone, especially this truculent sixteen-year-old. When he glanced at her, she stared him down.

He gave it one last try. ''Well, in two weeks, Carey's drama class is doing its big play, and parents are supposed to come. Do you think you could make that one?''

''I don't know, Will,'' his father said reasonably. ''It's too far ahead to make any definite promises, but we'll—''

''Forget it!'' Will cut him off with an impatient gesture and stood up, looking at both of them with undisguised hostility.

Once again Gwen felt compelled to defend Jim from his selfish, demanding son. ''What about you?'' she said. ''While we're at it, isn't there anything on your agenda you'd like to have us attend?''

''No,'' he said flatly. ''There's nothing I'm doing that would be more fun if you were there.''

"That's enough, Will," his father said angrily. "If you can't speak to Gwen or me without being rude or sarcastic, then please don't speak to us at all."

Will blinked. His gaze traveled around the dining-room walls over their heads while he considered his father's words. Then, his eyes on his father, he nodded. "I'll work on it," he said ambiguously, and left.

Jim pushed his plate away. "Gwen, love, I'm sorry. I've never known Will to act this way. I don't know about leaving you alone with them this week."

He sounded as if he were contemplating leaving her in a cage full of untrained tigers. Gwen, who had been wishing that she had her old apartment to flee to, had to laugh. "Don't worry about us, Jim. We'll be fine. Meg will be gone, but Lew and Carey are no problem, and I can handle Will."

Jim seemed convinced. Now all she had to do was prove it to herself.

# 7

**F**or the next two days, Meg was so busy getting herself and Cricket ready for the trek north that as far as the rest of her family was concerned, it seemed as if she had already left. Wednesday afternoon, while Gwen was defending a frustrating case in court, Will and Carey went to Lew's Little League game and out for pizza afterward to celebrate his team's victory and his own spectacular performance: four-out-of-five base hits; three stolen bases, including one to home plate; and two diving catches for outs in the first and fifth innings. They got home very late and very high on the last six hours and were unprepared for the angry reception given them by Gwen as they came in the front door.

Having forgotten Lew's game, Gwen had no idea where they were. She had been waiting since 6:30, fear alternating with fury as she imagined everything from car crashes to kidnapping, and their carefree arrival was the last straw. "Where in the name of heaven have you been?" she said furiously. "And why didn't you tell me where you were going?"

"I told you about Lew's game last Sunday," Will said, angry with her for spoiling their great mood.

"Didn't you see the note on the board?" Carey added anxiously.

"What note on what board?"

Carey showed her the board in the family room where messages were left for various members of the family. *Gone to Lew's game and out for pizza afterward. C, L, & W,* said the note in Carey's neat round print. Because he was making no attempt to hide his satisfaction at Gwen's embarrassment, Will brought all of her wrath down on his head a moment later.

"There's nothing to eat in the house," she said accusingly, giving him her laser look. "Who's in charge of the shopping?"

Will wrinkled his forehead in exaggerated bewilderment. "I don't know," he said innocently. "I thought you were."

"Will Schuyler," she snapped, "I will not tolerate your rudeness. Not to your father. Not to me. When I ask a question, I expect a plain answer—unembellished with irony, sarcasm, antagonism, hostility, or any other emotion you may be feeling at the time. Is that clear?"

Will's mouth was already shaping itself around a sharp

retort when Carey nudged him. "Will . . . don't," she whispered.

He looked at her unhappy expression and the tight thin line of Lew's mouth and abandoned what he had intended to say for something less calculated to annoy Gwen. "Sorry," he said, keeping his voice as neutral as possible. "What was the question?"

Gwen moderated her own tone of voice, and the conversation began again. "Who usually does the shopping?"

"Meg."

"Then we'll have to find someone else."

"I'll do it," Carey volunteered instantly.

Gwen, smiling, shook her head. "Will. . . .?" she said.

"Starting tomorrow, I won't have the car."

"You can use your father's until he comes back. Then we'll have to work out something else."

Will struggled with his thoughts for a moment and finally abandoned attempts to find a polite way of saying no. "I'll do it this week," he said slowly, "but I'm not planning on doing it forever."

"You are planning on living here for a while, though, aren't you?" Gwen said coldly. If this little monster expected her to wait on him hand and foot, he was in for a rude awakening.

"For as long as I can stand it," he said evenly, and they locked glances briefly. "I know," he added. " 'Leave us, Will.' Don't worry, I'm going." And he did, this time slamming his bedroom door behind him.

Carey and Lew had drawn closer together during this exchange and were watching Gwen apprehensively. Suddenly she was sorry. Sorry she had taken Will on in front of them. Sorry she had spoiled the exuberance of their mood. What a way to start the week, she thought sadly. So much for the last sixteen years of experience in understanding and handling people that were supposed to have seen her safely through this "difficult period of adjustment" everyone had warned her about.

On an impulse she smiled at the two stricken faces. "Don't worry," she told them far more confidently than she felt. "Will and I will get it worked out eventually." She was rewarded by a slight, tentative smile from Carey, and a gruff "Okay" from Lew. It did not occur to her until she was settling slowly into bed a few minutes later that she had not even thought to ask Lew how his game had gone. On a scale of one to ten, my friend, she told herself wearily, you can give yourself about one and a half for tonight's performance.

Up early the next morning for a run before breakfast, Gwen was the only member of the Schuyler family to wave Matt and Meg off to Craigie, and that only because they passed her on their way to the stable to load Cricket into the van. Meg leaned out the window to ask her to tell everyone good-bye, and as the car disappeared around a corner ahead of her, Gwen found herself wishing fervently that they were taking Will with them.

In spite of her assurances to Jim and the two younger ones, in spite of Sally Ryder's affectionate description of Will as someone who cared deeply about other people and as the possessor of an outrageous sense of humor, she could not see herself and Will coming to any understanding unless there was a dramatic change in his attitude. Others might see a different side to him, but she found him aggressive, arrogant, and far too used to having his own way. The less she saw of him, the happier she was going to be.

She was lingering over a meditative cup of coffee before leaving for work, wondering what the future was going to be like in this house where she was so much an outsider—and an unwelcome one at that—when Carey appeared in the doorway. She stared in surprise at her father's empty chair.

"Where's Dad?" she said. "Did he leave already?"

"He left last night. He's gone to Washington for a week."

"For a week?" Carey's voice rose. "But he was supposed to sign my drama-camp stuff and give me the check. I have to have it in on Saturday, or I can't go. I kept reminding him and reminding him, but he always said he'd do it later. Oh no!" she wailed. "What do I do now?"

"I can sign it," Gwen said hastily. "I'm one of your legal guardians now"—she was carefully avoiding that treacherous word *mother*—"and it will be perfectly official. The camp won't complain, I promise you."

"What about the money, though?"

"I have the checkbook. Just tell me how much it is, and that's all there is to it."

Carey pulled herself together. Between them they made short work of the forms, laughing over their shared memories of the unbelievable awfulness of chicken pox, and discovering that both of them were cowards about getting shots of any kind. Carey was on her way out of the room again when Gwen asked her when the drama camp began.

"Not for three weeks. Oh . . . that reminds me. Lew's going too—to sports camp, not to mine—and I bet Dad forgot to sign his forms. Maybe you'd better ask him."

But Lew, when asked at supper that night about his plans, shook his head and said he had changed his mind.

"Changed your mind?" Carey repeated in amazement. "Lew, you've been talking about that camp since last September!"

"I said I'm not going," he told her fiercely. "Mind your own business, why don't you?" The truth was, he did not trust his father or Gwen. He was not going to go away like everyone else and leave the house undefended. Someone was needed to stay at home and make sure nothing else got changed or thrown away while they weren't looking.

"Won't you be lonely here by yourself every day?" Gwen asked him.

"Maybe. But it's easier to be lonely at home than at some weird camp. Anyway, Sergeant Prado and I are going to all the ball games, even if Matt isn't here. That's better than camp."

"Who is Sergeant Prado?"

"You know him. He was at the party. He works with Lieutenant Ryder at Homicide."

"Oh, you mean Tony," Gwen said. Sensing that there was more to Lew's refusal than he was willing to admit, she added, "Well, if you change your mind—"

"I won't!" he said angrily.

Gwen let it go. It was almost too late for her to get through to Meg or Will, she thought resignedly as she watched Lew tracking down his peas and spearing them with sharp thrusts of his fork, but she and Carey were making progress. Given time, maybe Lew would be willing to trust her too.

By the end of the week Gwen had decided it was definitely too late for her and Will to come to an understanding. Convinced that Will was deliberately making life difficult for all of them, she wished many times that he would go to Craigie, or Timbuktu, or even, on occasion, hell.

When she was alone with his sister or brother, their conversation was relaxed and highly entertaining. The instant Will appeared, Carey and Lew retreated, answering questions in polite monosyllables and maintaining a careful neutrality, as if afraid that by appearing to take sides, they might precipitate another scene like the last one.

In spite of their efforts Gwen and Will had another confrontation Saturday morning over the question of keeping the house clean. Will flatly refused to help and told Gwen that since she obviously didn't want to do it any more than he did, she should hire someone else to do it for her. After this exchange he locked himself in his room and turned up his stereo so loud that the entire house reverberated to the beat of the bass.

He emerged once to take Carey somewhere—too late Gwen remembered the piano recital—and by the time he came back Lew had gone off with Sergeant Prado for the first of their expeditions to the ball park. Gwen decided she might as well get some work done at the office and left Will in possession of the house. When she returned home late in the afternoon, the house was silent and empty.

Will had left no word as to his whereabouts, but a note on the board told her that Carey had gone to the movies with a friend and would be home by nine o'clock. She had included the friend's name and phone number in case anyone needed her. Gwen's appreciation for Carey's thoughtfulness rose another notch or two.

Not knowing when to expect Lew and not wanting to start supper too early, Gwen went into the living room to wait for him. She found herself unable to concentrate on any of the magazines piling up unread on the table but did not pin down the reason for her restlessness until the front door opened and shut again with a thunderous bang.

Lew was back. As relief swept through her, understanding followed. All this time she had been waiting impatiently for his return. She had actually been looking forward to having some time alone with him. "Lew?" she called, before he could vanish down the hall to his room.

"Yeah?" He came only as far as the doorway before stopping, but he was grinning widely and his unpatched eye sparkled and danced with suppressed excitement.

She could tell by looking at him what the answer would be to her next question, but she asked it anyway. "Who won?"

The look of astonishment he sent her was identical to the one Meg had worn earlier in the week. It was a look that said plainly, *I didn't know you cared,* but he was so fired up that his enthusiasm burst out of him with explosive force. "We did! It was the greatest game . . . you should have seen it!" He stopped abruptly—had something in her expression turned him off?—and shrugging, turned to go.

"Wait, Lew," she said quickly. "Tell me about it while I get us some supper."

And for thirty-five nonstop minutes he did—play by play, breathless with excitement, his voice dropping as he reached a climactic moment and rising again with the remembered thrill of a successful rally.

Gwen, who had been to one ball game in her life and been bored to death, loved every detailed minute of it. He was a born storyteller. "Lew, that was fantastic!" she said, when the last ball had been hit to left field, leaped for, bobbled, dropped, and the winning run had slid safely across home plate. "You make me want to go and see a game myself."

"How about tomorrow?" he said instantly. "It's a doubleheader. Starts at twelve."

A doubleheader? Gwen hesitated. Oh help, she thought. What have I gotten myself into? Did she really want to spend a steamy afternoon and half the evening with the smells, the noise, and the crowds—and with Lew giving her a breathless rundown on everyone and everything that was going on? Of course she did.

"All right," she said emphatically. "We'll go. But you'll have to keep me posted on what's going on out there. I don't know very much about baseball."

"I'll keep you posted," he promised. "Oh boy, that's great!" As he carried his dishes out to the kitchen he added as if he had read her mind, "You can bring a book to read in the boring places, if you want."

Gwen was still laughing at this perceptive remark when Will, who did not announce his comings and goings with Lew's careless abandon, suddenly appeared in the kitchen. Lew muttered something and fled. Gwen felt her own lighthearted mood evaporating in the presence of his brother's brooding silence. While Will was throwing an assortment of things into the blender for his special evening meal, Gwen hastily finished drying the pans she and Lew had used and retreated to the living room. Surrounded by her own possessions, she felt on safer ground.

You coward, she told herself irritably. You and Will are tiptoeing around each other as if you were bombs—armed and ready to go off on contact. She had no idea how long they could live together on these terms, and she could foresee no solutions that would not cause a lot of unnecessary pain and unhappiness, to Carey and Lew especially.

You thoughtless, self-centered brat, she said silently to Will's back a moment later as he went down to his room. Do you think I can't see what you're doing? You're forcing Lew and Carey to take sides, to choose between us, and you have no right. They shouldn't have to choose, they should have both of us if that's what they want. If you cared about anyone besides yourself, you'd understand that. Why, in God's name, didn't you go to Idaho with your sister . . . ?

# 8

*Lying* on his bed in the dark, a new cassette blasting away unheard on the stereo, Will was asking himself the same question. When he was away from home—spending as much time as he could with Don at the boarding kennels where he worked or playing tennis with friends from last year's Lowell High varsity—he could kid himself that everything was okay. As soon as he came in the door again he could feel the tension and hostility. He would have liked to cool things down a little, get his relationship with Gwen back on a more impersonal level, but he didn't know how. And now Carey and Lew were being affected by his war with Gwen, the last thing he wanted to have happen.

A knock on his locked door startled him. Opening it, he was relieved to find Carey waiting on the other side.

"Sorry," she said abruptly, "but I have to talk to you, Will, and there's never a good time. I want to do it now."

He did not feel much like conversation, but it must be important or she wouldn't be so insistent. "Okay," he said, inviting her in. Turning the music down a little, he stretched out on his bed and left the comfortable reclining chair to her. "Okay," he said again, when she seemed reluctant to begin. "I'm all yours. What's on your mind?"

"You," she said succinctly. "And Gwen. Will, please . . . I don't know what's wrong, but you're. . . ." She hesitated, and Will realized she had been getting up the courage to have this talk for days. "You're spoiling it. You're not giving her a chance."

"What about her giving me a chance?" he said hotly, stung by this unexpected criticism from his closest ally, but Carey refused to be sidetracked.

"You're horrible when she's home, Will. You're different—not like you're really you anymore. It's scary. Lew and I hate it when you and Gwen are fighting. Please, Will, go to Craigie with Matt and Meg. You could still go. It's not too late. I heard them trying to get you to come. They really want you."

"And you don't?" he said bitterly. He felt as if she had thrust a knife between his ribs and was twisting the blade.

"Don't be stupid!" Carey yelled. "You know it's not that. It's just . . . we don't need you now—to take care of us like you used to have to. You know what I mean." What she meant was that she wanted him to feel free again, not to worry about them anymore, but he didn't understand. She wasn't doing any good by talking to him. All she was doing was hurting his feelings and making him mad, and her own feelings suddenly overwhelmed her.

"I don't want you making yourself sick because of us all over again!" she cried. "I don't want you being mad all the time and ending up leaving home or something. I want to have you and Gwen too. Will, if you go away this summer and come back in the fall, everything will be all right by then. I know it. Please . . . *please*, Will."

"I'll think about it, Care," he told her gruffly, not wanting her to see how upset he was. "Just get out of here and let me think about it for a while, okay?"

For a long time after she left, he wrestled with what she had said, knowing she was right. Even before she had come in tonight, he had begun to see what she was trying to tell him. They didn't need him. Carey and Lew were doing great on their own. Somehow they had gotten through to Gwen themselves, and all his efforts to run interference for them *were* spoiling things.

He had overheard them talking to Gwen several times. They sounded as if they were actually enjoying each other's company. Tonight, for instance, Lew and Gwen were laughing about something in the kitchen. When he interrupted them, Gwen had given him her laser look, and Lew had clammed up and disappeared—the way he used to do when Gwen was the one intruding on a conversation. It didn't feel so good to be the intruder, the unwelcome one in the family. Carey had been right about that too.

Wait a second, Schuyler! He caught himself sharply. Why all the gloom? Why aren't you sending up rockets, firing off cannons, dancing in the streets? Isn't this what you wanted? Isn't this what you've been praying would happen for the past six months? To get Gwen to pay attention to them, to get her to care? So how come—now it's finally happening—you're lying here trying to keep cool and calm and make your lousy stomach quit acting like Pompeii's last day?

You're free, you jerk! Don't you understand? You aren't responsible for anyone but yourself anymore. You don't have to worry about Carey needing something to share things with or Lew having someone around who's tuned in to him. It's just you on your own again. Freedom! It's the greatest! Right?

Wrong. He wasn't feeling great. He was feeling more like he did after a tennis tournament when he had blown the match for no reason, lost points he should have won, muffed his serves. Stupid and useless. A liability to the team instead of an asset.

Lew and Carey didn't need him anymore. Nobody did. And instead of the discovery being the enormous release he had looked forward to for so long, it felt as though the crew had mutinied and chosen a new captain, casting their old one adrift to float aimlessly around with no land in sight and nothing to tell him which direction he should go.

Even if he went to Craigie, what use would he be? Twelve lousy years he had been in school and what had he learned? Nothing . . . nothing that made him any use to anyone else. He couldn't even go out like Don Turner and get himself a decent job he could support himself on. He had a choice all right . . . some choice. Either he stuck it out in this house where he was the outsider now, the spoiler, and kept his mouth shut and himself out of the way as much as possible, or he went to Craigie and tried to make himself useful doing things he had absolutely no idea how to do.

Horses and bunkhouses. . . ? He groaned. They couldn't be worse than hassles and hanging around L.A. all summer, or could they? He had a sudden vision of Matt and Meg on the highway heading north, kidding around and talking about what they would do when they got there. If he were in the car with them, what would he be doing? Nothing. Just sitting there listening. Even Cricket would be more useful in Craigie than he would.

He had no choice. It was home or nothing. He wished fervently that Matt and Meg had never left. A second later the incredible selfishness of that thought hit him so hard that he sat straight up in bed and sent off another message. Direct-line ESP.

Have a great time, he told them urgently. I mean it, you guys . . . a great summer. You've earned it. Then, hoping to take his mind off himself and his problems and calm his stomach down, he started reading a three-inch-thick paperback he had been saving for the moment when he had no more homework to do and plenty of time on his hands.

# 9

At about the same time that Gwen was sharing supper and the ball game with Lew, Matt and Meg were turning off the main road from Boise to Craigie and heading down a country road. Matt had been driving the last stretch while Meg looked out the windows and asked questions about everything she saw. She was amazed that Matt knew the names of every dog they passed, and he laughed at her amazement. "What did you expect? City kids don't even know who their neighbors are, but up here everyone knows everyone else, *and* their dogs. We're almost there," he added.

"I can't wait to get out of this torture chamber," she said fervently. "Matt, can you believe it? We're really here!"

We really are, he was thinking. Back in Craigie. All those people to face. And the wall . . . the lousy wall. Even if he turned his back on it—refused to think about his family in those three dark drawers—its shadow was going to hang over him all summer. The Maitlands' gate was coming up on the left. In five more minutes he would be committed to this summer as irrevocably as if he were on a roller-coaster ride. No way to get off except at the other end. . . .

Knock it off, McKendrick! he told himself, dealing ruthlessly with the nervous flutters before they became a raging panic. You made the choice, you can live with it. He grinned at Meg. "Just remember, old buddy, it's your fault we're here. I never would have come without you.''

"Hedging your bets?" she asked impudently. "Okay, Big Bro . . . I'll take the blame if it's a disaster, but I get all the credit if it's as terrific as I think it's going to be."

"It's a deal," he agreed. Rumbling across the Maitlands' cattle guard, they started up the long drive.

"Eeyow!" Meg said, coughing and choking as she and Matt hastily rolled up their windows. "Are we making all that dust?"

When Matt stopped a moment later, the cloud of dust rolled over them like fog. "Out, slave," he said grandly. "That gate must be opened and shut behind me."

"Now I know why you wanted to drive this last bit," Meg grumbled. Holding her nose, she did as she was told and had just regained the safety of the car when a short wiry figure, crowned with a mop of curly, copper-colored hair, burst out of the house in front of them and was followed immediately and no less energetically by two other people.

"Hang on," Matt said as he drove the station wagon over by the barn and parked. "It's going to be like living through a hurricane for the next few minutes, but you'll get used to it."

Meg laughed. She had experienced Gary's unbridled energy during the wild spring vacation he had spent with Matt in L.A. over a year ago, and Matt had told her he got it all from his mom and dad. She thought she was prepared, but nothing could have prepared her for the exuberant warmth of the welcome they gave Matt. He was thumped and hugged and kissed, his hand pumped up and down at least fifty times, and all the time three people were carrying on nonstop conversations to which his shouted *yeses, nos,* and *I'll tell you later's* were providing a kind of chorus and two ecstatic dogs were leaping all over him, barking wildly.

While the Maitlands were busy with Matt, Meg went

stealthily around to the back of the trailer, grinning to herself. Although they weren't blood relations, Matt called them aunt and uncle, and they obviously couldn't have loved him more if he had been their son. Matt, you idiot, she was thinking happily. How could you ever have had any doubts about coming back here?

Her efforts to be quiet about opening the trailer door were thwarted by Cricket, who was pressing his great rump against it. The bar squawked as she slid it back, and an instant later everyone was swarming around her too. For a few breathless minutes she came in for a sizable share of hugs and handshakes herself.

Cricket was coaxed from his own torture chamber and allowed to run and roll in a corral while they all leaned on the fence, laughing at his contortions and bombarding Matt with news of Craigie and the ranch. It was not until Gary told her that Susan was responsible for cleaning out Cricket's stall and getting everything ready for him that Meg realized Gary's twelve-year-old sister had not been there to greet them.

After Cricket had been bedded down for the night, Gary's mom herded everyone into the house and gave them barely enough time to wash up and sit down at the table before she swept them all away on a flood of conversation. Her ideas leapfrogged off one another with bewildering speed.

"We'll all help you unload the car later, but right now what I want is to hear all about your trip up and your— oh, Matt, didn't Gary say you finally won that big Los Angeles newspaper award for running that you were after? That's wonderful! I've always known you had something special when it came to running. Remember, Frank, how he used to come tearing down Little Creek Road every day, slap our gatepost, and be off home again—just like clockwork? Six-thirty every morning for six years, and—"

"I must have missed a few mornings here and there,

Aunt Belle,'' Matt broke in, laughing at this vision of himself appearing day after day like some deranged wind-up toy.

"Not one," she said firmly, winking at Meg. Taller than either her husband or Gary, Aunt Belle had a face indelibly wrinkled by sun and laughter and blue eyes that twinkled and flashed as if she were constantly sending out messages through them in Morse code. She reminded Meg of someone's fairy godmother, disguised for practical, everyday purposes as a hardworking ranch wife, but unable to prevent her real identity from showing through.

"My turn, Belle," her husband said, seizing this split second of silence to get a word in. "We've been talking your ear off with our own news, Matt. Tell us about the trip. Any problems?"

"Only with Cricket." Matt exchanged grins with Meg at the memory. "He's not one of your more docile and obedient animals. Yesterday it took us nearly an hour to get him into the trailer, and I did all the work while Meg spent most of the time crooning gently in his ear."

"That's not what I was doing, and you know it," Meg said as everyone began to laugh. "I was telling him how horrible he was, and what I was going to do to him if he didn't get into the trailer that instant, and some other things I think I won't repeat," she added vaguely, bringing on another round of laughter.

"What is he, Meg?" Uncle Frank asked. He had a round freckled face like an Irish gnome's, just enough hair remaining to show where Gary's flaming mop had come from, and a note like leftover laughter in his rumbling voice that made him sound as if he were continually amused by everything going on around him.

"Half-Arabian, half-Thoroughbred," Meg told him. "Plenty of endurance, good sense when he wants to use it, a stubborn streak I haven't trained out of him, and a large dollop of mischief to top it all off."

"He's a beauty," Uncle Frank was saying as the screen door squeaked slightly.

Susan edged through it and slid quietly into the empty chair, as if hoping to escape their notice. Bits of straw were clinging to her long shiny braids. She must have been up in the hayloft when they arrived, Meg thought, wondering why she'd hadn't come down to see Matt.

"Look who's here!" Aunt Belle and Gary said to her simultaneously.

Susan took in Matt and Meg in one swift glance. "Hi," she muttered, helping herself to what was left of the meat and vegetables. "Sorry I'm late."

An instant of silence fell over the table. Meg caught the look Aunt Belle exchanged with Gary and the slight shake of her head.

"Hi, Sooz," Matt said. "Good to see you." His gaze lingered thoughtfully on her bent head for a second or two before he turned to Uncle Frank and continued the conversation with a description of Meg's skill at training and handling Cricket over jumps. This led them into a discussion of the horses on the Maitland ranch and then, when Matt shied abruptly from the subject of his own family's horses, to a more general discussion of how families around Craigie were faring this year.

After supper Uncle Frank and Gary, who was obviously bursting to get Matt to himself, insisted on taking Matt off to meet some old friends from the Maitland menagerie and see some of the changes they had made since he was last there. Meg shook her head at Matt's invitation to join them.

"I'm helping with the dishes and talking to Aunt Belle . . . about you," she teased, laughing at his look of dismay.

"Please, Aunt Belle," he was pleading as Gary pinned his arms to his sides and hustled him out the back door. "Only the good stuff . . . promise? Remember, Aunt Belle"—his raised voice drifted back to them—"I've got my reputation to protect!"

"Hmm," said Meg, as she and Susan cleared and scraped the dishes while Aunt Belle swished soap into a panful of steaming water. "That sounds promising. Were he and Gary really awful?"

"Wild," Aunt Belle said reminiscently. "And wonderful. The things they got up to—well, you can see all the gray hairs they've given me. Never a day they weren't up to something. Riding those inner tubes down the Big Creek rapids during spring thaw. Building the rope bridge across Little Creek. They never did master that one—fell in every time. Jumping out of the hayloft door clutching umbrellas for parachutes. Painting themselves and their clothes green and brown—for camouflage, they said. It was months before we cut the last speck of paint out of their hair." She chuckled at the memory.

"The worst times, though, were when one of them would come home alone. The sight of Matt or Gary racing into the yard, hair flying, face white as a salt lick—it was enough to give me heart failure the first few times. Got used to it, though. I had to. Between them they broke four arms, three collarbones, one leg apiece, and lord knows how many times they knocked themselves unconscious or cut themselves badly enough it needed stitches." Aunt Belle rolled her eyes toward the ceiling. "Somebody up there must have been looking out for those two every minute."

"Which one was the worst—the one who thought up all the things to do?" Meg asked.

"No way to choose between them," Aunt Belle said. "Both of them claimed the credit or took the blame for their schemes, whether they turned out good or bad. I often thought they had the same idea simultaneously, they were that close. Almost like twins. Some of the crazy things they dared each other to try . . ." She shuddered. "That parachute jump—that was one. Each of them as bad as the other, egging each other on. They'd try anything once, except . . ." Aunt Belle hesitated, glancing at Susan, who was putting away the dishes as fast as Meg wiped them and humming tunelessly to herself as if the conversation bored her.

"Except," she repeated more slowly, "when it came to Katie. When Matt had Katie with him, nobody—not even Gary—could get him to take a foolish risk. Never cared two pins for his own hide. Hated to have his father tell him he'd done something stupid, though. That was all Adam had to do to punish Matt, and Matt took it right to heart. Never made the same mistake twice. But I was going to say about Katie—"

Susan dropped the bowl she was holding onto the table with a crash. "Don't!" she said shrilly. "Just don't!" Whirling, she left the kitchen at a run. They could hear her feet pounding up the stairs.

Meg concentrated on the pot she was wiping dry. Aunt Belle said nothing for a moment, her hands motionless in the soapy water. Then she sighed and resumed her brisk scrubbing of the final pan.

"Susan and Katie were best friends too," she said. "Had some wild adventures of their own, trying to keep up with their older brothers. Susan is twelve now, a year older than Katie would have been if only . . . if only we . . . oh, shoot!"

Smiling apologetically at Meg, Aunt Belle reached for a paper towel and blew her nose. "Susan's missed Katie something terrible," she went on. "As much as Gary's missed Matt. But Gary's had letters and phone calls—times like this summer to look forward to. Even the hope that Matt might come back again someday to stay. Susan . . . well, I'm not sure she ever really accepted it, ever really believed Katie was gone. Until now. Now she'll have to accept it, and lord knows, it won't be easy."

Aunt Belle turned suddenly and took Meg's hands in her damp soapy ones. "Meg-chick," she said softly. "This summer isn't going to be easy for Matt, either— seeing old friends, working on his own family's ranch and all. You saw tonight how, after more than two years, he still shies away from talking about his family—sharing memories of them. I'm not surprised he came back—he never could turn his back on a challenge, no matter how impossible it sounded—but I'm glad you're here with him. He'll never ask, but he'll need all the help you can give him just the same.''

Meg stared at her, appalled. His family's ranch? They were going to be working on Matt's own ranch? But they couldn't . . . he couldn't . . . he never said . . .

The shock of her discovery was followed by a wave of disgust. How could she have been so blind—so stupid? How *could* she? Sometimes she thought she was the most self-centered creep she knew. Just like their father, Carey had accused her once, and Carey had been right. It was Meg's fault as much as their father's that Will had gotten sick. All the time he had been struggling to keep the routines going by himself so she would feel free to leave and go away to college, all the time he had been worrying about Lew and Carey and not telling anyone, she had gone right on doing her own things. Oblivious. Feeling sorry for herself because she thought no one cared about her. And now she had done the same thing to Matt.

Matt had never wanted to come back here. She could see that now. What was there here for him except a lot of painful memories? But he had come anyway, and why? Because *she* wanted to. Because it was such a great chance for her to escape from home.

Oh Matt, she thought miserably. I can't make you go through your whole life, remember the people and the places you've lost, hurt you all over again. Not for my sake. Why didn't you tell me? *Why didn't I ask . . . ?*

''What's wrong, Meg? What did I say?'' Aunt Belle was watching her with shrewd, understanding eyes.

''Nothing. You didn't—Oh, Aunt Belle!'' Meg burst out. ''It's my fault we're here. He never said anything about the ranch being his family's, and I didn't think about how hard it was going to be for him. I just wanted to come so badly, and he came because of that . . . because of me. What should I do?''

For an instant neither of them moved. Then, unexpectedly, Aunt Belle swept Meg into her strong arms for a fierce hug. "Meg-chick, you don't know how glad I am to hear you say that. If it's true, then he's chosen the best reason in the world to come back, and as long as he thinks you're happy then he'll be able to weather the bad moments ahead. Cheer up, love," she added, with a return to her usual whirlwind style. "Don't you regret coming for a single minute. The two of you will have a glorious time, I promise you. Oh, it'll have its ups and downs, but you have a summer ahead of you that you'll never forget. And maybe," she added, more to herself than Meg, "yes, I think for certain—it's going to turn out the best thing for him in the end.''

"You finished the washing-up yet?" Uncle Frank's cheerful voice came from beyond the screen door. "We're ready to unload Matt's and Meg's things if you are.''

The rest of the evening went by in a blur for Meg. Grateful for the darkness and confusion and the chance to pull herself together, she left Matt and Gary comfortably settled in a tent off the back porch with some silly remark about not letting themselves be frightened by things going bump in the night. But when she was alone herself, tucked into Gary's bed like a little girl by Aunt Belle, listening to the unfamiliar nighttime noises outside the opened window and to what sounded uncomfortably like crying from Susan's room across the narrow hall, she had to argue long and fiercely with herself before her own desire to cry was thoroughly squashed, and she thought she was ready for tomorrow.

All right, Matt, she promised him. You brought me up here to make me happy, and I'm going to be so happy you won't recognize me. I don't know if that's going to be enough to make the bad moments easier for you. I don't see how it can. But it's all I can do to make up for what you've done for me. Starting tomorrow, I'm giving you an Academy Award performance.

The blame and the credit for this summer. When she said she would take on both of them, she had spoken more truly than she realized.

# 10

**M**att had planned to run before breakfast on Sunday, but he woke to the smell of griddle cakes and bacon already cooking and thought with relief that it would have to be postponed. Later in the morning they had to go over to the ranch to talk to the owners about the summer. It would be easier seeing it again for the first time with Meg and Gary along to distract him from too much remembering.

Speaking of Gare. . . . Matt eyed the mound snoring gently in the cot next to his. Stealthily extricating himself from his own sleeping bag and dressing first, he unzipped Gary's bag with one swift motion. "Up, up, you lazy lout!" he bellowed.

Even when Gary was woken out of a sound sleep, his reactions were immediate and instinctive. The ensuing wrestling match brought the tent down on top of them and left Matt with a lump over his ear from the falling tent pole, but Gary did not consider himself truly avenged until he had dropped a handful of ice cubes down the back of Matt's shirt after breakfast.

Truce was called temporarily to allow Gary time to get ready for church. "You want to come?" Uncle Frank asked casually as the Maitlands were getting into their car.

"I . . . no, not yet," Matt said. Uncle Frank nodded and drove his family away without another word.

"They're nice," Meg observed.

"The best," Matt agreed, staring after the cloud of dust, his big hands curled tightly around the metal bar across the top of the gate.

Meg sucked in a gigantic mouthful of fresh air and let out a contented sigh. "Thanks for bringing me," she said, jabbing him lightly in the ribs. "I wish you had told me whose ranch it was before we came, but as long as you aren't sorry, I'm ready to have the time of my life."

"If I had told you whose ranch it was, would you still have wanted to come?" Her silence gave him all the answer he needed. "We both wanted to come," he told her firmly. "Don't worry. I'm not sorry, and I'm not going to be."

Getting her neck in a painful judo hold, he marched her to the barn to let Cricket and Aunt Belle's elderly mare out into the pasture for the day. They spent the rest of the morning wandering around the Maitlands' place, Meg asking a lot of questions about the old days, and Matt replying with such outrageous exaggerations that she could not believe a word he said. She got even with him by hinting that after supper last night Aunt Belle had already told her everything she wanted to know about him.

"Everything?" Matt repeated, advancing on her ominously.

Meg prudently put the pasture fence between them. "Everything," she said solemnly. "Matt, I never would have guessed you were such a— Help!"

Vaulting the fence, he was after her, chasing her through the pasture, in one end of the barn and out the other, across the plank bridge over the creek, and into the field on the other side, where he caught up with her easily and flung her down in the tall grass with a flying tackle. They lay there laughing until Meg caught her breath.

"You aren't even breathing hard, you rat," she said enviously.

"You're out of shape. A brisk run every day before breakfast would do you good."

"How about a brisk ride? Less agony, more fun."

"Lazy lump," he said, tickling her face with a long bit of hay. "You'll grow old and fat before your time."

"No way! Statistics say I'll outlive you by seven years," she boasted. "Wait a second . . . I hear someone yelling."

"Good. They must be back. Let's go get this introduction to our slave masters over with."

Gary had promised Hank Pomeroy, the L.A. brother, that they would be there by noon. They took the Schuyler station wagon, Matt driving while Gary kept up a constant monologue about people they both knew. As they drove under the crossbar and rattled across the cattle guard at the entrance to his own ranch, Matt seemed so engrossed in stories about his old buddies that Meg hoped he had not seen the sign overhead.

Hanging from the crossbar was a long redwood board with the letters POMEROY RANCH burned into it. Above it a rough rectangular patch, like a wound in the weathered wood of the crossbar itself, was all that remained of the place where Matt's father, dreaming of the future, had burned MCK RANCH into it twenty-one years ago.

They drove along the dirt road for a mile and a half, past a field in hay, a pond, a barn and corrals full of horses on the left, another small barn or shed for farm machinery on the right, and as they got closer to the house, three small A-frame cabins set in among the trees where the ridge began to rise steeply on both sides of the narrow valley. Rounding a corner, they were stopped by a yard gate similar to the Maitlands'. When Meg hopped out to open it, she stood staring for so long that Matt beeped several times before she remembered what she was supposed to be doing. Except for a new coat of paint, Matt's old home—a two-story white house—was an exact duplicate of the Maitlands'.

"When you're through gawking," Matt said with a grin as he and Gary drove past, "come on up to the house."

When Meg caught up with them again, they were shaking hands with a big, powerfully built black man whose craggy, rumpled face would have looked at home behind the wheel of a semitrailer. Gary had told them everything he knew about the Pomeroys on the way over, and Matt's reaction had been to ask how Craigie had responded to their first black family.

"Took a little getting used to," Gary had said. "Plenty of black cowboys in the Old West, but Craigie's never had a black rancher before. Everybody's been polite and all, but there's a kind of wait-and-see feeling."

Meg's initial reaction had been surprise, and then surprise that she should be surprised. She hadn't grown up in Craigie but in a part of the country where the parents of her black friends did everything from cleaning teeth to teaching in graduate schools. So why not ranching?

When it was her turn to be introduced, their new boss shook her hand and left it feeling somewhat disarranged. "Hank Pomeroy," he said. "Call me Hank. And you're Meg. Come on around the back. Got a lot to tell you in the next half hour. First job," he added, gesturing at it on the way by. "Get the addition painted."

Trying not to watch Matt for his reactions, Meg stared at the sizable new room extending back from the original kitchen. It took up an area into which, if this had been the Maitlands', the back porch, the tent, and another ten feet of yard could have fitted. There were plenty of windows and a large patio at the back to replace the porch, and once the raw new wood was painted to match the house, it would not look so stark and out of place.

Hank led them up the wide steps and through sliding glass doors into the room itself. "This is where everyone eats, everyone gets together after supper, and where everyone will have to entertain themselves on rainy days. Nice, eh?"

"Very nice," Meg agreed, to fill the silence emanating from Matt and Gary in waves. It *was* nice—walls paneled in light gray wood, built-in cupboards and bookshelves where there weren't windows, and a huge stone fireplace. Two long sofas, lots of large pillows, a card table, and some comfortable chairs took up half the room. The other half was dominated by the longest table Meg had ever seen. Made of thick wood planks stained dark and varnished like a ship's deck, it was surrounded by benches. A carved, high-backed chair stood at either end. Beyond it was the kitchen—everything in the same place as it was at the Maitlands', but all of the appliances bigger, shinier, and newer.

"How many people can eat here at one time?" she asked in amazement.

"Thirty," Hank said. "Built it myself."

"How many people are you expecting?"

"The five of us"—by *us* he must mean Pomeroys—"and five of you, and anywhere from twelve to twenty guests per week. We'll go into all that when I come up next weekend. I want to get you going on the essential jobs first."

Matt spoke for the first time. "Five of us?"

"Yeah. You three and two local kids I hired this week."

"I thought you said you weren't working here, Gare."

"I'm not."

"Who's the third one, then? You don't mean—?"

"If you mean Will," Meg blurted, "he didn't come."

"What the—! What do you mean, he didn't come?" Hank turned on Gary. "Didn't you tell him I was counting on his help?"

"Well, yeah, but he's not too good with horses—"

"To hell with the horses! I've got that end covered. I need someone to work on the building and repairs when I'm not here. Call him," Hank told Meg peremptorily. "Call him and tell him I'll pay his way up here. No, forget that. I'll bring him up myself next weekend. I've got to have someone, and he's it."

"I'll call him," Meg said, "but he's stubborn."

"I'm stubborn too. Give me your number. I'll call him myself when I get back to L.A." He glanced at his watch. "I've got to get going soon. Okay, down to business. This week is separate. Just you three—you still available?" he said to Gary, who nodded, "—doing the big jobs. I'm paying three-seventy-five since I'm not giving you room and board yet. Starting next week, though, you'll be living here—in a tent, if necessary—until I've got the bunkhouse finished. You'll be helping Peggy with the meals in the kitchen," he said to Meg as he spread some sheets of paper on the dining-room table and searched his pockets for a pen, "cleaning the cabins, keeping the kids amused, and you'll be—"

Kitchen? Cleaning? She couldn't have heard him right.

"Wait a minute," Matt said harshly, while Meg was still trying to clear her throat of a sharp-pointed obstruction that had suddenly filled it. "Meg and I came up here to wrangle horses and take people on trail rides."

"You're still with the horses," Hank said. "Here . . . this is the contract for the summer. Read it before you sign it."

Matt jammed his fists into his pockets, refusing the paper Hank was holding out to him. "We're both working horses, or it's no deal," he said flatly.

Hank seemed to be measuring him. He had a hundred

pounds or more on Matt weightwise, and for an instant Meg was afraid he was going to flatten Matt with one of his huge fists. Matt slowly drew his own hands out of his pockets and tensed, waiting.

# 11

"*Sit* down," Hank said, and there was enough barely controlled rage in his voice for them to do what he said. "Now, all of you, listen. I've been working on this project since last fall. I'm up to my ears in delays, setbacks, cost hikes—everything. I've put a hell of a lot of my time and money into this thing, trying to get the job done right and the summer moving the way it should. And it turns out everything stands or falls on five kids who don't know me from Joe Blow and don't give a damn what happens to my ranch.

"I've got to have two of you on the horses, two of you helping Peggy, and one of you working for me. Until this week I didn't have anyone. All systems go and not a hope of getting it off the ground. And then, like a miracle, I'm promised three fantastic kids from L.A. who can do anything and everything, and two days later I get two more from right here. One of them says she'll work with Peggy; the other one says it's horses or nothing. I don't ask why, I don't complain."

He looked at Meg, and his expression changed. "Look, Meg," he said. "I'm sorry about disappointing you. If I had the choice, I'd pick the horses too. But what

I need now, what I'm asking you to do, is the work with Peggy. You won't be working for her every minute, you know. You'll have time for the horses too . . . teach the kids to ride . . . whatever. But that's the way it is. If you quit on me, well . . .'' He shrugged helplessly.

Meg knew her cheeks were flaming and wished there was some way she could hide her reactions from Matt. He knew her too well. He was not going to believe her when she said she didn't care. But either they stayed and she worked for Peggy and made some money doing it— or they went home and she worked for Gwen and her father for nothing. Not much of a choice, but a choice all the same, and not that hard to make. Not trusting herself to speak, she reached for the other piece of paper and signed it quickly before Matt grabbed the pen out of her hand.

"Wait a minute, Meg. We don't—''

"I want to stay, Matt,'' she said. "If I can't have the job I want, I least I've got a job. Nothing else is changed.'' Her mouth tasted like ashes, and she clenched her fists under the table to make them stop trembling. Come on, Matt, she begged him silently. Sign it and let's go.

"Thanks,'' Hank told her almost gently. "You're a good sport, Meg. You've more than lived up to your advance billing. I'm sorry about the way it's worked out for you, but I'm sure as hell glad you decided to stay.''

Abruptly Matt snatched his own contract off the table, glanced over it, and scribbled his name angrily at the bottom. He shoved it at Hank and stood up. "Let's go,'' he said.

"I've got a few more things to tell you,'' Hank said evenly. "Bear with me. I'll be leaving for Boise in fifteen minutes, and you'll be on your own for the rest of the week.''

He spent the remaining time showing them where the paint, thinner, and brushes were located and which parts of the A-frames needed the protective coat of stain, add-

ing before he left that if they finished those jobs before
the weekend, they could start cleaning and repairing the
tack stored in the barn nearest the house. By the time he
had driven off, Meg had herself well in hand. When Matt
turned on her, taking up the argument where they had left
off, she was ready for him.

"Forget the stupid contracts, Meg," he said roughly.
"We don't have to stay. The whole thing's a mess. I'm
sorry I dragged you all the way up here just to—"

"Who dragged who?" she said with a laugh. "I'm the
one who wanted to come, remember, and I haven't
changed my mind."

"You don't want to leave?"

"Are you kidding? At home I don't get paid for doing
all that stuff. And like he said, I won't be working for
Peggy every minute."

"But you and I were supposed to—" He whirled on
Gary. "Did you know about this, Maitland?"

"Don't blame me, Matt," Gary said, backing away
from him in mock terror. "It's the first I've heard of it,
I swear."

"Who are the two kids he's hired locally, then?"

"I told you, I don't know. I haven't even talked to him
since I told him on Monday you were coming."

"All right," Matt said. "We'll wait and see who the
guy is on the horses—maybe we can work out something
with him. Meg, I'm really sorry."

"I'm not," she said, "and if I hear that word again,
you're going to get some more of those ice cubes down
your neck."

He stared at her for fully thirty seconds, looking for
signs of her real feelings in her face. Now that she had
weathered the initial shock, her defenses were in better
shape. She stuck her tongue out at him.

"Brat!" he said suddenly. "Watch yourself. I'm not
the only one who could be heading for trouble." But he
was grinning a little as he said it.

It's going to be okay, Meg insisted to herself, plastering a grin across her own face and hoping it would stick. Not perfect after all, but okay.

"Come on," Matt said suddenly, grabbing her hand and hustling her across the yard.

"Where to?"

"Just around. I want to see what else is changed besides the name on the gate, and this." He jerked his head at the addition as they went past.

So he did see the sign, Meg thought as she was whirled along on a dizzying tour of the ranch. He saw something that must have hurt him a lot worse than what just happened to me, and he didn't even show it for a second. Honestly, Meg Schuyler, the next time you feel like screaming "It's not fair!" go bury your head in a hole somewhere first, will you?

When she tuned in to Matt and Gary again, they were deep in the game of Remember-the-Time-When . . . ? Gary was making up for his uncharacteristic silence during their encounter with Hank, but when his enthusiasm for total recall included other members of Matt's family, Matt's face closed up. Cutting Gary off abruptly, he strode away. The other two had to run to catch up with him. When Matt did this a second time, Gary took the hint and confined himself to his own and Matt's doings.

Listening with growing delight, Meg found the barns, the shed, the creek-fed ponds, the wooded hills on either side of their valley, even the pasture fences coming alive—peopled in her imagination by two energetic little boys. One was tall and sturdy for his age with dark unruly hair and an all-out grin, the other skinny, red-haired, and freckled, and both were possessed of out-sized appetites for the adventurous and impossible. Wild, Aunt Belle had called them, and wonderful. She could believe it.

Matt suddenly broke off in the middle of a sentence

and eyed her suspiciously. "What are you grinning at?"

"You'll never guess," she said airily. "And I'm not telling."

Matt exchanged looks with Gary. Before she could run, they had scooped her up and hustled her to the edge of the small pond beside the vegetable garden. Choked with growth, the water looked muddy and uninviting. A couple of frogs were eyeing her morosely. Meg stopped struggling and said very calmly, "If I tell you, will you promise not to throw me in?"

"Promise," said Matt as they heard the crunch of tires on the gravel turnaround in front of the house.

"Okay, I was thinking what cute little boys you must have b— You promised!" she shrieked as without a word they started to hurl her in.

Gary, who had made no such promise, let her go in midair. Matt, at the last moment, didn't. Which is why, when they introduced themselves to Art and Peggy Pomeroy a moment later, Gary was wearing a smug grin and Matt and Meg were smiling sheepishly as they tried to ignore the water running off them and making muddy puddles in the dust around their feet.

As she offered Mrs. Pomeroy a damp hand the words on the career-center poster—*Always be clean, neatly dressed, and have your hair well groomed for your first meeting with a prospective employer*—were running through Meg's mind.

"Catch anything?" Art asked them with a grin. He was younger than Hank—in his late twenties, probably—and with his sweat-stained hat, long lanky body, and scuffed, down-at-heels boots, looked more at home on a ranch than his brother.

His wife laughed. "I won't ask you in," she said with the good-natured calm that—they were to learn over the summer was the way Peggy Pomeroy handled disasters both large and small. "Art has some things he wants to talk over with Matt. Why don't Meg and I sit out here and get acquainted while you three are getting things sorted out?''

She led Meg over to one of the four redwood tables on the patio outside the addition—a woman not much taller than Meg and not much older, her curly hair cut very short and an air of quiet confidence about her that Meg appreciated. She had an idea that Peggy would have everything organized and under control this summer, and she would not be expected to do it all herself. That in itself would be a welcome change.

They chatted for a while about Meg's family, and when Meg explained why Will hadn't come and said she hoped he'd change his mind, Peggy smiled wearily.

"If Hank has anything to say about it, he will," she said. "This whole thing has been Hank's idea from start to finish. I still can't believe he talked us into it."

Meg wondered if Peggy was feeling as steamrollered by Hank Pomeroy as she was, but it was not a question she could ask. "Well, it's a great place," she said instead. "No one could come here and not have a good time."

"I know, but it's going to take lot of work. I couldn't do it without you and Marcie."

"Marcie?"

"Marcie Trasker. Hank hired her sometime this week. You'll like her. Her father owns the drugstore and soda fountain in Craigie, and she baby-sits for me. I'm surprised she didn't ask for the job sooner, now that I think of it."

"Oh," said Meg. "Do you know who's helping with the horses?"

"No, I don't. She came one morning while I was out riding along Big Creek. Hank said she's a local barrel-racing champion, though, so I guess she's qualified to handle the horses."

"She?" A girl? Of all the unfair tricks! Horses or nothing, she had said. Blackmailed Hank into giving her

Meg's job. What makes her so high and mighty that she can't stoop to cooking and cleaning? Meg wondered, hating her already.

"Jase, love," Peggy said suddenly. "No more muddy paws on Meg's jeans, please."

Meg looked down, expecting to see a small dog, and saw instead the impish face of the youngest Pomeroy, Jason, who was not quite two years old. Having patted up all the mud from Matt's and Meg's puddles and spattered himself liberally in the process, he had come stumping over on small fat legs to see if the source of such exquisite pleasure had produced any more of the same. He regarded Meg with raised eyebrows and an approving twinkle in his brown eyes that give him an air of having shared a superbly funny joke with her. His muddy paw prints were visible on one leg of her jeans from the knee down.

"Nice," Meg said approvingly, finding his expression irresistible. She offered him her other leg. "Do this one for me too, okay?"

Head slightly to one side, Jason regarded her thoughtfully. Then he clapped both hands together, inspected each one closely, and announced in cheerful tones, "All gone," before trotting off to join his four-year-old sister Beth in their sandbox.

Meg had dried off and was feeling uncomfortably itchy by the time Art returned with Matt and Gary from their tour of inspection. Recognizing from Matt's tight-lipped silence that he was dealing inwardly with something difficult and painful, she refused Peggy's offer of cold drinks by saying she needed to get home and out of her mud-stiffened clothes before they had to be chipped off her. Promising to be back and ready to work by nine the next morning, they drove home in silence, arriving at the Maitlands' at a little past four. A police car was parked beside the house.

"For crying out loud!" Matt exploded. Too many demands had been made on his emotions and his self-control for one day. "What am I? Some kind of sideshow freak they're all going to come out and stare at?"

"Knock it off, Matt!" Gary said sharply. "Sheriff Hensley's the only one who'll come out to the ranch, and you know it. Everyone else will just wait until they bump into you in town." The close call with Hank Pomeroy over their jobs, and the tour around the ranch with Art Pomeroy asking Matt questions he could not avoid answering about his dad's crop-rotation schedule and how Adam McKendrick had dealt with the problem of water in the high pasture, had left Gary feeling guilty and depressed—emotions he was not used to handling. Now that he had seen what coming back to Craigie was going to cost Matt, he was beginning to realize that this was not going to be just one more summer like the old times after all.

He had thought it would be so simple. All he had to do was get Matt back to Craigie, and the place and the people would do the rest. Once Matt found he still belonged here, he would want to stay. But it wasn't going to be that easy. Not for Matt, and not for him either. In fact, if this summer was not going to turn into the biggest mistake of their lives—destroying the past and his and Matt's friendship along with it—he was going to have to work every minute. After today, he was not optimistic about his chances.

Matt brought the station wagon to an abrupt halt. Jerking the handbrake on with unnecessary force, he stared unseeingly ahead.

"Well, I hope he doesn't want to see me," Meg said lightly into the awkward silence. "Your Idaho ponds are revoltingly smelly—not like our pure Los Angeles water. I'm going to take a shower . . . *before* I get undressed." Getting out, she strolled across the yard, ignoring the crowd of curiously sniffing dogs that followed her to the kitchen door.

"Matt," Gary began slowly, "I'm really—"

"Don't!" Matt cut him off roughly. "Don't say it,

Gare. It doesn't help . . . just makes it worse. I'll survive, and I'll have a great summer, okay? Just don't—''
He gestured with one hand as if shoving aside something
he didn't want. "Don't say it, that's all. Don't even think
it. Deal?'' Dark eyes met blue ones, as they had done so
many times before. Message sent. Message received.
Over and out.

"Deal.''

"Let's go, then.''

But Matt's meeting with Sheriff Hensley was delayed
by several minutes as his own dogs, Poor Boy and Pat—
now members of the Maitland household—discovered
him coming home all over again and repeated last night's
joyously undisciplined welcome. Generous amounts of
Maitland yard dust were added to Matt's disreputable
shirt and jeans as he rolled happily on the ground with
them, and the commotion brought Gary's mom and dad
and the sheriff out to watch the fun. Shouting his hellos
over the dogs' clamorous barking, the sheriff finally
hauled Matt to his feet.

"Can't compete with a welcome like that one, Matt,''
Hensley said with his booming laugh, "but I'm glad
you're back, son. Real glad.'' He was shaking Matt's
hand and thumping him resoundingly on the back as he
spoke, and Matt managed a grin and a pretty convincing
"Thanks,'' in return. "Not the only one who feels that
way, either. Lots of folks looking to see you in town.''

"Yeah, well, I'll be in . . . sometime. Next week,
maybe. I don't know.''

"No rush,'' Hensley said. "Take your time. They'll
wait.'' He eyed Gary hovering protectively around
Matt's shoulder and grinned. "Don't know what I'm so
glad about, come to think of it. You two together again
and loose in my territory? Think I'll put in for an extra
deputy for the summer.''

"They're going to be working a twelve-hour day,
Tom,'' Uncle Frank said. "Won't be enough starch left

in 'em by nightfall for any Paul Revere midnight rides, or time to get themselves lost in the hills.''

"Hey, Dad!" Gary protested.

"Low blow, Uncle Frank," Matt added severely.

"Well, you have to admit you two have pulled some real beauts in your time."

"When we were kids, maybe." Gary's scorn for his own and Matt's behavior as kids made everyone including Matt laugh, and the sheriff left them shortly afterward with a few more thumps and handshakes all around.

"What's for dinner?" Gary asked his mom. "If I'm lucky enough to live that long."

"Stew, salad, rhubarb pie." She wrinkled her nose as they crowded together into the narrow kitchen. "Matt, is that you?"

"Yes, ma'am," he said guiltily.

"Would you believe it, Mom?" Gary reported gleefully. "He fell in the pond by their vegetable garden. Just fell right in. I told Art he'd better put up a fence. If the other guests from L.A. are as bad as Matt, they're going to be hauling people out of there day and ni—no, no, Matt. Help! I apologize. I was kidding, Mom," Gary confessed wildly. "I threw him in on purpose." But it was too late. He knew by the look in Matt's eyes that sometime, in the not-so-distant future, his good buddy was going to make him pay.

Way to go, Maitland! he congratulated himself. If he could keep that look in Matt's eyes instead of the other one, his plans for this summer might have a chance after all.

# 12

*The* sun and the birds were up at a little past five the next morning. Matt woke minutes later, yawning lazily. When he tried to stretch, he found his sleeping bag so twisted around him by his restless tossing during the night that he almost had to wake Gary and get his help to unzip it. By 5:30, he was dressed, warmed up, and on his way.

He dreaded making his first run, but he was also impatient to do it and get it behind him. Whether he started from the Maitlands' ranch or from his own, he was going to have a lot of familiar landmarks to ignore, a lot of memories waiting to spring at him like dogs guarding their territory and tear him apart. Wrenching his mind away from the ordeal ahead, and the wall waiting for him at the end of it, he forced himself to concentrate on the run instead.

*What a great day! A perfect day! Smell that pine-sweet, Idaho-summer air. Man, you don't get air like that in L.A. Six-seven-eight-nine-ninety. . . . Take a left. No, don't look at the gate, McKendrick. Forget it. She's not there. . . .*

Mentally he sang a few choruses of "Rocky Mountain High," which matched his mood and his rhythm, until the familiar sound of stones scattering under his feet with the glassy click of well-placed marbles reminded him again of other early-morning runs.

*Hawk up there, circling. Remember the day—? No! Forget it, I said. Just run . . . just run. Don't think about anything—not the ranch, not the duck pond, not the triple tree. Don't look for them, either. They aren't there. It's someone else's ranch now. Not yours. Not theirs. Just someone else's ranch, Nothing special about it.*

*They're dead, McKendrick. Gone. Get that through your thick skull. They're not coming back. . . .*

Jogging slowly around the last corner, he half expected to find the house of his nightmares, abandoned and rotting. Seeing it alive, familiar—exactly as it had been for the first sixteen years of his life—was worse.

A small blue bike lay on its side in the yard, and curtains were moving slightly at the opened windows. The smell of coffee and the faint sound of a radio indicated that someone was up, and the disgruntled squawk of chickens being rousted from warm nests as someone gathered breakfast eggs told him where that person was. Everything the way it had always been. Except for one thing. The woman coming out of the chicken house was not his mom. . . .

Matt relaxed his stranglehold on the yard gate, returned Peggy Pomeroy's wave with a quick lift of his hand, and went back the way he had come, running hard until he was through the gate and out on Little Creek Road. He was not going to make that run again until he moved over to the Pomeroy ranch to stay. From now on he would just keep running on Little Creek Road past the ranch.

It was a longer run anyway. Better. And Little Creek was just another country road, nothing special, no memories along it that would send their ghosts out after him. Except for the place coming up on the right, where, seven years ago, he had found Poor Boy. Or rather, where Poor Boy had found him.

When he heard Matt coming, Boy had scrambled frantically out of the narrow drainage ditch. He was crying and limping painfully—an abandoned pup with a broken leg that someone had probably lost out of the back of a passing pickup.

Now he was the one thing Matt could afford to remember. Boy wasn't a ghost; he was alive and waiting for Matt at the Maitlands' gate. He couldn't get over the fact that Matt was actually coming and going the way he used to. Each time they met was like the first one—the deafening noise, the leaping and slobbering, the heavy paws thudding against Matt's ribs.

"Okay, Boy, that's enough," Matt told the dog breathlessly, holding Boy's shaggy head in both hands and looking him in the eye. "I can't go through this routine every time I come in the gate, okay? Act your age. I'm here to stay . . . for a while, anyway. And I love you too." But he wasn't sorry that Poor Boy had been there to greet him after that first lonely run.

Matt, Meg, and Gary turned up at the Pomeroys' at nine o'clock that morning, dressed in scarecrow ensembles from Aunt Belle's rag-bag collection of threadbare shirts and irreparably torn pants, and ready to paint. The addition was one story high and had so many windows that the actual wall area was not that large, but they had to put two coats on it, so it was a two-day job. With Jason helping, it could easily have taken them all week.

Since there were no paintbrushes for him to use, Jason cleverly supplied himself with a dish mop from the cupboard under the kitchen sink. Before anyone noticed what he was up to, he had smeared white paint on the shiny glass surface of the back door, on his red wagon, on the Pomeroys' Australian sheepdog, and somehow on both the top of his own head and the seat of his pants.

Alerted at last by Beth, who was keeping paint buckets filled and stirred for everyone, Peggy arrived on the scene. Calmly thanking heaven for the invention of paint that could be washed off, she spent the next half hour hosing everything down to its original color and condition. The sheepdog retreated to the barn in a huff, but Jason sailed through it with his twinkle undimmed and his dignity intact. Consoling himself for the loss of his paintbrush, he climbed on the picnic table and twiddled the knobs on the portable radio until Meg begged Beth to take it inside before they all went out of their minds.

By contrast with yesterday, it was a good day. Matt decided that working with his hands was the best way to keep the thinking parts of him occupied and out of danger. He was responsible for the top third of each wall, while Meg and Gary worked on the lower two-thirds at a safe distance from his splattering brush. Gary kept an anxious eye on him all day, anticipating his revenge, and Matt decided to let his good buddy spend a few days imagining more horrible forms of punishment than Matt could ever actually inflict on him, before he evened the score.

By Wednesday of that week they had finished the addition and one of the three A-frames. Hank Pomeroy had built the cabins in places where they blended in with their surroundings. Once stained, they looked as if they had grown there along with the trees. Plumbing and framing for a fourth cabin had been completed, but he had run out of time on that one.

"Be lucky if he gets to it before next fall," Art said. "Too bad. He's got so many people wanting to come, he could have filled it easy."

"For the first summer we've ever done this," Peggy said emphatically, "we're going to have enough people on our hands as it is. Be nice if he'd finish the bunkhouse, though."

The bunkhouse was still just a raised wooden floor with pipes jutting up through it. Looking at it, Meg was doubtful whether Will would be able to help Hank after all. He *was* good with his hands. She remembered with a qualm the complicated model ship he had assembled with painstaking precision, complete with rigging and sails, which she—with an unintentionally badly aimed pillow—had demolished the day after he had finished it. But model ships and life-size bunkhouses did not seem to have much in common.

He should be up here, though. It was too good a sum-

mer for him to miss. She decided to call him again that
night. After her first attempt to reach him on Sunday
evening, when no one had been home to answer the
phone, the time had somehow gotten away from her.

# 13

**I**f she had not already intended to call Will, the letter
waiting for her when they got got back to the Maitlands'
would have sent her to the phone at once. It was from
Carey.

> *Hi*, [it began cheerily]. *Hope you're having fun up
> there. We're not. Meg, please make Will come up
> there with you. I tried to tell him he could go and not
> worry about us anymore, but he won't listen. He just
> lies on his bed listening to his music, or spends the
> whole day and half the night out with Don or someone.
> Meg, he keeps fighting with Gwen. It's awful. Lew and
> I hate it. He's getting all gray and quiet like he was
> before, and we're scared he's going to get sick again.
> Please come back and get him. Tie him up or some-
> thing. Make him go. He won't listen to us, but he'll
> listen to you and Matt. Good luck.*
>   *Love, Carey*
> *P.S. Lew says to tell Matt the Angels are doing great.
> He's been to three games already, one with Sergeant
> Prado and two with Gwen.*

With Gwen? Meg thought, wondering what was going on down there. Gwen fighting with Will and going to baseball games with Lew? She could not picture either one somehow.

*P.P.S. All he talks about is baseball. I'm going crazy! Good thing my drama camp's in two more weeks.*

Meg made a collect call immediately. The phone was answered by Lew, who hemmed and hawed about accepting the charges in his British butler's accent until Meg bellowed over the operator's polite twang, "Lew, quit fooling around and say yes! I need to talk to Will."

Instantly serious, Lew went off to get Will before Meg could even ask him how the Angels were doing.

Will's sudden deep growl startled her. "Hullo?"

"Hi. It's me. How are things?"

"So-so," Will said. "Everything's under control."

Oh it is, is it? Meg thought, but there was no point in making him defensive. "Good. Has Mr. Pomeroy called yet?"

"Some guy called and left a message while I was out. I thought it was something to do with school. Why? Who is he?"

"He's your boss for the summer. Listen, Will, if Lew and Carey don't need you, this man really does. He's desperate. When we told him you weren't coming, he practically had a heart attack. He really was counting on you. I felt bad about letting him down. And it really is work building things—no horses, I swear. He wants your help so badly, he says he'll even pay your way up here. Think about it, Will, please? We're having a great time. You'll love it."

Will was silent for a long time. Then she heard him sigh. "I have been thinking about it. I was going to call you at the end of this week." He paused again, and Meg began mentally scratching around for some other arguments to bombard him with. "Are you sure he wants somebody who doesn't know from nothing about building houses?"

"Positive," Meg said, crossing her fingers.

"I guess I'll come, then. I'm not doing any good around here. Everyone wants me to leave. Even Carey." He laughed, but Meg did not like the humorless sound of it.

"Will, do you mean it?"

"Yeah, I guess so. Have blender, will travel. I'm practically on my way."

"Call Mr. Pomeroy back fast. If he hasn't already given up on you, he'll figure out a way to get you here."

"Okay. Tell Matt hi . . . and Gary. I guess I'll see you guys soon."

"Great! Perfect! Will," said Meg in a burst of genuine relief and pleasure, "you've made my day!"

"Golly gee," said Will, his sense of humor not quite extinguished after all, and she hung up on him.

The prospect of Will joining them put everyone in a good mood and during supper sparked off another game of Remember-the-Time-When. . . ? This time, though, they focused on the week when Gary had spent his spring vacation in L.A. a year ago. For good reasons most of his adventures had never been shared with his parents.

Matt told all, avenging himself on his good buddy with a fiendish memory for detail that had Aunt Belle weeping tears of anguished laughter and Uncle Frank still chuckling long after they left the table. The only one who did not join in the general hilarity was Susan. Her sullen silence created a space around her that no one wanted to enter uninvited.

With each passing day Susan had become more miserable and resentful. At night the sound of her crying reminded Meg painfully of the days after her own mother had died. She had listened to Carey sobbing in her room next door until one night she had gone in and talked to her little sister about the mother they both missed so badly. Both of them had felt better after that, and if Carey had cried any more, she had managed to hide it from the rest of them.

But Meg's attempts to make friends with Susan were bluntly rejected. Aunt Belle, who seemed to miss very little that went on in her family, told Meg to wait awhile and be patient. It was something, she thought, for Susan and Matt to work out between them, and she would be surprised if Matt let it continue for long without doing something about it.

Aunt Belle was right. Later that same night when Matt, Meg, and Gary were playing cards, they needed a fourth. "Hey, Sooz," Matt said, "I need a partner. Want to play?"

Sending him a look of hate and fury, Susan stormed out through the kitchen, slamming the screen door behind her.

Matt fiddled with the deck in his hands for a minute, then placed them neatly in front of Gary. "You deal," he said. "I'll be back in a minute." After a pause Gary and Meg began a mindless game of Pounce to fill in the time until he returned.

Matt was coming out the back door when he heard the thump of Susan's feet as she jumped off the porch. Knowing it wouldn't stop her, he did not waste time calling her name but took a flying leap off the porch himself, catching up with her before she reached the barn and grabbing first one arm and then the other as she fought him furiously.

"Quit it!" she shouted, kicking and scratching. "Let me go!"

He carried her inside the barn instead and slid the big door shut behind them so she couldn't run away again. With the door shut, the barn was almost black inside, and he knew from experience that some things are more easily talked about in darkness. "If I let you go, will you calm down and talk to me?" he said.

"No! I'm not talking to you! I hate you! You can't make me stay in here. *Mom!* Let me go, you big—"

"Not until you promise me you'll talk. I'm not going to go on living with your family if you're going to be storming around the house all the time refusing to talk to me."

"Good! Don't stay, then! I don't want you around here anyway. I'll be *glad* if you go!"

This was getting them nowhere. He knew she hated him, and he knew why. He wanted her to tell him herself, to get it out where they could talk about it. "You didn't used to hate me. We used to be pretty good friends. What happened?"

What happened, McKendrick, his inner voice told him harshly, is that you got Katie killed. Sooz was Katie's best friend. Why shouldn't she hate you? A lot of people do, and she's got more right than any of them.

Suddenly he did not have the stomach for this conversation after all. To hell with it. Next week he'd be over at the Pomeroys', and without him around all the time Susan could get herself back to normal. He released her abruptly and started for the door, but Susan's furious outburst stopped him.

"What happened? *What happened?* You know what happened! You took Katie away and left her in that terrible place when you knew she hated the dark, and she got killed. That's what happened. And then you come back here, and you laugh and fool around with Gary and make stupid jokes about everything as if what happened doesn't matter! As if you don't even care! I hate you! I hate you! I wish *you* were dead!"

She flew at him, punching and kicking while he stood silent and unmoving, making no attempt to fend her off. In the darkness he closed his eyes, guilt and remorse blazing through him again as unbearable and devastating as if it were only a moment ago that Sheriff Hensley had woken him up to tell him his mom and dad had died in a car crash, and the nightmare had begun. . . .

He was back in the Maitlands' kitchen, yelling at Aunt Belle and Uncle Frank—begging them not to send Katie away. . . .

He was back in the locker room—doors crashing shut around them, making what Gary had just told him hard to hear, harder to believe. "They're sending Katie to the deaf school, Gare? Your mom and dad? But they can't. She doesn't want to go. I told them I won't let them. Didn't they believe me?"

He was back on the bus to Boise—sick and scared and furious. Why? Why hadn't they understood? He and Katie needed each other. It had been rough losing their mom and dad; it was too soon to lose each other too. Katie beside him, punching him to get his attention, pointing at things outside the window she wanted him to see. Vibrating with excitement, as if they were having a big adventure instead of running away from a situation they couldn't handle, heading for L.A. and something better, or worse. . . ?

He was hitchhiking from Boise again—remembering the cold, the wet, the frustration of being ignored. The people who stopped—some nice, some too nosy. The weirdo who drove the last stretch to L.A. and left them standing on the corner in the bleak warehouse district. The relentless hunger as his wallet flattened to absolute emptiness. Katie—eager, determined, tugging at his hand to get him moving, finding the door ajar and a place to sleep inside the condemned and vandalized old theater.

He was back in the morning of that last terrible day— "It will be a long walk, Kat. Maybe all day. I can't count on finding a job right away. Maybe you should wait here." Katie clenching her fists, breathing too fast, scared but not admitting it. He knew the signs. He gave in, told her to come. She knew him too, knew he wouldn't have asked if he didn't have a reason. "Okay. I stay here. Bring me hot dogs when you come back." Positive he could do anything.

He was walking again, looking for Help Wanted signs, asking, being turned down. Walking, and looking, and asking. Walking . . . walking . . . Back to the theater empty handed. Scared and hungry. So hungry he hurt. Fighting off the two guys who came after him. Relieved to find out they were cops. Walking out of police headquarters while no one was watching. Back to the Palace Theater. Searching frantically in the dark. Where was she? Where was she . . . ?

He was back in the morgue, with the numbered drawers. One of them opened. The sheet whipped away from the small body. He couldn't believe it. Didn't want to believe it . . .

*Katie . . . oh God. I never should have left you there alone. . . .*

"Sooz?" he said slowly after a long, long time. She had stopped hitting him and retreated to the hay bale in front of Cricket's stall. He could tell where she was by her hiccuping sobs. "If I tell you something—something I've never told anyone else—will you keep it a secret?" She did not answer, but her crying was no longer so violent and uncontrolled. She could hear him at least.

He lowered himself onto another hay bale across from her and leaned back against the stall door. Fixing his eyes on a thin streak of moonlight coming through a crack high on the opposite wall, he drew in a shuddering breath and let it out again slowly before beginning, haltingly, to try to make her understand.

"You're right . . . about what I did. And you're right about . . . about what happened. It was my fault. I left her there alone, and because of that she died." He had to take another long breath. "But you're wrong about one thing, Sooz. I do care. There's no way I can tell you how . . . how much it hurts. Knowing I killed her. Knowing she's dead . . ." Tears welled up and slid coolly down his hot skin. "But I care. I want her back as badly as you do. I want her growing up . . . making friends . . . taking care of her animals. All those things she was going to do . . . she was meant to do, if only . . . if only I hadn't— Oh God!'' He was crying now himself, breathing raggedly, swallowing hard, trying to get himself under control.

The narrow bale rocked slightly. He could feel Susan's thin body trembling against his. Swiping futilely at his tears, he dropped an arm across her shoulders.

Gradually she relaxed against him. "I'm sorry," she whispered. "I'm sorry, Matt, I'm sorry."

"Don't," he said quickly. "Don't. It's okay. I'm glad we got it all . . . out. But, Sooz, you see why I can't talk about it . . . tell people how I feel?" She didn't answer, forcing him to go on. "If I let it show all the time, it would be worse. A lot worse. Me breaking down. Everybody telling me they're sorry. I couldn't . . . I couldn't stand that either. You see what I mean?

"Things happen sometimes. They hurt so much, you think you can't take it. You want to die. But you don't. You go on living. You have to let other people live too, Sooz. You can't always be reminding them you hurt like hell, making them feel sorry for you. It helps, makes it easier, if you've got other people around to, you know, care about, joke around about with . . . to belong to. It helps.''

Giving her a small squeeze, he tried to make his voice lighter. "So now you know my secret. I have to trust you not to tell anyone else about it, either. Okay?"

"Not even Mom?"

"Not her, not anybody. Not even yourself. Just forget it. Go on living.''

"I can't forget. But I won't keep reminding you either,'' she added quickly as she felt him stiffen. "Not even when it hurts like hell."

"Oh lord," Matt groaned. "Don't let your dad hear you talking like that. He'll wash your mouth out with soap.''

She giggled. "I'll tell him you told it to me. Remember that time you and Gary were saying bad words in your foxhole, and I heard you and went and asked Mom what they meant?''

"Do I remember? Boy, were you a little brat! You wrote them all in Katie's notebook, and she asked *my* mom what they meant. They were spelled pretty weirdly, but Mom knew what they were, all right. I must have brushed my teeth about twenty times before I got the taste of soap out of my mouth.''

They sat together on the bale for a long time, not saying much, just keeping each other company and thinking their own thoughts. When they finally rolled the door back, it was nearly as black outside as it was in, except for the sky—as star-splashed as if Jason had been at work with his dish mop and the leftover paint from the addition. In L.A. for too long, Matt had forgotten how fantastic the Craigie night sky was. As he looked up at it, his pupils contracted slightly as if he were staring into a lighted room. For a moment he could not see through the velvety darkness ahead.

"Everyone's gone to bed," Susan whispered. Only Poor Boy was up, pushing his cold nose into Matt's free hand and whining anxiously as they approached the darkened house. "Good night, Matt.''

" 'Night, Sooz,'' he said softly. Stooping, he fumbled his way into the stuffy tent and felt his way to his cot. His groping fingers located his sleeping bag and discovered it had been rendered useless by what felt like a hundred feet of clothesline and at least a thousand knots. Gary. Getting revenge for Matt's getting revenge on him at supper tonight.

Protesting violently that he had not done it, that Meg must have done it, that never in a million years would he waste his precious time and energy on such a stupid stunt—Gary was wrestled out of his bag by a stronger and more determined Matt, and left muttering threats and curses and fumbling with the knots in the dark. Matt zipped himself comfortably into Gary's warm bag and fell asleep with uncharacteristic ease.

But sleep was his enemy, stripping away his waking defenses against remembering and pursuing him through dream after dream with the memories he could not bury deep enough to kill.

# 14

*M*att woke in blackness, fighting off an attacker. Striking out with wild sweeping blows, he connected and heard his assailant grunt, but something heavy fell across his chest. His flailing arms were caught and pinned to his sides, and the shouting voice finally got through to him.

"Matt, for crying out loud, wake up!"

He stopped struggling instantly. "Gare?"

"Who did you think it was, you jerk? Matt, are you okay? You've been yelling for your dad and screaming "No, no!' and thrashing around like you had snakes in your bag."

Another nightmare. Oh lord . . . he ought to have expected that. They were bad enough in L.A., but coming back here . . . he should have been ready for them. "Sorry, Gare," he said hoarsely. "Just a lousy dream, I guess. Did I do any damage?"

Silence. Gary was counting his wounds. "Just a couple of sore ribs and a fat lip is all. And scared out of my skin. What was the dream about?"

"Nothing. I don't remember."

"Sure you don't. Come on, Matt. Nobody forgets a nightmare that fast. Spit it out, old buddy. You know what Mom says—if you tell someone about a lousy dream, it won't come back and haunt you any—"

"Forget it, I said!"

While Gary rustled around getting back into his sleeping bag Matt tried to steady his violent breathing, slow down his hammering pulse. It had been a bad dream, one of his worst. He had dreamed one like it before, at the beginning of the week.

"Listen, Matt." Gary's quiet voice came out of the blackness beside his head. "This is the second one you've had since you've been back. At the rate of two every five days we'll all be basket cases by the end of the summer. They aren't your own private nightmares anymore, old buddy. As long as I'm sharing sleeping accommodations with you, they're going to be mine and Will's too, when he gets here. And if you yell like you did tonight, you're going to have Mom and Dad and probably Susan and Meg out here too. Is that what you want?" They both knew the answer. "Okay, then. If you can think of a better way to get them out and off your mind, okay. Otherwise it's Mom's old remedy. Just forget I'm here," he added. "I'll be asleep in five minutes anyway. Tell it to Poor Boy."

Matt gave him a lot longer than five minutes, but he knew Gary was right. He had to get rid of these lousy dreams somehow. Aunt Belle's remedy was probably worth a try, especially after he had just proved to Susan that she'd feel better if she talked things over and got them out in the open. It was easier said than done. Reaching under the sagging cot, he wound his fingers in Boy's shaggy coat to give himself the comfort and courage he needed. Finally, unable to postpone the moment any longer, he began.

"It was a dream, Boy . . . about the time I got lost in the hills. I was pretty small . . . five or six. In the dream I'm a little kid again. Scared. Yelling for Dad. Wanting him to find me. Then I hear him far away, calling me.

He's riding Tripoli, and I can hear them coming closer, crashing through the brush. He stops, yelling my name, and I yell back. I'm so glad to hear him, I can't wait for him to get to me. I start running toward the noise. And then . . ." He stopped, the dream image vivid and horrible. He could not bring himself to put it into words.

"Say it," came the whispered command.

"And then . . . then they break through the trees, out into the clearing where I am, and they're . . . Oh God . . . Dad and Tripoli, they're not . . . They're both . . . dead. Just bones and . . . and skulls."

The musty, cobwebby smell of the canvas tent, the shrill sounds of tiny night creatures outside, Boy snuffling and whimpering under the cot as he chased rabbits in his sleep—all of them were smells and sounds from his past, familiar and comforting. For a long time Matt lay staring into the dark, one hand kneading Boy's rough fur; the other fist clenched and flung over his face. He thought Gary was asleep until he heard his breath released in a long sigh.

"Matt?"

"Mmm?" he grunted, pretending to be almost asleep himself. He had done all the talking about this he was going to do.

"You know what I remember about your dad?" Matt was silent, not wanting this either. Gary went on anyway—try and stop old Gare when he had his mind set on doing something. "He was so big—so tall, you know? Like a real giant. When we were little kids, not even up to his belt buckle, I used to tilt my head back to look at him, and all I could see was his nose and the scar under his chin. Unless he was talking to me. Remember how he used to go down on one knee so we could look him in the eye?"

Matt remembered. He fought it, but his father's face hung there now in front of him—the black shaggy eyebrows, the dark deep-set eyes and laughing mouth, the tiny scar under his chin, and the mustache he'd cultivated until Katie's deafness was discovered. He'd shaved it off so she could see his lips, and it had taken one whole summer for his upper lip to tan the same color as the rest of his face. . . .

"You remember the way he used to rest his hands on your shoulders and look at you without saying anything?" Gary was saying. "Just wait for you to tell him what had happened?"

"Yeah."

"That's what I remember most about him—feeling his big hands on my shoulders and coming through them a kind of vibration, like guitar strings. As if I was feeling how he felt about me, you know?"

"Yeah, I know."

"Sometimes it felt like he was laughing. You couldn't tell by looking at his face, but you could feel it coming through his arms and hands."

"And when he was . . . not mad, exactly," Matt went on slowly. "He never really got mad, but . . . well, disappointed maybe. When we had done something really stupid or dangerous, you could tell because nothing came through. I hated that. Like he had cut himself off from me, not wanting to share himself for a minute or touch me, even though his hands were on my shoulders."

"Yeah." Gary was quiet for a while, and Matt thought with relief that he was through. But he wasn't. Not quite. "He was a great guy, Matt. You were lucky to have him."

"Gare—!"

"I know, I know. Enough said. Don't worry, I'm asleep already. Have been for hours."

They were both silent then, but neither one slept for a long time.

**15**

*B*y Saturday morning they were through with the painting and had gotten a good start on sorting and cleaning the tack. They were sitting around outside the barn door, trying to assemble some complete bridles from the miscellaneous pieces they'd salvaged from the pile dumped in the dusty tack room, and keeping an eye on Jason, who was doing some fancy assembling of his own, when they heard a car door slam. A moment later a cheerful voice called out, "Hi, Jase, what are you doing?"

Meg glanced up and saw Matt's pleased grin of recognition before she turned herself to look at the visitor. A girl about her own age, but taller and rounder with straight dark hair in bangs and a ponytail. A turned-up nose and a couple of crooked front teeth gave her a decidedly tomboyish air.

"Well, hey, Marcie! Great to see you!" Matt said, and there was no doubting that he meant it.

Meg felt an ominous stirring inside her. Something sharp and painful was waking for the first time.

"Hi, Matt," said Marcie, obviously equally glad to see him. "I heard you were coming back, but I thought it might be one of Gary's whoppers."

"Would I joke about a thing like that?" Gary said indignantly.

"You'd joke about anything," Marcie said. "I stopped believing a word you said after you promised

93

that rubbing those shiny green leaves all over my face would get rid of my freckles.''

"Oh hey, that's not fair," Gary protested. "I just got the wrong kind of leaves, that's all."

"And I got poison oak like I've never had it before or since."

"Well, so did I."

The three of them grinned at each other. Suddenly Meg felt excluded, out of place. She was a stranger here, and so was the Matt McKendrick she had known so well back in Los Angeles. The Matt who was standing here now—in dusty boots, faded jeans, and a blue denim work shirt; sweat sticking his hair in dark points to his tanned skin, and a pair of reins draped loosely around his neck; sharing nearly sixteen years' worth of memories she had no part in—this was Craigie's Matt. Gary's and Marcie's Matt. Someone she didn't know. For the second time since they'd arrived—not sure what she was afraid of—she wished fleetingly that she could go home and take him with her.

"Oh hey!" Matt suddenly remembered her. "Marcie, this is Meg. Meg, meet Marcie Trasker, the Third Musketeer. You haven't heard as much about her yet, but *she* was the one who got us into most of those predicaments we're so famous for."

Oh lord . . . worse and worse. Why couldn't she have been dull and mousy? "Hi," Meg said, firmly pulling herself together. "I guess you and I are going to be partners on KP duty this summer."

"You're working here too?" Matt said. "Hey, that's great! Things are really looking up. Now, if I can just persuade the guy who's working the horses with me to get lost, maybe—"

"The guy? Don't you know who it is?" Marcie shot a quick look at Gary.

"I don't know either," he said hastily. "Don't look at me."

"I know it's a she," Meg put in, "but I don't know her name."

"A she?" Matt reacted exactly the way Meg had to the news. "Then why . . . ? I thought, when Hank Pomeroy told us the fourth person said it had to be horses or nothing, that it must be a guy. Meg was supposed to have that job, Marcie, and this girl talked Hank Pomeroy into giving it to her instead. Blackmailed him. Horses or nothing! Wait till I— Who is she?" he demanded.

Marcie looked unhappy. "Matt, look, don't get so mad. Things are different now. She probably didn't know—"

"Who is it?"

Marcie seemed so uncomfortable that Meg, with some idea of diverting Matt from this relentless interrogation, gave him the rest of what she knew. "Hank said she's the local barrel-racing champion. Does that ring any—"

"Lisa!" Matt and Gary exploded together. Matt kept going. "Anyone but her! I might have known. Whatever-Lisa-Wants-Lisa-Gets Lomax." He drove one fist furiously into the palm of the other hand. "Well, two can play at this game. I'm not spending the summer trying to work with that spoiled— I'm telling Mr. Hank Pomeroy that it's Meg on the horses, or he can find someone to take my place."

"Matt, for heaven's sake, relax," Meg said irritably. "We've been all over this before, and there's nothing we can do about it. I'm doing something I don't like, with someone I do," she added, grinning at Marcie, "and you're doing something you love with someone you hate. If that's the way it is, we can live with it."

She had barely finished delivering this stirring speech, which she was not entirely sure she believed herself, when she became aware of someone standing not fifty feet away in the open doorway of the addition, listening to their conversation. It was not Peggy Pomeroy.

Meg's mouth fell open slightly. She blinked. The other

three turned to see what she was staring at, and as if on cue, the girl came down the steps toward them like Scarlett O'Hara making a grand entrance.

"Lisa!" Matt hissed angrily, seeing the spoiler of Meg's summer, the spoiler of many moments in the past, the spoiled only daughter of a wealthy Craigie family, who had never been told no in her life.

"Lisa?" Meg echoed feebly, and her heart really sank. Lisa had to be the most beautiful girl she had ever seen. Oh lord, she thought, and she was only half joking, it's *not* fair!

Lisa was about five feet two inches of slim graceful elegance. Her hair, a natural blond so light it shimmered like silver in the sun, was feathered back on the sides from a center part and fell lightly over her shoulders the way Meg's might have done if she could have persuaded her ridiculous curls to lie down and die. Her dark blue eyes were framed in thick black lashes, and her lightly tanned skin had a naturally healthy glow. *Her* nose never turns red and peels in the sun, Meg thought glumly. The only makeup she was wearing was a pale pink lipstick.

"Hi," she said coolly to Matt, who was towering over her, scowling darkly and looking anything but glad to see her. "Welcome back."

"What the hell do you think you're doing?" he demanded. "Blackmailing Hank Pomeroy into giving you Meg's job!"

"Meg's job?" She glanced at Meg, appraising and dismissing her as no threat. Meg had been given that look by the class beauties before. "Was it your job? I'm sorry. He asked me what I wanted to do, and I told him."

"Horses or nothing!" Matt stormed. "That's what you told him. Who do you think you are, laying down ultimatums? Meg came up here this summer to work with the horses and get away from the cooking-and-cleaning bit she's been stuck with for two years at home. The job's hers. You can work in the house.''

If Matt wants Lisa to change her mind, thought Meg—watching Lisa's mouth tighten and the blue eyes darken dangerously—then he's going about it the wrong way. You don't tell this girl what to do.

"I'm doing the horses," Lisa said with a remote, infuriating smile. "Why don't you work in the house and let Meg have your job if you don't like the arrangements? Oh, by the way," she added, having silenced him completely, "Mr. Pomeroy wants us all inside to go over the schedules." She preceded them across the yard, a small but striking figure in immaculate pale blue jeans, fitted western-style shirt, and well-worn but shiny boots.

Meg watched her go, feeling scruffy and adolescent in a pair of Will's outgrown jeans, a floppy T-shirt, and her shaggy pony tail. She also felt unsteady, as if the earth had shifted under her feet. A subtle change had just occurred in the way she thought about herself and Matt.

In the last two years Matt had become as close a member of their family as if they, like the Ryders, had formally adopted him. He had started off as Will's friend and rapidly filled some major gaps in everyone's lives. Lew's nickname for him, Big Bro, was used by all of them as a kind of accolade in recognition of his special status.

She and Matt had gone out alone now and then—most memorably to the senior prom—but most of the time they'd done things together with the whole family. She hadn't thought of him as ''hers''—the other three would never have let her get away with it—and it hadn't bothered her when he'd double-dated with Will a few times. As far as she knew, it hadn't bothered him when she went out with other guys either. The possibility of losing him to someone else had never occurred to her.

But that was L.A., and this was Craigie. The rules had changed. First Marcie and now Lisa . . . Suddenly anything was possible, and she was surprised at the strength of feelings she didn't know she had. As she followed the others into the addition she was wondering gloomily if taking more time over her appearance would make any difference. Probably not. Matt had seen her at her worst too many times to be dazzled now.

# 16

**A**rt and Peggy Pomeroy were already seated at the long table when they trooped in. Everyone was given a pencil and a small pad to take notes on, and Art proceeded to give them an outline of the weekly schedule.

"Guests arrive Sunday afternoon each week," he said. "Hank or I will meet the plane in Boise. A couple of times one of you may have to come along in Peggy's wagon to bring back the extra guests. They'll unpack, have supper with us, and after supper we'll all show 'em around, give 'em an idea of what they can do and where things are.

"Monday—and this is where you start taking notes," he added as he saw Meg doodling horse heads on her pad. "Breakfast at eight o'clock sharp. Trail and arena riding from ten to one, with a box lunch for the trail riders. Afternoon they can swim, hike, help out around the ranch. Anyone thinks they need to go to town—one of you can take them. You're going to have to sort all this out yourselves—who's going to be responsible for the odd jobs each day—but you can do that later.

"Supper's at seven every night. Monday, after supper, we'll have a hayride. Any of you play guitar?"

There was a general shaking of heads. Gary, unexpectedly, nodded.

"You want to play for us, then? Three . . . maybe four nights a week? We'll pay you."

"Sure, thanks," Gary was obviously delighted to have an excuse to hang around the ranch with the rest of them.

"Good. Okay now, Tuesday. Breakfast trail ride—means a lot of work for everybody. Home by eleven. Then you take everyone who wants to go to the lake for the day. They can fish, water-ski, rent boats, sail or whatever. After supper the kids can play games, the adults do whatever they want.

"Wednesday—expedition day. Take 'em rafting on the Salmon River. Anyone who stays home entertains themselves. After supper a campfire. Thursday and Friday will be a repeat of Monday—trail and arena riding, box lunch, swimming . . . all that—except that Friday night we'll barbecue supper and have a last campfire. Thursday night they can go into town for the square dance or a movie.

"Saturday morning the guests leave for Boise before noon. You clean up, get things ready for the next group, and the rest of the time until Sunday afternoon is yours." Art leaned back in his chair and surveyed them expectantly, waiting for some reaction.

"Sounds . . . busy," Meg said finally. "I'm still not clear on what Marcie and I are supposed to be doing, though."

"We'll go over that together in a minute," Peggy promised, "when Art and the other two go down to see about the horses."

No one had any other questions, so they split up. Gary volunteered to continue the tack-matching game with Beth and Jason while Meg and Marcie went with Peggy to the nearest cabin to see what needed doing in all three before they were ready for occupancy.

Still fuming over Lisa's high-handed attitude, Matt followed her and Art down the road toward the lower barn and the corrals where they kept the horses. They were halfway there when he saw the horse. Big, gleaming black—even from this distance he knew who it was. But it had not been there yesterday.

"Where did that black horse come from?" he said to Art. "The big one in the near corral?"

"Ask Lisa. She rode him over this morning."

"You?" Matt stopped short. "He's yours? That's the Black—my old horse. Where'd you get him?"

"At the auction," she said. Her voice was warmer, without the cutting edge it had had before, but Matt did not notice.

The auction, he was thinking. Where everything his family ever owned had been sold. Everything. All he had left was the money that was going to help him get through college. And Lisa—who always got anything she wanted—Lisa had the Black.

"You haven't changed, have you?" he said bitterly. "Still the sweet, lovable kid you always were. Not only did you grab Meg's job, which means she's stuck in the kitchen and I'm stuck with you, but you're going to let me watch you ride my horse all summer, and probably ruin him in the process!"

Lisa started to say something sharp in reply, remembered Art, and changed her mind. Whirling, she strode off ahead of them, slashing at the blue camas growing alongside the road with the quirt in her hand.

"Mr. Pomeroy?" Matt was determined to give it one last try, but the man beat him to it and silenced him on the subject for good.

"It's Art," he said. "Just Art. Listen now, Matt. Hank told me about the trouble over the jobs, and I'm real sorry about the mix-up. But while the guests are here, you're going to have to put a good face on the situation. Nothing kills enthusiasm for a return visit faster than a lot of bickering and backstabbing by the people running the place. If there are bad feelings between you two, either get 'em out in the open and get rid of them now, or bury 'em too deep for anyone else to guess they're there. Got it?''

Matt swallowed. Art was right. This was a private feud between him and Lisa. It went back a long way, and he had no right to let it interfere with a job he was being paid to do. "Right," he said gruffly. They did not speak again until they ducked through the fence and went to inspect the horses.

There were sixteen horses and a Shetland pony, besides the Black and Lisa's quarterhorse, Good-bye Charley, which she had brought over as well. Planning to put on a real show for the guests, Matt thought bitterly. Art had four more horses for his own use in an adjoining corral. Two of them worked to harness and could pull the wagon for the hayrides, and the other two were his own and Peggy's. Matt would have to pick one of the sixteen for himself to use regularly, and he and Art were discussing the horses' good and bad points when Lisa broke in.

"Matt?"

Just in time he softened his tone. "What?"

"You can use the Black. I—"

"No, I don't want him. He's yours now. Thanks anyway," he added for Art's benefit. He felt more like hitting her. Once, he almost had.

On a twenty-mile endurance ride she had refused to ease up on her straining horse. When Matt grabbed the reins from her and brought both of their horses to a halt, she had hit him with her quirt. The slash across his neck had hurt, and when she hit him again, he wrenched it from her hand and nearly hit her back. Instead he had hurled the quirt as far as possible into the scrub and dragged her, screaming and scratching, off her horse. Tying a rope around her waist, he had taken her and her exhausted horse home again, the two of them walking all the way.

Something in his expression must have revealed his thoughts. Giving him a look that said plainly, *I hate you too*, Lisa turned her gaze back to the horses while Art was finishing up his commentary. He left them shortly afterward with a promise to help with the trail clearing, but he was a working man himself and the job of running the ranch came first. They would have to do most of the extra work themselves.

Ten of the horses had come with their own tack. Matt and Lisa started with those first, riding them in the corral to see what their dispositions and their gaits were like. Once they had the trails cleared, they could take the horses out on them and see how they behaved.

"You haven't forgotten much," Lisa said while they were exchanging the first pair of horses and raising and lowering stirrups.

Matt shrugged. "I've been riding in L.A.," he said, checking the cinch and swinging into the saddle.

"What's it like in the big city for a boy from the country?"

Everything she said had such a sarcastic edge to it, he thought, as if she were slicing him into little pieces. He had no interest in making polite small talk. "Okay, I guess."

"Will you stay? There, I mean?"

"Where else would I go?" he said irritably. What business was it of hers? "Back here?"

"You're here now, aren't you?"

He could not deny that, so he said nothing, urging the pinto he was riding into a jog and then a lope. In an arena, at least, this horse seemed responsive and reliable. Too bad he was so small—not much over thirteen hands.

They marked each halter with the horse's name and wrote the names above the saddle racks as well to make it easier to match them up every morning. Saddling up two more, they each rode one for five minutes, then swapped mounts again. Both of these were plodders, the kind who would go exactly where the other horses went because it would mean the least expenditure of energy on their parts. Okay for nervous adults or kids with more enthusiasm than sense, they decided.

While they were saddling up the third pair, Meg and Marcie drove by on their way into town for more cabin-cleaning supplies and stopped for a moment to watch.

Meg eyed the motley collection milling around the corral. "Which horse are you going to be using, Matt?" she asked, and Matt thought how typical it was of her that she could so easily put herself in his place and ask the question uppermost in his mind—something Lisa Lomax would never learn to do in a million years. Meg whistled suddenly, softly and admiringly. "How about that one?" she said.

He knew without looking which one she had chosen for him. Under any other circumstances he would have chosen that one himself.

"He's Lisa's," he said shortly.

"Matt could use him if he wanted to," Lisa said mockingly, "but he's too proud. He can't take anything from me."

You are so right! Matt thought savagely, tightening the cinch so hard that the horse he was saddling grunted and swung its head around to take a bite out of his arm. "Watch it, you!" he growled, loosening and tightening the cinch several times to see if the horse, a nondescript roan, had a habit of nipping. But, treated with the proper courtesy, the roan returned the favor. Matt rode him without further incident. This horse might be bony and ugly, but he had nice movements, and he was plenty big enough—sixteen hands at least.

Watching him from a distance while Lisa was working him out, Matt decided that he and the roan would make a good pair. He was feeling kind of bony and ugly himself at this point. Tomorrow he'd take him out on the trail first thing and see how he—

The clangor of a bell shattered the stillness of the valley, shattered his absorption with the horses, took him back in time with a jolt that for an instant made the world around him turn gray.

*Come home*, that bell had said for eleven years of his life. *It's time for lunch . . . time for supper . . . time to go to town. Come home, I need you.*

For eleven years, whenever he had heard that bell, he had dropped everything and come. No matter what stupid mistake he had made during the day that he was going to have to face up to, no matter what important job he was doing that he wanted to finish—when he heard that bell, he went home. Otherwise his dad would have thought he couldn't come—that he was hurt or lost somewhere—and would have left the ranch and the hungry livestock and ridden all night and all day until he found him.

"Matt?" He did not recognize the voice or the face for a second. Lisa was staring at him anxiously. "Do you feel all right? You look terrible. Too much sun probably. You should wear a—"

"Lunchtime," he said curtly, turning his back on her and her unwanted concern by dismounting and rapidly removing saddle and bridle from his mount.

He did not offer to help her with the roan, who was too big for her to unsaddle easily, but set off at a rapid jog for the house, using the time alone to pull himself together. For the rest of the afternoon he worked on the horses with a fierce concentration that invited nothing but the most essential conversation from his partner, who retaliated by retreating behind a brisk, businesslike facade herself. Each of them had tried out every horse in the string by the time Lisa had to leave for home.

She rode off on Charley, leaving the Black behind. Matt was glad to see her straight back and shining hair gradually disappearing in the shadows under the trees across the valley as she took the shortcut over the ridge. Distributing flakes of hay and topping off the water trough for the trail mounts, he was climbing through the fence on his way to find Meg and Marcie and Gary when he was stopped by a snort and a low nicker.

# 17

**A**ll afternoon he had kept his mind fixed on the job he was being paid to do, refusing to acknowledge or even think about the presence of the Black in the adjoining corral. After two years the horse was not going to remember him. But he remembered the Black. He remembered every scar, every swirling cowlick, every ticklish place on his shining hide, and every way he had of responding to the person who rode him.

Matt glanced over his shoulder. Lisa was out of sight. He reached out and rubbed the hollow place under the Black's hard cheekbones. "Hey, old buddy," he crooned softly. "Remember me? Had some good times together, didn't we? How's she been treating you?"

Not bad by the look of him. Not an ounce of excess fat on him, and his coat so shiny and well groomed, he looked like a candidate for the Grand National. It did not occur to Matt that Lisa might have been taking some trouble over the Black for his sake. He felt only grudging admiration for her skill at handling horses until, as his gaze swept over the Black's lonely corral, he realized that Lisa had left without feeding or watering her horse.

Swearing furiously, he ripped into another bale of hay as if it were Lisa herself. "That spoiled little—! A lot she cares about your comfort or your condition. I should have known she wasn't responsible for the way you look." By the time he was heading up the road toward the house, the sense of satisfaction brought on by the productive afternoon was gone and he had worked himself into a royal rage.

The other three were sitting at one of the picnic tables, drinking some of Peggy's home-brewed iced tea. Meg took one look at him and sighed audibly. "Watch out, everybody—Big Chief Thunder Cloud is on the warpath again."

"Knock it off, Meg," he growled.

She ignored the warning. "If you're going to look like that for the rest of the summer, I *am* going home. I'm going to be too tired to fight with you every night, and anyway, Marcie and I are having fun already. On second thought, why don't you go home instead?"

Matt looked into her eyes—those incredible eyes that could change from green to blue depending on what she was wearing, and sometimes on her mood. Right now they were green and sending out angry sparks, but he knew that the instant he let his own grin break out, she would relax the thin, disapproving line she had made with her mouth and grin back at him.

*How many times does she have to tell you, you self-centered creep? If she can live with a job she hates, you can live with a person you hate. Forget Lisa. Don't let her ruin Meg's summer any more than she already has.*

The corners of Meg's mouth were twitching. He tried to hang on to his scowl and make her break up first, but she always outlasted him, and this time was no exception.

"Did anyone ever tell you you'd make a terrific teacher?" he said mischievously, appealing to Gary and Marcie for support. "Remember old Twitchy in kindergarten? What a witch! She had that same grim gray line for a mouth and those beady glaring eyes. Had us all scared out of our minds—poor little kids.''

"Not you," Gary countered while Meg was looking around for something to stuff in Matt's mouth and silence him permanently. "She kept putting you down and you kept popping right back up again. That day you kicked her, I thought she was going to kill you for sure!"

"I remember that," said Marcie. "I was so scared, I sneaked into the big girls' bathroom and cried for the whole recess. I was sure she was the Wicked Witch of the West, and when we came back in she was going to have turned you into one of those horrible flying monkeys."

"Yeah," Gary agreed. "But there he was—big as life, not a mark on him, head down on his crossed arms. That was her 'thinking it over' position, wasn't it? You couldn't sit up again until you were ready to say you were sorry."

"That's right," Matt said. "I wish I could say I never gave in to her, but I couldn't stand hearing all of you whispering and rustling around. I had to look up, and she got me . . . *zap!* The old bag. She still there?"

"She sure is."

"Poor Beth gets her next year." Marcie sighed. "There ought to be a law."

"Meg?" Peggy Pomeroy was standing in the opened door. "Oh, there you are. Hank just called. He's got all kinds of crises brewing and won't be up until the end of next week. He asked me to tell you that it's all settled, though, and he'll be bringing Will with him. I told him what you've all accomplished, and he's really pleased." She glanced back into the kitchen before continuing. "Art says that starting tomorrow you'll be clearing trails and getting the horses settled down and ready for riding. You're all planning to move over here permanently tomorrow night, aren't you?"

They looked at each other, and Meg asked the question for everyone. "Gary and Marcie too?"

"Of course, if your families don't mind."

"Mine won't," Gary said. "As long as I pull my weight around the ranch, I can sleep where I want to. We've got a tent and three cots, if you need them."

"I think we will. We—" There was a crash behind her, and Peggy rolled her eyes. "I'll talk to you about it tomorrow. I've got Jase bathing in the sink, so I'd better not— Help!" Another crash, accompanied by delighted shrieks, and she was gone.

"How about your family?" Meg asked Marcie. She had not considered the nights before. Lying alone in her tent, listening to Gary and Matt and Will fooling around next door, would be no fun at all.

"I don't know, but I'm sure going to ask."

They considered the new dimensions that had just been added to the summer in pleased silence for a moment, and then Gary hit them with a great idea of his own.

"Hey, you guys, it's Saturday night! Next week I'm back in chains, hitting the books. What say we do the town tonight? Take in all the famous night spots. Visit a pleasure palace or two in Idaho's world-renowned Sin City."

"Wow!" said Meg. "Sounds exciting. Where is this place?"

"Four miles that-a-way," Gary said with a flourish.

"You mean Craigie?"

"None other than. You've just seen it in daylight. Looks like any other hick town, right? But Saturday night . . . like wow, man! You ain't got nothing in L.A. comes even close!"

"I'm game," Meg said, laughing. "Marcie?"

"I can't wait. This I have to see."

They all waited. The silence became uncomfortable.

"You in or out, Matt?" Gary said lightly.

"I—yeah, sure. Okay," he said with a shrug that said clearly, *I have to get it over with sometime.*

"Okay," Gary rushed on, before Matt could change his mind. "Synchronize watches. Home to change . . .

six minutes to town. Meet you at your place, Marcie, at six.''

"Make it six-thirty," Meg told her in an undertone. "I have to wash my hair."

"Me too," Marcie whispered. "Stall them as long as you can."

Meg stalled them masterfully by taking possession of the only bathroom at the Maitlands' with a shower and refusing to acknowledge Matt's and Gary's pleas to hurry it up, or their threats to break down the door, until she was dressed and ready to go. They arrived at the Traskers' at 6:35—Gary fuming and Meg looking, Matt thought privately, terrific. He was glad he had her with him on this first sortie into town. He had come tonight because he could not hide out on the ranch forever, but no matter what Gary or Tom Hensley said, he was not looking forward to facing Craigie after what happened.

Katie was dead. It didn't matter who killed her; the facts were still the same. He had run away with her and left her alone, and because of those two things she had died. Craigie would hate him still. It was just a question of how much.

Marcie's mom and dad wanted to catch up with Matt themselves, so it was nearly seven by the time the four of them were strolling along Craigie's main street toward the pizza parlor. Meg and Marcie were laughing helplessly at Gary's attempts to recast everyone they saw into their secret Sin City identities, but in spite of the unexpectedly warm welcome given him by the Traskers, Matt was wary and silent at first. It took Gary's transformation of a tiny white-haired old woman into the owner-trainer of a team of champion mud wrestlers to break Matt down and get him laughing along with the rest of them.

When they opened the door of the pizza parlor and the noise and the warm spicy smells rushed out to meet them, Matt stopped short. He looked as if he were going to turn around and run. Like a well-drilled team, the other three surrounded and swept him through the opening into the crowded room, engaged him in a lively discussion of what to include on their custom-made pizza, and hustled him into a booth before he had any more time to worry about the reception he was going to receive from his former friends and neighbors.

Still friends, Gary could have told him. Still friends. He would never have persuaded Matt to come home to Craigie or brought him in here if he hadn't known that was true. He had been at the town meeting last spring when Sheriff Hensley had stood up to tell everyone that Matt had been cleared. All of them, the sheriff had said, himself especially, had done Matt a terrible injustice. Craigie agreed, but Gary knew Matt would have to find it out for himself before he would believe it. That was why they were in Papa Luigi's on a Saturday night—so Matt could meet half the town and get it over with.

Gary had not been wrong about Craigie. The steady trickle of people stopping at their booth to say hello to Matt had swelled to a torrent by the time they finished eating. Older members of the community confined themselves mostly to welcoming him home and wishing him the best, although one grizzled old rancher, whom Gary would gladly have taken out back and beaten to a pulp, commented when Matt stood up to shake his hand that it looked like he wasn't going to be as big as his dad after all.

"Looks that way," was all Matt said, but he threw a look across the table that Gary, although he ignored it, correctly interpreted as meaning he'd had about all he could take.

It was harder to shake off the kids, who squeezed into the booth with them and draped themselves over neighboring tables to the obvious annoyance of Papa Luigi's staff. Gary finally brought the reunion to an end by announcing they'd have to run for it if they were going to make the last show at the movie theater. By the time they were settling into their seats, the four of them were alone again.

The film itself was a comedy that Matt and Meg had already seen, but it didn't matter. Meg was so highly tuned to Matt's mood that she could not concentrate on anything but his tense, silent presence beside her. They were twenty minutes into the action when he sighed, shifted to make himself more comfortable, and draped an arm across her shoulders. One more hurdle safely cleared. Moments later Meg found herself laughing helplessly at dialogue she had found only mildly funny the first time around.

Although Gary would not be available to work until after church the next morning, over private custommade shakes at the Traskers' old-fashioned soda fountain, the others settled on ten as rendezvous time at the Pomeroys. Heading home, Matt found himself thinking that a roller-coaster ride was a better description of this summer than he'd realized. Up and down and no way to duck out or get off when things got rough. And no way of knowing whether there were going to be more ups or downs . . .

# 18

*S*unday turned out to be a milestone day—the first of many. As soon as they were up and dressed Matt and Gary took their tent down and loaded it with the cots and Matt and Meg's gear into the Schuyler station wagon. After breakfast Matt drove everything to the Pomeroys' while Meg rode Cricket over. It was the first time Cricket had been ridden since his arrival, and he behaved very badly, pretending terror at discarded beer cans and windblown paper bags. Sweating and exasperated, Meg left him in the Black's corral—Matt promising to keep an eye on them while they got acquainted—and spent the rest of the morning working in the Pomeroys' vegetable garden with Marcie and Peggy and the two little ones.

Lisa arrived at 10:30 on Charley. Matt did not give her time to dismount before he tore into her for leaving the Black uncared for when she went home the day before. When he stopped criticizing her skills as a horsewoman and her selfish, irresponsible attitude toward horses and the rest of the world long enough for her to get a word in of her own, she reminded him furiously that he had said he would feed and water yesterday. "I took it for granted you'd do the Black too."

"Don't ever take it for granted I'll do your jobs for you."

"My mistake,"she said coldly. For the rest of the

morning they worked on matching tack with horses in stony silence.

After lunch everyone went down to the corrals to choose and saddle horses for the afternoon's work. Gary arrived on his trail bike while they were sorting themselves out. He was as good on a horse as any of them, but Marcie preferred wheels, so he took her behind him on his bike. With Meg on Cricket, Matt on the roan, and Lisa on a nervous gray mare, they set out to ride some of the existing trails and see what was needed to make them usable by riders and hikers.

They rode up the old fire trail to Chapman's Lake first and found that the spring thaw had left it badly rutted in places. Dragging a couple of dead trees aside, they decided that after one morning's work with pick and shovel, Art should be able to get up it in his pickup, making it a pleasant trail for the breakfast ride. A flat open space near the small lake would make a good place to build the barbecue pit Hank wanted for the evening campfires, minimizing the fire danger in the dry summers.

"One down, three to go," Matt said as they headed back down the road with Gary and Marcie in the lead.

"How about the ridge trail?" Lisa suggested. "It's in pretty good shape—at least the part I use every day—and Dad won't mind." Her father, no longer in the cattle business himself, owned pasturelands in the next valley that he leased to other ranchers in the area. His property and the Pomeroys' shared a boundary line along the top of the ridge.

"Might as well have a look at it," Matt said, and they headed across the Pomeroys' valley and up the hill on the other side.

The trail was fine to the top of the ridge, where it headed downhill and out onto the flatlands, and also branched left and right, running along the property line beside the post-and-wire fencing. Here the trail was overgrown and the fence in need of repairs, but a spectacular view of the entire Craigie area was visible farther along the ridge to the left, so they pushed on, Gary stopping frequently to disentangle his Honda from the undergrowth.

While they were waiting at one of these enforced stops, Lisa's mare, unable to stand the noisy bike and the close quarters, reared suddenly and bolted back the way they'd come. An instant later, crouching low over the roan's neck to avoid overhanging branches, Matt was racing after them.

"Gary!" Meg yelled. "Shut that thing off!"

"What?"

"Lisa's horse bolted. Matt's gone after her." She jerked her head back down the trail. "I'm going too."

"Oh lord!" Gary said. "Listen, we might as well keep going on this so-called trail. If I follow you guys, I might spook the mare again. Tell Matt we'll head for the high pasture and come down that way. We'll see you at the ranch."

"Okay," Meg said. Turning Cricket with difficulty in the narrow space, she followed the fence line as fast as she could on the haphazardly cleared trail. She neither saw nor heard anything of the other two up to the point where the main trail crossed the one she was on and ran down both sides of the ridge.

Down to the right, the trail to the Pomeroy ranch was rugged and winding. If she were in Lisa's position, and the mare had given her any choice, she would not have gone that way. Straight ahead the undergrowth looked undisturbed. Meg turned left, down toward the flatlands, keeping her fingers crossed.

She had been calling Matt's name for several minutes, her voice sounding thin and lost in the hot heavy atmosphere of the woods, when she emerged unexpectedly from the trees and saw them a long way off—stick figures on a rolling green landscape. They had both dismounted, and Matt was running his hands over the mare's chest and forelegs. While Meg watched he picked up one leg and then the other, examining the hooves. She was urging Cricket toward them when Matt remounted the roan and gave Lisa a hand up behind him. Leading the mare, they came toward her at a slow walk.

"Are you okay?" Meg called out as she cantered up.

"Watch it!" Matt shouted as the mare reared again. Fighting to hang on to its reins, Lisa was almost dragged off his horse. "Careful, Meg," he added more calmly, but she felt like a fool as she fell in silently behind them.

The mare was limping badly. They made slow progress to the start of the trail. At this rate, Meg realized, they were going to waste the rest of the afternoon getting home. She rode up alongside the roan, keeping a safe distance from the skittish mare. "Matt, Gary said to tell you he'll keep going along the ridge until he gets to the high pasture trail and come back to the ranch that way. You won't have to worry about the mare meeting up with his bike again."

"Good."

His silence was daunting. He couldn't be mad at her for spooking the mare, could he? Behind him, Lisa was flexing and stretching her arms to relax her tense muscles. Whatever else had happened, she had obviously not been thrown off. Her shirt and jeans, both a soft peach color, were as immaculate as they had been when she'd arrived that morning.

She rode that idiot horse all the way to the flatlands, Meg was thinking, and probably ran it around in circles until it had to stop or fall down. No big deal for Lisa Lomax, champion barrel racer. If it had been me, I would probably have gone flying into the nearest bramble patch when the mare first bolted.

She had been run away with twice in her life and had ridden the horse to a standstill both times, but whenever she compared herself with Lisa she was finding it hard to imagine herself as anything but second best. Reminded that they had more pressing problems than her rivalry with Lisa to solve at the moment, she made what she thought was a sensible suggestion.

"Matt, there's no point having all of us held up. Why don't you and Lisa ride home and get another horse and let me lead the mare back? You know where the other trails are, so you're both more useful at finding good ones than I am."

"It doesn't matter," he said shortly. "There won't be time to ride any more trails today."

"It matters to me," Lisa contradicted him. "I have to be home by five. We're having company for dinner."

"Tough," Matt growled.

Lisa stared at the back of Matt's sweat-stained shirt, her nostrils flaring. If looks could kill . . . Meg thought.

"You don't understand," Lisa said tightly. "I have to be home on time. I have no choice."

"*You* don't understand," Matt told her. "You never have understood. Seems to me we've been through this before. In this situation, Ms. Lomax, the horse comes first."

Lisa clenched her fist. For an instant Meg thought she was going to hit him, but she let it drop slowly back on her own leg instead. Then she looked at Meg. "I'd like to take you up on your offer. If you wouldn't mind lending me Cricket, I'll—"

"Don't do it, Meg," Matt interrupted roughly. "She's ridden western all her life. She can't handle your fancy English style."

Bull! Meg thought. Lisa could ride anything any style. Matt's attitude puzzled and annoyed her. She had never thought of him as a grudge bearer, but if he was treating Lisa this way because of the mix-up over the jobs, she wanted him to know she didn't like it. "Go ahead," she told Lisa. "Just don't let him tell you he's scared of old newspapers or barking dogs, because he's not."

"Thanks," Lisa said crisply as Meg gave her a leg up and raised the stirrups a notch. "You've saved my life. I mean it. I'll bring him back early tomorrow . . . in top shape,'' she added for Matt's benefit. He had ridden ahead for several yards before stopping, his rigid back mute evidence of his smoldering rage.

Meg watched Lisa ride off on Cricket, handling the unfamiliar reins with a firmness that reassured her. Cricket was in good hands—literally, she thought with a grin as she ran to catch up with Matt.

As she stood beside the roan her head was level with Matt's knee, but he made no move to help her mount. ''I need a hand up,'' she said impatiently, and he reached for her without speaking—dragging her up, handing her the mare's reins, and moving off again before she was securely settled.

Putting up with his silence as long as she could, she yielded at last to a mischievous impulse and began counting his ribs—a trick that, because he was so ticklish, usually broke down his resistance in two seconds flat. Trapping the roving hand, he pinned it against his side with his elbow. When she slid it out and started counting again, he grabbed the hand and jerked it forward roughly, banging her nose against his hard back and bringing tears to her eyes.

''Hey!'' she protested. ''That hurt.''

''Then cut it out.'' He did not let go of her hand.

''And if I don't want to?''

''Then you can get off and walk.''

The tone was the same one he had used to Lisa, and Meg strongly resented it. ''You're in a great mood,'' she said sarcastically. ''What did I do to make you so mad, or should I ask?''

Matt had apparently been waiting impatiently for the chance to answer that question. ''You let Lisa walk all over you, that's all. She snapped her fingers, like she's done all her life, and you stepped right into line like everyone else. Sure, Lisa, take my horse. I understand. You just lamed one and you can't be bothered to get it home and see it's properly cared for. You've got more important things to do.''

"Let go of my arm," she said furiously. When he did, she flung herself off the roan's bony rump and landed off balance, falling and hurting her wrist but managing to hold on to the mare's reins. Scrambling to her feet, she flicked her hair out of her eyes and glared up at Matt.

"Just because you have some old feud going with Lisa, Matt McKendrick, don't expect you can snap *your* fingers and I'll go along with *you!* The way I see it, Lisa did a great job of staying on a bolting horse. She knew the horse was in good hands, and she had to get home. It made no sense for her to go all the way back to the Pomeroys' when she was late and halfway home already, and why she had to get home is none of my business. If she said she had to, she had to.

"I'm sorry you find it such a burden to share your horse with me, but don't worry about it. You go on. The mare and I will get back just fine without you. Go on," she said again, but he stayed where he was, sitting loose-limbed and silent on the big roan, staring down at her and blocking the trail. Dwarfed by his additional height, she felt as powerless as someone Beth's size. "Matt . . . move!"

"No," he said. "Not until you get back on this horse."

"I'm not getting back on that horse."

"Yes, you are."

"No, I'm not."

They glared at each other, matching scowl for scowl.

Suddenly Matt laughed. "I wish you could see yourself," he said. "All you need is a slingshot, and you'd make a great David. Which I guess makes me Goliath, doesn't it?" She refused to be mollified, even if he was making jokes at his own expense. "Okay," he said finally, "I apologize. I was wrong—not about Lisa, about you—and I'm sorry. Okay?"

She did not really want to coax the mare the rest of the way home by herself. "Maybe," she said, not letting him off so easily. "I'll think about it."

She gave him her hand, but when he started to pull on it, she screamed and doubled over, clutching her wrist. He dismounted in one swift motion.

"What happened? Meg, what's wrong?"

"It's okay," she gasped.

"Let me see."

"There's nothing to see. It's okay," she insisted. "Give me a leg up instead."

He boosted her up and mounted himself, swinging his leg over the roan's neck. They moved off down the other side of the ridge toward the Pomeroys', the mare plodding docilely along behind them. Meg put her arms around Matt's waist, tucking her thumbs into his belt and leaning against him.

"Did I do that? Hurt your hand, I mean?" he asked after a while.

"No. I did it when I . . . um, dismounted, if you can call it that, with such grace and coordination."

"I'm sorry," he said, gently rubbing her sore wrist with his free hand.

"It's better already," she reassured him, not minding that he cared, but embarrassed at being fussed over when it was her fault it had happened.

"That reminds me," he told her sternly, as if reading her mind. "Don't ever get off a horse that way again. Not unless you know him backward and forward—no pun intended," he added as she gave an exaggerated groan.

"I won't. I was mad at you and I wasn't thinking."

"Horses and tempers don't mix," Matt said firmly.

In his tone Meg could hear echoes of other voices telling him the same thing. "Yes, sir. Sorry, sir," she said, grinning to herself, and they made the rest of the journey in a companionable silence that was a great improvement over the other one.

## 19

*The* mare's limp was diagnosed as a strained chest muscle by Art, who was obviously relieved that it was the local barrel-racing champion and not a terrified guest who had been riding her, and the roan received a double handful of grain for his stalwart performance. The horses having been seen to, Gary, Meg, and Matt set up the two tents beside the embryonic bunkhouse and then went back to Gary's for a final feast with his family.

Marcie's parents had agreed to her sleeping at the ranch, and the Pomeroys had asked her and Gary to bring their families back with them after supper for what might be the last chance for neighbors to get together before the end of the summer. It was a large friendly group that gathered on the patio as the west ridge spread its lengthening shadow across the valley. Gary was strumming softly on his guitar, and conversation grew more sporadic as everyone relaxed in the peaceful warmth of the evening.

"How about giving us some of your songs, Gary?" Art suggested finally. "Kind of a trial run?"

Gary needed no persuading. He led them in a number of old standbys, entertained them with hilarious imitations of well-known country-and-western singers, and came around at last to some of his favorites by John Denver.

"Try this one," he said. "It has a story that I'll have to sing to you, but it's got a great chorus. Goes like this." He played a chord and sang it for them once before taking them through it a couple of times themselves. "It's a song about his uncle," Gary explained. "A great old guy who knew what the important things in life were. Okay? Here we go:

> "Had an uncle named Matthew,
> Was his father's only boy.
> Born just south of Colby, Kansas,
> Was his mother's pride and joy.

"Here's where you guys come in—

> "Yes and joy was just a thing that he was raised on,
> Love was just a way to live and die,
> Gold was just a windy Kansas wheatfield,
> Blue was just a Kansas summer sky."

Gary sang a couple of verses that told of the memories the singer's uncle had shared with him, of the times when

> "Growing up a Kansas farm boy,
> Life was mostly having fun,
> Riding on his daddy's shoulders,
> Behind a mule, beneath the sun,"

and they sang the chorus again.

It *was* a great chorus, Meg agreed. She liked the idea of love and joy not being rare occasions but a natural part of his everyday life, of gold not representing money but the beauty of a field in wheat, and blue not sadness but the brilliance of a summer sky.

Then it was Gary's turn again, and he told them of the hard times, how his uncle lost his farm and his family but had not let their loss destroy him too. He had come instead to live with the singer's family, to share his memories of the good times, to become the singer's friend.

It was at this point, while they were singing the chorus again, that Meg felt her first misgivings. Matt was sitting on the steps of the addition, leaning against the glass door with Susan Maitland on one side of him and Beth on the other. The sudden stillness of his position told her something was wrong, but not until Gary began his solo part again did she realize what it was.

"So I wrote this down for Matthew," Gary sang in his warm tenor. "It's for him this song is sung—"

No, no! Meg thought wildly. Not you, Matt. It's nothing to do with you. But the events described in the song had a strong resemblance to his life, and the coincidence of the names being the same underscored that fact.

"Riding on his daddy's shoulders—"

Matt was leaning forward now, elbows on his knees, intent on shredding a leaf to bits and keeping his face and his feelings hidden from the rest of them. Meg had a sudden image of him as a small boy on his own father's shoulders. Oh lord, she thought desperately as they began another chorus, will this stupid song never end?

Everyone was singing loudly. Can't they see how he must be feeling? Meg wondered angrily. And Gary—the idiot! He knew Matt better than anyone else there. He had shared that life. How could he have done this to him?

After Gary had led them through the final, triumphant chorus, Meg was ready to call a halt to the evening, but during the awkward silence that followed someone asked for "On Top of Spaghetti." Gary plunged into it eagerly and took them back to safer ground.

Afterward, when the Maitlands and Traskers had gone home, Meg maneuvered the lineup outside the bathroom so she and Gary were the last ones there. "Gary!" she began threateningly the moment he emerged with toothbrush in hand.

He groaned. "Don't say it, Meg. I've put my foot in it before, but this time . . . lord! Don't worry, that's one song you won't be hearing again."

"How could you?"

"Would you believe—all the time I was learning it, it never hit me how much like his life that story was until I saw him sitting there tonight remembering? I was afraid if I stopped in the middle, it would just make things worse. Meg . . ." His voice changed, and the expression on his lively freckled face grew serious. "I never would have done that to him on purpose. It's different for you. You've only known him since . . . since the accident and Katie's murder. For you, those are the important things in his life. You can't forget them, and he can't either.

"But for me, the important things—the things I remember about him, the way I think of him as really being—are the things that happened *before* his parents died. The good times . . . like the song said." Gary was silent for a moment. Then he shook himself and grinned at her, getting his defenses back in working order. "Besides," he added, as if this were going to explain everything, "I never called him Matthew in my life."

He's right, Meg was thinking as they shared the flashlight on the way back to the tents. Matt's life didn't start the day he came to Los Angeles. It began a long time ago, and he must have packed a lot of good times into his first sixteen years, or he wouldn't be the kind of person he is. She wished he could have those years back in his memory at least, wished he was not so determined to pretend they never existed. If it weren't for Gary's persistent remember-when games, someone who didn't know Matt would never guess he had been here before.

Keep it up, she told Gary silently, wishing she had been part of the old days herself. Make him remember. Those times were too good to forget.

*20*

**O**n Monday they felt as though they had more than
enough time to finish the trails and settle the horses, to
get the cabins ready, and to bake and freeze and can
foods. They worked nonstop from dawn until dark—
Matt up first and running five to eight miles; Meg and
Marcie up next to help Peggy with breakfast; Lisa arriving every morning as Gary was leaving for summer
school and leaving promptly at 4:15 every afternoon;
Gary back in time for supper each night. After supper
everyone helped around the ranch until the sun went
down and then rolled into bed and slept solidly until the
rooster and Matt got them up again the next day. By
Friday afternoon they were not quite done.

Lisa had left for the day, and Matt was up on the east
ridge cutting some low-hanging branches that might
prove hazardous to inexperienced trail riders. Meg and
Marcie were shelling peas for supper at one of the picnic
tables when Hank Pomeroy drove into the yard in a long
blue van with POMEROY RANCH, CRAIGIE, IDAHO painted
along the side, and parked over by the barn.

"Will's here!" Meg stripped the pod she had just split
open of its row of peas and dumped them into the bowl
before leaping up to greet him. An unfamiliar figure came
slowly around the back of the van, and for a sickening
instant Meg thought Hank had brought the wrong person.
"Will . . . ?" she said, appalled by his appearance—
gray, Carey's letter had said, and she wasn't exag-

gerating—and by the way he leaned wearily against the side of the van as if needing support to remain on his feet. His hair was badly in need of cutting, she noticed, and the mischievous glint in his brown eyes that she had grown up with had been extinguished. He looked like a survivor from a World War II prison camp.

Thinking it was the only thing she could safely kid him about, she came up with a casual remark about his needing a haircut. It turned out she was wrong.

"Lay off," he told her shortly. "I've had about all the remarks I can take on that subject already. When I want it cut, I'll cut it."

"Sorry," she said. "How was the trip?"

"Pretty grim. Nonstop except for meals. Hank doesn't fool around, does he?"

"No," Meg agreed with a laugh. "Were you able to eat all right?"

"I'm sick of milk and crackers and bananas. Otherwise . . ." He shrugged.

"Well, hey, it's great to see you! Come and meet Marcie."

Using her own enthusiasm, she tried to imbue him with a spark of his old good-humored zest for life. She could tell he was making an effort as he was introduced to Art and Peggy and the children, greeted warmly by Gary and Matt, and shown around the ranch after supper. Finally, though, he took her aside and begged her to show him where he was sleeping. Hank was expecting a full day's work out of him tomorrow, and he did not want to fall apart on the first day. He was exhausted. When Matt and Gary joined him in the tent an hour later, even their muttered conversation and occasional laughter did not disturb his sleep.

Saturday, the day before the first group of guests would be arriving, Matt, Gary, and Art began clearing the last trail. Lisa met them on the ridge and went home from there, so they did not see her at the ranch at all. Meg and Marcie moved most of the furniture out of the cabins while Will and Hank put down the carpeting they had brought with them, and then moved everything back in again—a job that took most of the day. Hank then took Will up to Chapman's Lake in Art's pickup. By the time the bell called them home for supper, they had dug a good-sized hole and constructed a cinder-block cooking pit.

Meg was glad to see there was no lack of things for Will to do that he was able to do. On Sunday morning he put railings on two sets of cabin steps that Peggy thought were too steep to be safe in the dark. When he was finished, Art suggested he cut up the dead wood that had been cleared off the trails by the others and bring it back to the woodpile.

Hank returned from Boise with the guests around four o'clock that afternoon, and everyone was caught up in the massive confusion and excitement of Week-One-with-Guests. By the time Meg realized she had not seen Will for several hours, he was rolled in his sleeping bag and dead to the world. She kept her fears to herself, but she could not help feeling anxious. Had they brought him up here too late for it to do him any good?

Later in the summer, when they had more experience, they would call this first group the Gung-Ho-ers, but at the time they were not sure they could survive from one day to the next, let alone for ten weeks. There were six adults, three teenagers, and four children under ten in this group. Determined to cram a lifetime of ranching experiences into one week, all of them wanted to do everything there was to do.

Ask if anyone wanted to collect the breakfast eggs, and at six o'clock the next morning eight people would be rummaging through the henhouse with excited cries. Mention a trail ride, and everyone would be milling around the corral wanting to choose their own mount and saddle and bridle it themselves. Suggest a hike, a swim, or a softball game, and a crowd would gather instantly, ready for action. On the Fourth of July they put on their own picnic with games, races, and a touch-football competition that finished everyone off. After supper they all went to town and watched the fireworks over the lake.

On the day that everyone went rafting on the Salmon River, Meg volunteered to stay home with Beth, Jase, and two three-year-olds too young to go. While they were napping peacefully on the big pillows in the Old Addish, as the addition was now referred to, she fell asleep briefly herself.

Will woke them all later in the afternoon when he came in with a load of wood for the fireplace. He had no responsibility for the guests' welfare and was dividing his time between sawing and stacking firewood and replacing rotted fence posts with any of the cut wood that was suitable for the purpose. Because he was still on his special diet, he was feeding himself and tended to keep odd hours that seldom brought him into contact with the others. They had seen little of him all week.

"You're looking better than when I saw you last," Meg said approvingly. His face was tanned, and there was a spring in his step. A sweatband around his thick hair was keeping it under control. "How's everything going?"

"Just what the doctor ordered," he told her with a trace of his former lightheartedness. "Ten weeks at hard labor is going to kill or cure me. Either way it'll be an improvement over the last few weeks at home. How are you surviving?"

"Just barely," she said, laughing. "I don't know whether I can keep up this pace all summer, but it's fun . . . I think. We don't see much of you, though. You aren't feeling lonely and unwanted, I hope?"

"No. It's a nice change, in a way. Maybe later I'll have more time. Hank's getting me started on the bunkhouse tomorrow, so I'll be working on that for a while. You know something, Meg . . . ?" He hesitated, changed his mind about sharing whatever it was, and turned away.

"What?" she demanded.

He thought about it for a moment. "Well . . . I'm not exactly looking forward to tomorrow. I mean, I've played it by ear up to now, managed to look strong and intelligent"—Meg gave him the obligatory snort—"and figure out how to do the things he wants done without asking a lot of stupid questions. But I don't know if I can work that with this bunkhouse thing."

He actually sounded as if he thought Hank might put him on the next plane to L.A. if he didn't turn out to be a master carpenter. "Will, honestly," Meg said, plucking an ace of diamonds out of Jason's smiling mouth and offering him the delights of a tennis ball instead. "He doesn't expect you to know everything. He'll show you how to do it. You know that."

"It's not that simple, Meg. What if he shows me, and I can't do it? What if I'm all thumbs and can't cut a straight line or match up the corners?"

Meg was so flabbergasted by Will's uncharacteristic lack of confidence that she could only stare blankly at him.

"I know, I know," he went on after a pause. "I'm crazy. Forget I said anything. I'll manage somehow," he concluded gloomily. "I don't have any other choice."

While she took Jase and the little girls outside to play in the sandbox, he made himself an early supper. She heard the pickup drive away a short time later, and eventually the distant growl of the chain saw biting into wood, and wondered what had been happening at home to so thoroughly undermine Will's confidence in himself. She hoped he was wrong about the bunkhouse, but he had her worried.

# 21

*Although* Thursday and Friday were crammed with non-stop activity with guests, Meg could hear the sawing and hammering going on behind the barn and see the progress Hank and Will were making when she turned in at night. Occasionally, when Will came to the house for his meals or to repair another wound—he seemed to be cutting and mashing himself a lot—she would be there too.

Once she asked how he was doing and was encouraged by the thumbs-up sign he gave her, even though the thumb was adorned by a decidedly unhygienic bandage. And at night, as she and Marcie lay in bed laughing at the day's misadventures or talking about people they knew and places they wanted to go, more and more frequently she could hear Will exchanging insults and inaudible conversation with Matt and Gary next door. Good, she thought, relieved. It's not too late after all.

On Saturday morning, although they were looking forward to some peace and quiet and a chance to get themselves better organized and prepared for the next group, they all felt strangely let down as the van drove away. They had made some friends in that short week, and to have them go out of their lives again, probably forever, was not a nice feeling. Beth said it for all of them when she burst into angry tears and fled to the barn, where she hid in the loft until lunchtime.

Will was hard at work on the bunkhouse by the time Hank left to take the guests to the airport. Meg and

Marcie planned to spend the morning and part of the afternoon cleaning the cabins, washing and drying sheets, and remaking beds. Gary was helping his dad on the Maitland ranch, and Matt and Lisa were cleaning tack and going over the horses for saddle sores and other potential trouble spots.

The two of them had made it through the week without open disagreement mainly because Lisa had managed to keep her mouth shut when the guests were around and let Matt tell her what to do. Living at home and not at the ranch had put her at a disadvantage. Because he ate with them and was around in the evenings, the guests knew Matt better and obviously thought he was in charge. She had no intention of letting another week go by, however, with her playing the role of dull-witted stable hand while Matt gave the orders.

It gave her a small psychological advantage to look down at Matt when she was talking to him, so she did not bring up the subject until she was safely mounted on Charley and ready to leave for home.

"I want to get something straight before the next group of guests arrives," she said.

He was saddling the roan, preparing to ride up to the high pasture and take a look at the troublesome water hole for Art, and did not bother to stop what he was doing or look at her. "What?"

"I don't like the way you went around arranging everything this week and giving orders. I'm not working for you, and I don't intend to be treated as if I am."

He turned, surveying her from under his dark brows as if she were some lower life-form he found barely tolerable. "How do you intend to be treated?"

"Like your equal. Partners. As if I'm as good as you are at this job." Which I am, she was about to add, but he beat her to it.

"I'll believe you're as good at this job when I see you caring enough about anything besides yourself to put yourself to some inconvenience over a horse who needs your help. Until then the arrangements can stay the way they are. They suit me and the horses just fine." Swinging himself into the saddle, he turned the roan and started up the road.

Spurring Charley after him, she jerked the reins out of his hand. "Wait just one minute, Matt McKendrick! I've had all I can take from you, and I'm not taking any more. I'm going to tell you how I feel for a change, and you can listen whether you like it or not.

"I took this crummy job because I heard you were coming back, and I wanted a chance to make friends—oh, don't worry, that's over," she said bitterly as he gave an incredulous laugh. "You've done a great job of killing that idea in the last two weeks. I'm sorry about taking Meg's job—I like Meg—but I didn't know it was her job when I took it. I said it had to be horses or nothing because I've been running our house for my father and my two brothers for the last year myself. Why do you think I can't live here like the rest of you? Why do you think I have to be home exactly at five every night?

"And as for the Black, I bought him because he was yours, and I didn't want some hotshot cowboy getting hold of him and ruining him. I brought him over here for you to have this summer because I thought you'd want him. You can ride him or not. I don't care what you do, but when the summer's over, I'm selling him to the first person who comes along. I look ridiculous on him anyway. He's much too big for me." She glanced past Matt at the Black himself, who was looking curiously at them over the fence. Matt turned to look at him too. She waited until he turned around again before she finished what she had to say.

"As for the job—for the rest of the summer it's strictly business between us. We work together because we have to, and I don't give a damn what the guests think. If you don't want them to know how much we hate each other, then you're going to have to be nice to me for a change. I'm through pretending!"

She flung the reins at him without waiting to see how he was going to react and took off at a gallop for the ridge trail and home. The summer's promise of escape from her demanding, all-male household, and of friendships she badly wanted, had soured on her like so many other things in her life.

She did not even have college to look forward to in the fall. When her exhausted mother had finally given up the fight with the spreading cancer, her father had begged her to wait. "Don't go yet, Lisa," he had said. "We need you at home." And she had agreed to stay, even though she was afraid that if she waited she might never go at all.

She was passing the partially built bunkhouse when a desperate voice penetrated the angry confusion of her thoughts.

"Hey . . . help! Whoever that is, can you give me a hand?"

Glancing around, she saw the lean, muscular back and sun-bleached hair of Hank Pomeroy's helper from Los Angeles. Sweat was trickling down his spine, and he seemed to be supporting the entire bunkhouse wall on one bare shoulder.

"What do I do?" she said, on the ground a second later.

"That ladder . . . bring it here," he gasped. "Brace it . . . against this end."

She wrestled the heavy ladder into position as quickly as possible. "All set," she said, stepping back out of the way. "I hope."

"Me too," he said, cautiously easing himself out from under his load. It creaked ominously but held, and he let out a huge sigh as he turned to thank her.

For a moment, as he stared openmouthed, she was afraid that he knew who she was, that Matt had warned him about her. She knew what Matt thought of her—Lisa the rich, Lisa the spoiled, Whatever-Lisa-Wants-Lisa-Gets Lomax. But then, as the boy grinned suddenly and engagingly, she knew he had been paying a compliment to her looks.

She was heartily sick of being admired for her looks and hated for everything else, but somehow, after the last two weeks in Matt's bruisingly critical company, a compliment of any kind felt good. She smiled back.

"Are you real?" he asked. "I mean, I'm not hallucinating, am I?" Her smile must have faded, because he was instantly contrite. "I'm sorry. Maybe that didn't sound quite right. I just meant that I've been praying for someone, anyone—any shape, any size, so long as they were more than four years old—to come along for the last eon or two, and . . . well, look who I got!" Rubbing the place where the wood had dug a deep crease into the flesh of his shoulder, he grinned again.

He sounded so genuinely pleased with his good luck that Lisa felt pleased herself. They could not, however, stand around all day grinning idiotically at each other. "Is it going to be all right?" she asked, looking doubtfully at the framework looming over them.

"It will be when I get the nails in where they belong," he said. "Hold the ladder for a second, will you?" He hammered vigorously for the next couple of minutes, gave the framework a tremendous thump with the heel of his hand, and was pronouncing it strong enough to withstand an earthquake when the bell rang for lunch.

"Aren't you going to eat?" Lisa asked, moving reluctantly toward Charley. The boy was settling himself against the trunk of a nearby oak.

"I've got mine here," he said, gesturing at a brown paper bag. "What about you?"

"I don't usually eat lunch."

"Well," he said after a thoughtful pause, "if you want to not eat lunch with me, you're welcome."

It took her a second or two to figure that one out, but since she did not have to get home right away, and since she was enjoying this friendly, relaxed conversation, she settled her own back against the tree. For a while they watched Charley tearing up clumps of grass that had been liberally seasoned with sawdust.

The boy seemed in no hurry to get to his lunch. Leaning back, he closed his eyes, soaking up the sun and flapping halfheartedly at a fly that persisted in landing on his nose. "Are you one of Hank's slaves this summer too?" he said finally.

"Yes. I work with the horses. How come I haven't seen you around?"

"Wherever there are horses, you won't see me around," he said emphatically. "Horses and I have nothing in common. I leave that side of things to Meg."

"Meg?" Lisa's heart sank. But, of course, if he had been recruited in L.A., it was perfectly possible that he and Meg knew each other.

"My sister Meg. You must have met her by now. She's the horse freak in our family."

"Then you must be Will." You're not *too* dense, Lisa, she thought. Who else could he have been? And the discovery made her feel as if a door had slammed and left her outside looking in. Again.

"Right." He seemed preoccupied with extricating his lunch from the bag. "I'm sorry," he said, glancing at her almost shyly. "I don't think I can play the Rumpelstiltskin game with you. Guessing the names," he added when she looked blank.

"Oh . . . um, Lisa," she told him, wishing she had the nerve to pretend it was something else. She was certain he must have heard about her from one of the others by now, but if he had, he was doing a good job of pretending ignorance. "How long will it take you?" she asked to keep the conversation going. "The bunkhouse, I mean."

"I don't know. I'd like to get it finished before Hank comes up again next weekend, but it's the first thing I've ever built that's bigger than I am." He laughed again, and she liked the sound of it—gruff and explosive, as if he couldn't hold it back. "It might finish me off first."

"I have some spare time," she said suddenly. "On Mondays and Wednesdays in the afternoons, and Saturdays. If you could use someone to hold up the other ends of things . . ." Her voice trailed off, as he seemed by his silence to be rejecting the offer. "Well, I guess I should get going. I'm keeping you from your work."

"No," he said quickly. "Don't go . . . unless you have to. I was thinking, if you really have the time, there are a lot of things that would be easier if there were two of us."

"Like propping up the walls?" she said. She was not good at teasing people. They always took her seriously and accused her of being bitchy, but Will seemed able to laugh at himself so easily that she took a chance. He did not disappoint her.

"Precisely," he said with a grin. "More fun if there are two of us trapped at the same time." While he ate his lunch the two of them entertained each other thinking up different kinds of work they could do as a pair—hiring themselves out as statuary for the front steps of public buildings, or as port and starboard lights on ocean liners—until Will looked at his watch and announced that it was work time.

"Tell me when it's three," she said. "I have to be home on the stroke of three-thirty, or I turn into a pumpkin. Up until then I'm all yours." And in spite of the good time they had doing it, they accomplished a lot before she left.

Matt, Meg, Gary, and Marcie had been planning on going into Craigie again that night and taking Will, but he was too busy helping Hank wire the bunkhouse and getting instructions on how to put up the roofing and the interior and exterior walls. Hank would be leaving on Sunday's flight—he was building bigger things than bunkhouses in L.A.—and Will wanted to be sure he knew what he was doing before Hank left him on his own.

"I can't eat pizza or popcorn anyway," he said

when Hank told him to get the lead out and go with the others.

But in the end they decided it was too much trouble to go anywhere. They had had enough people and entertainment to last them for a while, and it was starting all over again tomorrow. They wandered down to the duck pond and collapsed on the grass, talking about everything and nothing until someone discovered that Will had gone to sleep.

During the ensuing debate over whether to be insulted by such rudeness (Gary's and Matt's reaction) and throw him into the pond, or to have pity on his weakened condition (Meg's and Marcie's position) and carry him back to the tent, Will woke up and stealthily withdrew. Putting a safe distance between himself and the other four, he challenged them from the darkness with as rude an assortment of raspberries as anyone had ever heard. They chased him and each other back to the tents with banshee wails and cries of real pain as they tripped over clumps of grass and other hazards in the dark.

# 22

*I*n contrast to Week One, Week-Two-with-Guests was almost dull. Two of the cabins had been rented by four older couples without children. All of them enjoyed going on the trail rides and excursions or wandering around the ranch, but self-sufficient as they were, they seldom asked for extra time or entertainment from their hosts. If it had not been for the family in the third cabin, no one would have had much to do.

Cabin Three was a young couple with four children all under ten. Anxious to make the most of the week, the father was first in line at the corral in the morning, first in the van when an excursion was planned, and first to offer his services to Art when the subject of riding fences or looking for strays came up. His wife was always left behind with the children, and she wore a perpetually harassed look. This week was not going to be a vacation for her, but she obviously needed one as much as her husband.

Meg and Marcie finally persuaded her that they were there for the express purpose of entertaining her family. While they gave the children rides on the pinto, taught them how to swim in the duck pond, and took them into town for special ice-cream concoctions at Marcie's parents' store, their mother spent long hours chatting with Peggy Pomeroy, helping in the garden, and reading mystery novels in the hammock under the pine trees. By Saturday the anxious lines between her eyes had smoothed out, and before she left she thanked Marcie with tears in her eyes.

Meg and Marcie hoped that the week was going to keep her going for a while, but Meg, reminded of her own family, had her doubts. She wished she were old enough to tell the husband to shape up fast. If he didn't start showing them now that he cared about them, in about nine more years none of them would know or care whether he was around or not. By then, she could have told him, it would be too late for him to do anything about it.

Saturday night found the five of them down at the duck pond again, planning on a swim. Will had enjoyed a productive week with Lisa's help and was still glowing from Hank's approving reaction when he arrived that afternoon and discovered how much Will had accomplished while he was gone.

The other four were bored and restless. The week had been neither as hectic nor as satisfying as the first one, and they could see that there would be no way to anticipate what a week would be like. No matter how well they planned ahead, the character and pace of each week would depend on the guests themselves.

They heard someone coming down the road before they saw the shadowy form of horse and rider. There was no mistaking the shining fall of hair catching the moonlight. Lisa. A sudden silence fell over the group.

"We're over here," Will called out.

"For crying out loud!" Matt exploded at the same instant. "Who asked her to come?"

They turned, staring blankly at each other.

"What's that supposed to mean?" Will demanded.

If Matt had been in a better mood, he might have passed it off as a joke, but Lisa had been living up to her promise all week. After their confrontation on Saturday he had decided to quit making life harder for her than it already was, but his resolve was too new and fragile to stand up under her caustic tongue. From Tuesday on he'd been hard-pressed to hide their mutual antagonism from the guests. Now, edgy and irritable, he responded to Will's tone instead. "Just that I have to put up with her all day, and I don't feel like having her around when I'm not being paid for it."

Will rummaged through his pockets and produced a rumpled dollar bill, which he flipped onto Matt's chest. "I don't know what the going rate is," he said in the deliberately offensive tone that only Gwen and his father had ever heard him use until now, "but consider yourself paid."

"Forget it, Will," Matt growled, flicking the money away. It fell between them on the grass, looking strangely black and white in the moonlight.

Lisa dismounted and dropped Charley's reins over his

head. While he was nibbling at the grass on the hill behind them she made her way through a silence so prickly with embarrassment and hostility that she might have been picking her way through a grove of cactus, and dropped down beside Will with a carefully casual "Hello, everybody."

Outside of Will's "Hello again," a faint assortment of "Hi's," was the only response. Matt's silence seemed louder than all the rest of their greetings put together.

After a moment Gary said hollowly, "Anyone for a swim?"

No one stirred. Conversation was dead. Suddenly Matt stood, his moon shadow spreading ominously over them. "I feel like a hike," he said. "Anybody want to come?"

It was such a blatant rejection of Lisa that Will, who had begun to simmer down, found himself speechless with sudden fury. What did Matt think he was doing? Before he could think of a scathing remark, Lisa was on her feet.

"Don't bother to go on my account," she said coolly. "I was just leaving."

An instant later Will was standing too. "Wait," he told Lisa, stopping her with a hand on her arm. "I want to know what's going on? We said we were going to swim tonight, and all of a sudden Matt's playing cute and coy and inviting selected members of the club to go somewhere else. Why?"

"Ask her," Matt said.

His face was in shadow, but Will could see his eyes glittering. "I'm asking you," he said threateningly.

"And I'm not giving you an answer."

Meg had been listening to all this nonsense with some irritation, but the ominous curve of their shoulders and the taut stillness of their bodies as they challenged each other had suddenly become anything but nonsense. Matt and Will fighting? And over Lisa, of all people? "Will, for heaven's sake—"

"Shut up, Meg!"

"Don't tell *her* to shut up!" Matt said instantly, and Will—hearing the emphasis on the *her* as another un-called for slap at Lisa—hurled himself furiously at Matt with some idea of throwing him backward into the pond or grinding his face into the muddy bank until he apologized.

He underestimated his opponent. Instead of standing still waiting for him, Matt sidestepped his attack and tripped him, sending him sprawling into the mud himself. Will gazed up at Matt, looming over him like a gunfighter from the Old West about to teach the upstart kid a lesson in manners, and forgot the four inches, the fifteen months, and the twenty-five pounds Matt had on him; forgot that Matt still had a reputation for being pretty good with his fists, while he himself had not had a fight with another guy since he was eight years old.

Thinking only of Lisa—of the good times they'd had this week and the lousy way the rest of them had just treated her—Will launched himself at Matt once more and brought him down with a crash that knocked the wind out of both of them. He found it possible to hit Matt when he had him pinned under his own body, but Matt did not stay trapped for long. They rolled downhill—punching, kicking, and grunting unintelligible insults—toward the pond.

It was at this point that Lisa emerged from her state of frozen shock and endeared herself to them all. "Honest to God!" she exclaimed suddenly. "This is ridiculous!"

The other three watched openmouthed as she ran after the two writhing shadows. Darting back and forth to avoid their kicking legs, she waited for the right instant and gave Will, who happened to be on top, a tremendous shove. He and Matt went over the edge of the bank and into the pond together. Lisa, her momentum taking her farther than she had intended, went right in after them.

The others rose and raced to the spot where splashings, watery gurgles, and shouts were rising into the night air. Matt, Will, and Lisa, having disentangled themselves, were facing each other in a small circle, their expressions a blend of bewilderment and shock. Lisa was treading water, but the other two were standing on the bottom.

"Truce," Lisa said firmly. "Come on, you two."

Matt and Will looked at each other. Will's bleeding nose was contributing some vital nutrients to the life of the pond, but Matt appeared undamaged. "Truce," they agreed, shaking hands underwater.

"Truce?" Lisa said again, but without the authoritative inflection she had given it the first time. She was looking at Matt, but he was flicking water at Will and did not seem to have heard her. "Matt, please?"

# 23

**M**att stared at her without responding for a long time. Too long. Meg was getting ready to dive into the pond herself and hold his stubborn head underwater until he had to give in, when he glanced around at the rest of them and then back at Lisa. Reaching out, he carefully removed a piece of pond grass from Lisa's silvery hair. "Truce," he said lightly.

Meg's first rush of relief was followed immediately by a sickening stab of jealousy. Knock it off! she told herself fiercely. You of all people should know what Lisa's going through at home. The last thing she needs is to spend every day fighting with Matt and being ignored by the rest of us. . . .

Into the silence that had somehow descended on them,

Will dropped a small but potent bomb. ''Good thing I've got my bathing suit on under my jeans,'' he said with such earnest relief that it was a second or two before anyone realized the remark was a classic Will Schuyler Special of a variety they had not heard in a long time. Lisa and Matt immediately set about submerging him semipermanently, and the other three threw themselves into the pond, fully clothed, to help.

By rights, after that momentous celebration, Week-Three-with-Guests should have been a dream—perfect in every way. By the time they had struggled halfway through it, they all agreed that rights have less to do with the way things work out than luck and fate. The only word for it was *disaster*.

It was the largest group they had catered to so far—seven adults, four teenagers, and six children under ten. On their arrival the first question—asked by a pugnacious little boy with black piggy eyes and a sneering upper lip—was ''Where's the TV?'' and things went downhill from there.

Will had driven the Pomeroy station wagon to Boise to pick up the overflow of guests and baggage. When it appeared that one of the bags had been left at the airport, he was subjected to a string of verbal abuse from the woman to whom it belonged and told to go back and get it. Tight-lipped and silent, he turned the car around and headed for Boise. After he left, the bag turned up inside the van where the woman's husband had put it under a seat and forgotten about it. Will had to be paged at the airport until he got the message to come home.

No apologies were offered. He would not have accepted them if they had been. For the rest of the week he refused to have anything to do with the guests, dedicating himself entirely to the completion of the bunkhouse. Because he and his bunkhouse were the one fixed and stable point in the mounting chaos of that week, they became a refuge for the others when life with this group of bored and boring complainers became intolerable.

Although at the end of the previous week, Matt and Lisa had agreed that only one of them at a time was needed to take a group on the trail, they both went on all the rides with this bunch to give each other moral support. The rides out and back were a constant barrage of complaints ("My horse won't go."), demands ("Get me a stick and I'll show this animal who's boss!"), and remarks, of which "Is that what we rode all the way up here to see?" was typical.

Gary did everything but strip naked and dance to get them interested in his songs. They remained mute and bored. During the hayride one woman sneezed so violently that she made Art stop and let her off, and Marcie was chosen by a surreptitious drawing of straws to accompany her home.

The guests did not want to leave the ranch to go on expeditions, and they did not know what to do with themselves when they remained behind. The teenagers spent a lot of time by themselves in the woods until Matt caught them smoking and drinking beer late one afternoon and really let them have it. He did not care what they did to themselves, but he wasn't going to let them set the hills on fire. He told them they would be safe from detection in the equipment-shed loft, and fortunately they had sense enough to believe him

But the younger ones took the prize for the most obnoxious. Everything for them was either yucky or dumb. They would not swim in the yucky pond or eat the yucky food or go on any dumb hikes or play any dumb games. Beth took to following Meg and Marcie around to avoid their bullying, but Jase did not know meanness when he met up with it. Sailing through his days—a tiny indomitable tug in a harbor full of ocean liners—he accepted their surreptitious pinches and pokes and the deliberate bumps that sent him sprawling as serenely as he accepted hugs and smiles from the people who loved him.

Finding themselves unable to entertain this group, Meg and Marcie were reduced to defending the ranch and its occupants from the little monsters. Led by the piggy-eyed boy, the mob took pleasure in trampling the gardens and tormenting the animals. Thursday they had a tomato fight with Peggy's early crop, and on Friday they got into the canned fruits that were stored in the barn near the house. Having broken open several jars to find out what was in them, they went off and left the mess on the floor. Jason wandered in after them, and before Peggy had arrived to check on what he was doing, he had cut his hand on a jagged piece of glass.

She and Marcie raced into town with him, and Meg would have been left to organize the barbecue supper alone if Lisa had not called home at once and told her father it was an emergency. Between them they managed to put on a pretty good spread, but when one of the guests remarked after supper that it would be good to get home, it was all they could do not to shout "Amen!"

After paying lip service to the final campfire, they all sneaked away to the duck pond, where they lay around regaling each other with their favorite incidents and remarks of the week and cackling hysterically until it was time to drive Lisa home.

Saturday morning Matt was up earlier than usual for his morning run. Today was Meg's eighteenth birthday, and they hadn't decided how to celebrate it. The trouble was that in spite of Gary's efforts to invest it with sin and sensation, Craigie was basically a small town with the standard family-type entertainments, and none of them seemed momentous enough for such a once-in-a-lifetime celebration.

Matt had mentally considered and discarded four or five possibilities by the time he was jogging up Little Creek Road toward the ranch once more. Skirting the cattle guard and heading up the road past the duck pond, he was grinning to himself over the memory of his fight with Will when it struck him with almost physical force how much his perspective on the ranch had changed.

He was no longer fighting off old memories. New ones

had gradually replaced them. The duck pond was now the place where they got together on Saturday night to talk, where he and Will had fought over Lisa, and where Meg and Marcie had taught half a dozen little kids to swim. The Black was in the corral the way he had always been, but Cricket was there now too, and both horses nickered at him as he ran past.

Instead of his dad's green Chevy truck, the equipment shed now housed Art's red pickup. On the field beyond the shed they had celebrated the Fourth of July with such enthusiasm that after the football game several people had to be carried back to the house to recover. What used to be the ridge trail was now Lisa's way home.

As Matt came around the last corner he saw that the house and barn, familiar though they were, had changed subtly as well. They were becoming a part of this summer instead of staying reminders of the past. The big blue van with its Pomeroy ranch logo was parked by the barn; the Old Addish, the patio, and the barbecue area were partly visible from the yard gate where he was standing; and out in back, although he couldn't see them from here, were Will's bunkhouse and the garden pond he and Meg had fallen into on the first day.

Suddenly Matt whirled and ran back along the road again, looking—really looking—at the ranch. It was true. His perspective had changed. He had done a good job of holding off those unwanted memories. Maybe too good a job.

It wasn't his ranch anymore. He wasn't seeing the ghosts of his parents and Katie everywhere he looked. He wasn't seeing them at all. Was that what he wanted? To forget them completely, forget the life they had shared here, the good times they'd had? Did he want to pretend they had never lived?

Going to L.A. the way he had, right after they died, all he had taken with him was the image of his parents' bodies in the morgue. And then Katie's. For more than two years, transplanted from Craigie to that setting where there were no familiar places to remind him of the times when they had all been alive together, no friends from his past to share their memories of his family, he had not been able to remember them himself as anything but dead.

But pretending they had never lived, refusing to admit they ever existed—that was crazy! He would be killing them himself if he did that. How could he have been so stupid? Reaching the gate at Little Creek, he stopped, staring blindly at the familiar landscape while his mind ranged through his past, hesitantly at first, and then with increasing joy.

Suddenly he turned. He knew exactly what he wanted to give Meg for her birthday. She, of all people, would understand. Sprinting along the road for the fourth time that morning and racing down the shortcut behind the barn, he hesitated outside the girls' tent for a second. Realizing there was no way of knocking, he tiptoed inside. They were both enveloped in their sleeping bags like hibernating bears, but the curls spilling out of the top of her bag identified Meg for him.

"Hey," he whispered into the dark hole. "Wake up." Blinking sleepily, she emerged from her warm cave, and he put a finger on his lips. "Quick, get dressed. I've got something to show you. It's a birthday present."

With no idea that his sweaty windblown hair, his incredulous grin, and the glow in his eyes made him look as excited as a small boy, he left her alone. Hustling into her clothes, Meg tried to imagine what could have made him so happy. She decided that Poor Boy and Pat had produced puppies, and he was planning on giving her one. The last thing she was going to need in an L.A. apartment was a hound of superior intelligence and size like Poor Boy, but if that's what it was, she would love it anyway and worry about the details later.

Matt led her around the back of the barn and made her stop. "Look straight down the road at the top of the trees. You see where they make a V?" She nodded, perplexed. "We called it the Gap. If you were watching— No," he corrected himself. "If *I* was watching that spot, I could see the dust rising, and I'd know Mom or Dad was coming home." He swung her in a half turn. "Look up the hill. You see that huge old pine— bigger than any of the others?" She nodded again.

"When I was small enough, I used to climb to the very top of it and watch Dad working on the pickup at the equipment shed, or watch the Gap. When I saw the dust signal, I had to get down the tree and race through the woods, the corrals, and the pasture to the road"—he was jogging along now, holding her hand tightly so she had to run to keep up—"and end up right here. If I got here in time, Mom would stop and pick me up so I could open and close the yard gate for her. She'd tell me what she'd done in town, and I'd tell her if anything important had happened while she was gone.

"The duck pond," he said when they reached it. "We used to go skinny-dipping in it on summer nights when it was too hot to sleep. And the lower corral . . . this is where we kept the new or unbroken horses. I broke my leg here once—lost my concentration on a crow-hopping pinto and went flying into the fence. Dad dragged me out of there—me yelling bloody murder—and ran for the house and the pickup. My mom drove—it felt like she was going ninety and hitting every pothole between here and Craigie—and Dad and Katie stayed in back with me. Wrapped me in a blanket, and Dad hung on to my leg and Katie my head while the rest of me went crashing and banging all over the place. But nobody said a word about my losing my grip until I had the cast on and it stopped hurting. Then I thought they were going to tease me about it for the rest of my life."

Across the road from the corral was a tree stump. Three living trees grew out of it, but the center of the stump itself had rotted out and was hollow inside. Big enough for a small child to fit into.

"One of Katie's favorite places to hide," Matt explained. "She never got any farther than this when she was furious with somebody and running away from home—" He faltered, and Meg knew he was thinking about the one time when she had gone farther. He caught himself and went on. "And Pat always had her pups here too.

"Last stop, for now anyway. I've got a lot to show you, but we've got all summer." He took her out the gate on to Little Creek Road and turned her around. "I started running out this way when I was nine, like Aunt Belle said. Not every morning, but near enough. And one day when I got back here, I found Katie in her nightgown and bare feet, running down our road trying to catch up with me. I had to carry her home because her feet were all bruised and cut, and she pounded on me all the way. She was mad because I hadn't waited for her.

"After that I used to dress her every morning and let her run with me—not past the gate, though, until she was a lot older. She used to swing on the the gate until she saw me coming, way down the road, and then she'd take off for home herself. After a while I really had to go all out to catch up with her. Hey . . . maybe that's where I got that good old last-lap kick that's been coming in so handy ever since!" He laughed, delighted with this discovery—something he hadn't known about himself and his family until he let himself remember them.

Meg did not know what to say. Bursting with happiness because he was so transparently happy himself, she wanted him to know she treasured his present because she understood he was giving her something—memories of his family—that he treasured himself. She wanted him to know how glad she was that he had finally linked up his old life and his new one—Gary's and mine, she thought with delight—and was feeling terrific about being one person again. Whole, and not hurting anymore. But she didn't know how to say any of those things without trespassing on territory too private and personal.

"I'll race you back," she said instead. "Only you

have to give me a head start. Promise?'' He nodded, grinning at her while he jogged rapidly in place as if he couldn't wait to get moving. "Okay, count to one hundred by ones. And no cheating . . . no matter what happens. Okay?''

"Okay, okay," he said, laughing. "Get going."

"Lean down," she said, hoping she was not going to embarrass both of them by crying. "I love your present," she whispered. "Thanks." And then—because he was so close and smelled so warm and sweaty and healthy, and there was a ladybug in his hair, and the morning was so clear and pinkish gold and perfect, and she felt so fantastic herself—she kissed him hard on the mouth and fled up the road yelling, "One hundred by ones, and no cheating, remember!"

Five hundred by ones would not have given her enough of a lead to beat the California state high-school record holder for the 3200 meters, especially not in the high-flying mood he was in. He caught up with her as she reached the shortcut to the tents and bunkhouse. Grabbing her hand, he veered off the road and down the path. Arriving breathlessly at the tents a moment later, they enraged the other three by rousting them out of bed with glad cries and enthusiastic descriptions of the fabulous day they were wasting. It was breakfast time before they were all on speaking terms again.

# 24

*The* question of how to celebrate Meg's birthday was settled by Marcie when she told Art that Peggy needed a break from the hassle of running the ranch. She suggested he take Peggy with him when he and Hank drove the guests to the airport and have an entertaining night in Boise before picking up the next batch of guests on Sunday. Art thought it was a tremendous idea. Peggy was harder to convince, but when Marcie and Meg insisted they would be insulted if she didn't trust them to take superb care of Beth and Jase, she gave in with a laugh and went around for the rest of the morning whistling cheerfully to herself.

They lined up dutifully to wave the guests off, Beth swinging happily on the yard gate and making rude faces at the departing children. Just before the van was obscured by the dust cloud, they saw the piggy boy's finger raised in an unmistakable gesture, and it was all they could do not to reciprocate. With guests gone, the birthday celebration could begin.

As a present from everyone, Meg's responsibility for cleaning cabins and changing beds was divided among the rest of the crew. She was left to rock gently in the hammock with Jase, who had not recovered his natural ebullience after yesterday's encounter with the piece of glass.

Will was also excused from his share of the cleaning up so he could iron out the last few kinks in the bunkhouse in preparation for the formal christening ceremony planned for the afternoon. Like an artist with an unfinished painting, he had become so possessive about his creation that he had put padlocks on both doors and refused to let anyone except Lisa inside before he had completed it to the last detail.

By 1:30 the cabins and the horses were prepared for the coming week, and their time was their own. A massive shopping list was drawn up, and an expedition into town was organized. Home again by 3:30, everyone except Will assembled in the kitchen to construct the cake. Meg would have preferred to be involved in the cheerful confusion as too many cooks crashed around looking for things in cupboards and drawers, but she reminded them of her presence occasionally by reading choice snippets out of the weekend newspaper that someone had brought back with the groceries.

"Oh, hey!" she said suddenly. "Oh, wow! This judge can't be real. Listen to this." She read them an account of a judge who had refused to sentence three high-school boys for raping a fifteen-year-old girl. He said that because the girl had worn a miniskirt to school, she had asked for it. By the time she finished reading the article Meg's voice was shaking with fury. "Either this idiot approves of beating up people with other parts of your body like fists or feet, or he's not too intelligent. How did he ever get to be a judge?"

Always ready for a good debate, Gary took up the challenge at once. "But, Meg . . . having sex is something that, in the right circumstances at least, is a lot of fun. People enjoy it. You can't say that punching or kicking people is ever a socially approved activity."

"Oh yes, you can. When it's boxing or karate—then it's a sport. But using your fists or your feet to beat someone up because you've lost control of yourself isn't okay. It's assault and battery. And that's the same difference between a friendly game of sex, and rape."

"Ummm . . . ," said Gary, unable for once to think of a snappy comeback. Everyone laughed at the succession of expressions crossing his mobile face. "Round one to you," he said finally, "but I wasn't ready for it. Now if you want to tackle the burning question of nuclear energy, I'll—"

"Not that again," someone groaned, and Matt stuffed Gary's mouth full of marshmallows, holding it closed with difficulty while he yelled at Meg to read something noncontroversial like the baseball standings. The battle that followed was interrupted by the arrival of Will.

"Ta-dah!" he trumpeted. "Ladies and gentlemen, the bunkhouse awaits your presence at the official ribbon-cutting and champagne-christening ceremonies!"

Mindful of the hazards of broken glass, they poured a large bottle of ginger ale into eight plastic sandwich bags and threw them at the sides of the ten-by-twenty-foot bunkhouse until it was thoroughly christened. Lisa and Will then wound lengths of glossy gold ribbon around it, and when Beth had snipped her way through the last strand, Will finally unlocked both doors and invited them in.

They were all prepared to tease him about his obsession with his work. Instead everyone found themselves impressed with the results and amazed at the workmanship. The most anyone could manage beyond admiring remarks like "Wow!" and "I can't believe it!" and "Hey, you guys, look at this!" was an incredulous "Will, did you really do all this yourself?"

The bunkhouse was two separate rooms—each with its own entrance, each containing four built-in bunks with two drawers in each one, and a small bathroom with shower. They were carpeted in the same tweedy blue material Hank had used in the cabins, and the interior walls were of paneled wood, liberally sprinkled with shelves and clothes hooks.

"Will," Meg said, after inspecting the girls' side and finding it the mirror image of the other, "this whole thing is fantastic! I can't believe it! You really did this all yourself?"

Will's grin was so broad, he couldn't talk properly. "Well, some of it Hank had to do—like the plumbing connections and the window on your side and most of the wiring and the right-hand drawer in the bottom bunk over there and—"

"Help!" said Meg. "Never mind already. Stop him, somebody!" And Gary and Matt happily obliged.

Supper was barbecued at Chapman's Lake. The first course having been cooked and eaten, Marcie got the present giving going by producing hers with a flourish— all the makings for do-it-yourself sundaes from her father's ice-cream parlor. After everyone had tucked as much of this splendor as possible into stomachs already full of superb, made-to-order hamburgers, Meg was given permission to open the others.

Gary's was a rock—a smooth gray rock the size of a softball on which he had written in felt pens of many colors: *Souvenir of Craigie, Idaho—Sin City of the Western World*. On a forgotten shelf of the sporting-goods store, Will had found an enormous T-shirt—jelly-bean green with a life-size horse's head on the front. Even after she had washed it and shrunk it in the dryer, Meg could tell it was going to come to her knees and would make a great nightshirt. She thanked both of them profusely.

Lisa gave her a silver-and-turquoise necklace, producing it almost shyly, and was visibly relieved at Meg's unfeigned delight. Beth presented her with five handpicked ponytail holders, one of which Meg immediately used to replace the rubber band she was currently using. Matt's present was a class photograph of himself, Gary, Marcie, and Lisa in first grade. The original was one of Aunt Belle's prized possessions, but she had let him borrow it and have a copy made. Marcie had fat pigtails and an impish grin, Lisa and

Matt were missing their front teeth, and Gary had his arm in a cast.

Gary then produced some mail from Los Angeles, which, he said, he had been saving for her birthday in case everyone else forgot.

The postcard from Lew read:

*Dear Meg, Happy Birthday and all that jazz. How does it feel to be an old lady? Just joking. The Angels had a bad week on the road but they'll be home all next week and I'm going to at least three games. They've won every game I've been to, so I can't let them down now. We've got a new housekeeper. She's weird. I've got glasses now. They're weird too. Good joke. What do you call a bull who swallowed a bomb? Abominable. Get it?*

    *Good-bye, Lew.*

Carey's letter was only slightly more informative:

*Dear Meg, Happy Birthday. Hope you're having fun. I'll give you your present when you get home. I made it at camp. We go home this week, but I wish we didn't have to. I'm having a great time. Our tent got Slobs of the Week Award last week, and we might get it this time too. Everybody stayed up all night last night except for Stephanie. She says she didn't go to sleep, but nobody makes noises like that when they're awake. I had good parts in two plays and I'm not scared of acting in front of crowds anymore. Not too scared anyway. I got in trouble doing imitations, though. Have you ever noticed some grown-ups don't have a very good sense of humor? Lew says we have a weird housekeeper. I can't wait to see her. She can't be any worse than Mrs. Dresden. How many teakettles did she burn up? Three? Say hi to Will and Matt and don't get poison oak. I did and I can't tell you where.*

    *Love, Carey.*

By the time these gems had been read aloud and laughed over, it was almost dark. Jase had gone to sleep in Marcie's lap, and Beth was curled up on Matt's, sucking her thumb and staring glassy-eyed at the dying fire. Loading the remains of the feast into the pickup, they drowned the last embers and headed contentedly toward home.

# 25

**S**unday morning everyone overslept. After a large breakfast they all scattered on various errands. Meg was sitting on the steps of the Old Addish, sewing up a three-cornered tear in a favorite shirt, when Gary returned from church. Except for Beth and Jase in the sandbox, she was the only one in sight. He dropped down beside her, leaning back against the door and watching her work.

"I've got some shirts needing repairs," he said after a while. "If I bring them over, will you fix them up for me?"

"Nope," she said, biting off the thread and examining her work critically. "But I'll show you how to do it yourself, if you want."

"No, thanks." Tempted to get a rise out of her after yesterday's one-sided debate, he added mischievously, "That's women's work."

"Bull!" Meg said, rising to the bait. "Anything you need to know how to do so you can take care of yourself is a survival skill—nothing to do with men's work and women's work. Unless you want to be tied to some female's apron strings for the rest of your life."

She's done it again, Gary thought with a secret grin. I can't argue against that either. But this time he was not going to be outmaneuvered. "Okay," he said suddenly, "but I bet you don't know any more about cars than I know about sewing, right?"

"Right."

"So how come? That's a survival skill too. If your car breaks down on a lonely road and you can't figure out what's wrong and get it going again, you could be in real trouble."

"I'm not arguing with you. You want to teach me how to fix broken-down cars?"

"Sure," Gary said, detecting a challenge in her tone. "Come on."

It developed that Meg had never even changed a flat tire. Using the Schuyler station wagon as a guinea pig, she and Gary were hard at work when Matt and Will returned from the weekly trip to the dump. The two of them hung around offering useless advice and laughing enormously at their own jokes until Gary and Meg gave up in exasperation. Taking Beth and Jase, they all went down to the duck pond for a swim.

Marcie had spent the day with her parents but was back before the guests were due to arrive. She spoke for all of them when she confessed that she was not looking forward to the days ahead. "One more week like the last one, and I'm heading for a cave in northern Canada."

But Week-Four-with-Guests turned out as unpredictably as all the others. The station wagon arrived right behind the van, and they watched in mounting horror as Under-Tens spilled out of the doors like rabbits out of a magician's hat.

"It's the Invasion of the Little People," Will said in dire tones.

There were six adults and eleven kids—"Count

them,'' Matt said, appalled. "Eleven!"—all age ten or less.

"Eeyow!" said Meg to Marcie.

"Give me strength," Marcie said to the sky above.

"Lots of luck, you guys," Gary said gleefully.

Braced for the worst, everyone was delighted to discover that this group was as enthusiastic as the first week's guests had been. Because the children were all so young, they needed more supervision and did not go on excursions to the Salmon River and the lake, but they were eager to ride, swim, play games, climb trees, and go on nature hikes with Marcie. It was like running a day camp, and Matt and Lisa were pressed into service on nonriding days as the hares in a hare-and-hound chase and as captains of an ongoing game of Capture the Flag. On the last day they organized a minirodeo with Art and Peggy as judges.

Will also led a crew in the construction of a raft for the duck pond, a paddle-tennis table for the patio, and finally a tree house. He had to abandon this last project when Hank arrived mid-week with the news that if they could finish the fourth A-frame cabin in the next four weeks, he had a good group that wanted to come for the last week and stay over Labor Day weekend.

He and Will went to look at Cabin Four and see where they had to begin. On the way over Hank made one of the comments that Will had learned to interpret as the compliments they were meant to be. "I'm getting a hell of a lot more work out of you than I anticipated," he said. "If you and the weather hold up, we could get some work done on the main house before the summer's over. On a ranch," he added, in a tone that suggested he had learned this from bitter experience, "the last ones to have any money spent on their comfort are usually the human beings. But as long as I have the know-how and the money, that won't happen around here.

"Art and I grew up on a ranch like this one," he explained, "and my dad couldn't understand why I wanted something else out of life. Had some god-awful fights on the subject. Dad knocked me out a couple of times, but I kept growing on him until the day I faced him down and told him I was leaving. Never saw him again. He died a year later, and the ranch went to pay off his debts. Art tried city life for a few years, but he hated it. Not like me. Soon as he had enough money saved, he started looking for a ranch of his own. This is his second, and it's my guess he's here to stay.

"Well, let's see what we need to do to this place before I turn you loose on your own." He began ticking off a list of jobs, and Will felt a surge of pride that filled the void created by his sudden loss of confidence at the beginning of the summer. It was pride in himself and his rapidly developing skills; pride in his workmanship. He *was* good at this job. He loved it all—the smell of freshly cut wood; the satisfaction of making a good join out of two separate pieces; the soft feel of wood that had been sanded and rubbed; and above all, the permanence of the results. The practical, beautiful, usefulness of them.

This kind of work had reason to it, and purpose. Not like yard work, or housework, or homework. They had a purpose, maybe, but they were things someone else wanted him to do. This kind of work was different. It felt good. Hank's confidence in him added to his growing sense of fulfillment, and Hank's revelation about his father and his own choice for himself gave Will the germ of an idea.

For the remainder of the week, while working with Hank, he turned the idea around in his mind, looking at it from different sides, examining the possibilities. On Saturday night when they were all gathered on the grass beside the duck pond, Will sounded the others out on the subject.

"Now that you guys are through with high school," he said casually, "do any of you have the foggiest idea what you're going to do with the rest of your lives?"

They were slow to respond. The week had been fun

but physically exhausting for all of them. Matt finally threw out a comment that got things going.

"There's always ranching," he said slowly, as if he were thinking it through, "or something to do with people. Not manufacturing or selling."

"Did you ever think about being a policeman—a detective, like Tony and Lieutenant Ryder?" Meg asked.

"Yeah . . . but you never see anything but people at their worst. Pretty depressing."

"What about teaching . . . or coaching?"

"Not much better."

Laughter followed this remark.

"Seriously, though," Matt went on, "that's a possibility, I guess. Or maybe . . . well, I've thought about working with deaf kids."

"So have I," said Meg. "I like kids. I like working with them like we did this week. But there are too many teachers for the regular kids already. By the time I get there, who's going to need me except the special kids—the ones who are different? What about you, Marcie?"

"I wasn't sure before this summer, but now I am—a ranger with the National Park Service. You get people, and you get the earth itself. It's perfect." She glanced expectantly at Lisa. "Your turn," she prodded after a moment.

"I haven't the foggiest," Lisa said, and only Will, who knew about the promise she had made her father, could understand the bitterness in her voice.

"Is it my turn yet?" Gary asked. A chorus of "Yeahs" and "Um-hums" gave him the go-ahead. "I not only know what I'm going to do, my children," he said grandly, "but when summer school is over, I'll be launching myself on my lifetime career."

"You're really not going to college?"

"Why waste the time and money when what I need to know is right down the road at Mr. Lomax's Honda dealership?"

"Mr. Lomax?"

"Honda dealership?"

"You're not going to stay on your dad's ranch?" Matt said, surprised. "Does he know?"

"Yeah, he knows. We've talked about it a lot, and anyway, I won't be moving out for a while yet. But I'm a machine man. Machines and I understand each other. I've been working for Mr. Lomax for the last two years. Starting in September I've got a permanent job with him—mechanic, salesman, and someday a dealer myself. That's what *I'm* doing with the rest of my life."

Perfect! Will was thinking. Fantastic! I need to have a heart-to-heart with Gary, and the sooner the better.

"Will? Hey, Will, are you asleep again?" Matt was leaning over him threateningly. "It's your turn."

But his plans were not ready for public exposure. "I don't know," he said vaguely. "No people, though. I've had enough people hassles. I think I'll spend my life contemplating some nice, uncomplicated mechanical object."

"Like your navel?" This unexpected contribution from Lisa broke everyone up and turned the conversation to other things.

Will grinned into the darkness. For a long time he had been drifting in a panic. Suddenly, as if he had caught that legendary Seventh Wave, he was moving again. He knew where he was going—what a difference that made in the way he felt!—and he promised himself he would get there, no matter what the cost.

# 26

*W*eek Five everything was planned and executed with such ease that it seemed as if they were all on vacation themselves. The guests were a nice mixture of ages and interests and included several serious runners. One of them knew of Matt's reputation in high-school track, and Matt's morning run before breakfast became a regular part of the guests' schedule.

Meg had been running as far as she could with Matt every morning since her birthday, but the first day out with the guests, she nearly killed herself trying to keep up with the more competitive pace. For the rest of the week she contented herself with leading a group of the youngest runners to the end of the drive and back. One morning her group got such a late start that they reached the gate in time to see their parents and brothers and sisters coming back along Little Creek Road. They were still a considerable distance away, but the little ones swarmed up on the gate and along the fences, waving wildly.

"Hey, everybody," Meg said suddenly. "Let's race them back to the house. See if we can beat them, okay?"

Of course it was okay. It was a fantastic idea! Instantly the road was filled with eager children racing to be the first in their families for once, instead of the last. Meg, bringing up the rear sheepdog fashion, glanced back and saw that their challenge had been accepted. The group on Little Creek was going all out. "Run!" she screamed. "Here they come!"

Matt caught up with her between the shed and the shortcut and threw her a grin as he sprinted past. About twenty yards behind him, a father and his teenage daughter were coming along pretty strongly too, but the rest of Matt's team was spreading out as the runners gradually dropped behind. Her team still had a chance to get home first, and she raced after them yelling encouragement. Far out in front she could see two figures—a wiry little black boy named Tyrone and Matt himself. As they rounded the last turn before the gate the smaller one was fifteen feet ahead of his pursuer.

Meg had to stop once to scoop up her youngest charge, who had fallen and skinned her knee. The two of them were the last to reach the house, where an excited crowd was milling around the yard—children telling parents how they had managed to beat them, the older ones laughing and promising that next time would be a different story. Suddenly a small body crashed into her, and a voice shouted, "I won! I won!"

She looked down into two dark eyes glowing with the thrill of victory. "You were terrific, Tyrone!" she told him. "Absolutely terrific! What did Matt say?"

"He said I was terrific too!" Tyrone shouted, racing off to find someone else to share his great news with.

She would have liked to kid Matt a little about the race, but he was part of a large noisy group, and because she had to take a quick shower before she started work in the kitchen, the opportunity slipped by. Because of that missed moment, for the remainder of the week she found herself watching for him, looking for times when she could have him to herself. There weren't many.

Matt was in demand not only by the guests but by Art Pomeroy. Knowing he was on sensitive ground after that first day's painful tour of the ranch, Art had been hesitant about involving Matt in the running of the ranch itself. But since Meg's birthday, when Matt had begun to open up, Art had increasingly come to rely on him as a knowledgeable partner. Sometimes in the early morning or late afternoon, he and Matt rode out to check on the livestock or explore the practical requirements of some improvement Art was thinking of making, and after supper they often sat together discussing ranching in general.

No longer reluctant to speak of his family, Matt seemed grateful for the chance to share his memories and experience. The word *dad* cropped up continually in his conversation with Art, while with Gary's mom and dad and the five of them, he talked freely and affectionately about his mom and Katie. He felt at home at last in this place that was both old and new to him, familiar and unfamiliar. He belonged here again, as he had belonged once before.

*Belonged here* . . . Meg did not face up to the meaning of those words until the guests were piling into the van on Saturday with shouted good-byes and thanks for a great time.

"They make a handsome pair, don't they?" she heard one guest say to another. Looking around, she saw Matt and Lisa riding through the yard gate on the Black and Charley. Lisa was talking animatedly, and she heard Matt laugh.

They *were* a handsome pair. For one piercing, pain-filled moment, she wanted to stop everything, turn time back to that Monday morning in L.A. when Matt had told them reluctantly and unwillingly of Gary's impossible plan for the summer. I wish we'd never come up here, she cried in silent agony. I wish we'd never come back.

An instant later shame scorched her from head to foot. Never come back? Never let Matt remember the good times, shake loose from the nightmares and the pain of losing everyone he loved? Never feel whole and happy again? *Meg Schuyler, how selfish can you be?*

Cheeks flaming, she headed for the nearest cabin and threw herself furiously into the job of getting it ready for the next day. What was wrong with her? How could she have made such a disgusting wish? How could she even have thought it? It was a good thing for everyone else that she couldn't make things happen by wishing for them.

She couldn't change anything, and she wouldn't if she could. It was Matt's life. He had a right to choose how he wanted to live it. And where. After what he had been through, he had earned that right. And there was no doubt that he was going to have a choice to make. The Maitlands were as much his family as the Ryders. They loved him too, and they'd been part of his life for much longer.

She was glad he had a choice, she really was. She was not going to make it harder for him by letting him know how she felt, but it was no use pretending she wasn't scared.

How could she have wanted this so badly, prayed for it to happen, and feel so terrible now that it finally had? At the beginning of the summer she had been miserable because he was hurting. Now she was miserable because he wasn't.

You never stop thinking about yourself, do you? she told herself scornfully, but she had no control over her reaction. It shook and chilled her like a physical shock. What if he decided to stay in Craigie for good? What if she had to go back to Los Angeles without him when the summer was over, never see him again? Oh no, she thought helplessly. Matt, please . . .

Her share of the work done, she shook her head at Marcie's invitation to spend the afternoon in town, took the station wagon, and headed north, east . . . anywhere where she could be alone. Not entirely alone, though. She hadn't gone far when she realized that what she'd been looking for when she started driving was her mother.

How many times had she gone on some errand with her mom in this same old comfortable elephant of a car—just the two of them—and talked, knowing they wouldn't be interrupted? Talked about books and movies, dreams for the future—her mom's and hers both—problems at school, kids in trouble. She'd shared with her mom all nine months of Suzanne Dearborne's unwanted pregnancy, and the agony of her decision to give the baby up for adoption. Even though they agreed Suzanne had done the right thing, they had both cried. . . .

She was crying now. Sobbing helplessly, she turned down a dirt road, pulling over and parking the car so she wouldn't run into anyone. After a moment she moved out of the driver's seat and slid across to the passenger side of the car.

*You're not here. I know it . . . but I need you. I want you back so badly. . . .*

"Everything's changed," she wailed. "Everything's different now. He's not just a friend anymore. Mom, I love him. . . . I don't know what to do."

There were no easy answers. There never were. When at last she slid back into the driver's seat and headed for the ranch, the pain was still with her, but she thought she had buried it deeply enough so that no one, especially Matt, would know it was there. He had done the same thing for her when the summer began. She was determined to do it for him now.

# 27

*T*he week that followed, Week-Six-with-Guests, was another easy one for everyone except Meg. Matt's birthday was going to fall on the Thursday of that week. Sunday, after lunch, Lisa gave him an early birthday present.

"I'm switching jobs with Meg this week," she said out of the blue. "Happy birthday, Matt."

If Meg had been watching Matt's face as he struggled not to look so pleased that it would be an insult to Lisa, and failed utterly to disguise his surprise and delight, she would have understood the general laughter and felt better herself. As it was, she was covering her own mixture of shock and panic and the impulse to shout "No, no, I can't!" with an elaborate pretense of concern over what Jase was up to in the garden. By the time she was ready to face the others, Matt had his own expression under control again. She thought with a pang that he was no more enthusiastic about Lisa's offer than she was.

"Don't let him boss you around," Lisa told Meg firmly. "He thinks he's the only one around here who knows horses. If you aren't careful, you'll find he's giving the orders and you're doing all the work."

As it turned out, since Meg did not know the horses or the routines, she found it necessary to let Matt tell her what to do—and safer. With the guests around, it put a businesslike distance between them and made it easier for Meg to avoid the kind of conversation that might catch her off guard and betray her feelings.

On the trail rides she observed him from a safe distance—watching the natural sway of his long muscular body in response to the horse's movements, the breeze riffling through his dark hair, the skin crinkling around his eyes when he squinted into the sun or grinned at someone. She noticed the rugged bones of his knees standing out sharply under his tight, faded jeans, and the gradual curve of the strong running muscles in his thighs. She saw his hands, hard and callused and deeply tanned; his fingers curling gently around Jason's small pudgy ankles as he carried him on his shoulders; his knuckles standing out whitely as he hoisted saddles on and off the horses' backs. Absorbing every detail of his appearance, every inflection of his voice and laugh, she stored up memories of him as if she knew he would not be coming back to Los Angeles.

When he teased her, she wanted to cry. When he brushed against her accidentally or tried to roughhouse with her, she turned away, fighting the urge to throw her arms around him and beg him not to stay in Craigie.

Because it gave her a chance to be alone with him without having to talk, she ran with him every morning as far as she could. At meals and in the evenings she kept her distance, letting Beth and the guests vie for the privilege of sitting beside him or on him as the little ones often did. Once, watching him wrestling with four Under-Tens at the same time, she was reminded of a lion playing roughly and affectionately with its cubs. She wished she were Beth's age again, when loving him was not so full of pain and unanswerable questions.

His birthday created a welcome diversion. Because it fell in the middle of the week, it could not be celebrated with all the pomp and fanfare that Meg's had been, but he told them many times that what they did, with one exception, was perfect.

To start with, using a discarded sheet from Aunt Belle's bottomless rag bag, Meg and Marcie made a huge banner that read HAPPY EIGHTEENTH, MATT! and was signed by everyone on the ranch. When Matt vanished on his run down Little Creek in the morning, Will and Gary emerged from the trees and hung it from the crossbar. Everyone then hid in the trees again until he came back, leaping out with cries of "Surprise!" and "Happy birthday!" and ran with him back to the bunkhouse in a noisy swarm. Gary and Will had worked out a surprise of their own for him there. Before he knew what was happening, they tripped him and were carrying him with the help of an enthusiastic group of Under-Tens toward the garden pond.

In the end he was thrown in, but not without taking most of the Under-Tens and Will in with him. Gary, naturally, was left smirking on the edge of the pond, and Meg was pretty sure she knew what Matt was thinking as

he hoisted himself up on the bank. Gary was long overdue for the same treatment himself.

"Let me know when it's Gary's turn," she said to the
dripping Matt a moment later, and he promised her
grimly that when the time was right, she would be the
first to know.

The rest of the day was business as usual, but after
supper most of the guests went into town for the square
dance or the movies. When Will returned from chauffeuring duty, they gathered on the patio for cake and
presents.

Lisa had already given Matt her present, and the
Pomeroys' was the cake itself, decorated by Beth in icing
of three different colors, with Matt's name in wobbly,
two-inch letters. Carey and Lew had sent him a giant
blue and silver balloon that said *Way to Go, Big Bro!* and
cost Meg and Will a small fortune to have filled with
helium at the card-and-gift shop downtown. There was
still an impressive pile of gifts on the table.

Meg had ordered Matt's present from a local silver-
smith before she had begun wrestling with her private
fears. It was such a Craigie kind of thing that she was
sorry she had ever had the idea, but she gave it to him
anyway—a sterling-silver belt buckle engraved with his
initials.

"Beauty, Newk!" he said admiringly, using a phrase
picked up from a guest who had done a lot of traveling in
Australia, a phrase that in a lot of situations they found
expressed the right amount of delighted approval without
sounding too corny or sentimental.

Marcie's present was a photograph of all of them that
she had taken with Peggy's help and not without a great
deal of difficulty. She had gotten no cooperation from
Matt, Will, or Gary until she bribed them with a promise
of unlimited goodies from her father's store—a promise
on which she cheerfully reneged as soon as the picture
was safely in the camera. The instant she set the camera
on the picnic table, she had been thrown in the garden

pond. Meg and Lisa, their attempts at rescue proving unsuccessful, had followed her in.

Will and Gary had joined forces and bought Matt a black Stetson hat that suited him perfectly and that, Will explained, would clearly identify him in future as the bad guy. Matt set the hat at precisely the right angle on his head and scowled ferociously at each of them. "Anyone who gets this hat wet or crumpled for any reason is going to take a long time to recover. Get it?" They got it. In future the hat, at least, would be treated with respect.

Aunt Belle and Uncle Frank had sent over with Gary a handmade redwood sign. MCKENDRICK was carved into its polished surface. Matt looked at it for a long time, tracing the grooves of the letters with his forefinger. Glancing up, he realized the others were watching him and forced a grin. "Now *there's* a name," he said, but Meg was pretty sure he had been wondering whether that sign would ever hang from a crossbar at the entrance to his own ranch.

In fact, he had been thinking about this morning's conversation with Uncle Frank, who had been waiting for him when he arrived at the Maitland gatepost on his morning run.

"Wanted to be the first to congratulate you," Uncle Frank had said with a twinkle. "There were times there I wasn't sure you were going to make it to eighteen."

"Yeah, well . . . here I am."

The words hung in the air, carrying another meaning. For a moment they had simply looked at each other. Then Uncle Frank had reached for him, enfolding him in a rough embrace.

"Matt," he had said after a moment. "Belle and I. . . . You know Gary's plans. And Susan—she's restless, wants to see the world. This place . . . it's yours, whenever you want to come home."

*Come home . . . come home. . . .* All the way back to the Pomeroys', his running feet had kept time to those words. *Come home . . . come home. . . .* No matter how often he changed his rhythm, he had not been able to shake them off. . . .

The other presents, which Gary had been hiding at his house for the last three days, were from the Ryders and Tony. Matt opened a card from Tony enclosing clippings on the Angels and a promise to take him to the first home game after he returned; a card from Mrs. B. promising a royal homecoming feast with all his favorite foods; a miniature but remarkably versatile camera from Sally with instructions to take some pictures and share the summer with them in the fall; a portrait of Matt with Jenny on his shoulders drawn by Jenny herself; and a trophy from Michael that said *World's Greatest* on it. With felt pens he had added one rainbow-colored word— *Brother*.

Ryder's present was a small, intricately carved wooden box. Something inside was rattling, but no one could figure out how to open the box and find out what it was. After everyone had tried and failed, Matt groaned suddenly and announced that he couldn't stand the suspense. Leaving the sliding door open so they could listen, he went inside and made a collect call home. The Ryders were apparently expecting his call, because they heard him say, "Yeah, well, you were right. I wanted to thank everyone for the great presents. . . . No, not yet. Oh? Oh, okay."

They waited impatiently for another twenty minutes while he talked to each member of his family and gave them bits and pieces of the summer. When he came back outside, he told them it was a Chinese puzzle box. "The thing that's rattling is a present from Sally and Ryder. I can't have it, Ryder says, unless I get the box open."

The box looked old and fragile, not like something you could buy for a couple of dollars in Chinatown and break open if you couldn't get into it any other way. He turned it gently around in his hands. "There aren't any cracks," he said, frustrated. "I can't even tell which side is the top."

"Let me try again," Gary said.

Matt shook his head. "I have to figure it out—so I can tell Sally and Ryder I did it."

"Well, go for it then," Marcie said encouragingly.

"Yeah, Matt, go for it," Gary echoed. "Turn it around a couple of times. Yay! That's it! Use that thumb, man. Great moves, fella, keep it up!"

Everyone immediately got into the spirit of Gary's play-by-play, and the peaceful evening was shattered by shouts of encouragement and congratulations. Through it all, Matt remained cool and calm. Suddenly his fumbling fingers pushed, pressed, and pulled in all the right places. The top of the box slid partway open. Matt peered inside, while the others waited in breathless silence. "Wow!" he breathed. He looked around at the row of expectant faces. An idea struck him, and he grinned wickedly.

A second later he was standing on top of the picnic table, holding the box out of everyone's reach. Before anyone could react, he had closed it, smiling serenely at the cries of "Hey, Matt!" and "What did you do that for?"

"Listen, my children," he said, waiting until they were quiet. "We are going to play Gollum's game. You get three guesses. If you guess right, I'll tell you all about it—and you want to know, believe me. If you don't guess what it is . . ." He paused dramatically. "Gary goes into the garden pond."

Gary was outraged. He was also outnumbered. Everyone else thought it was a great idea and were ready with all kinds of ridiculous suggestions, but he demanded and got the right to veto guesses that weren't serious enough. Even so, they could not come up with the right one, and a rigid Gary, arms folded cross his chest like a dead Viking, was carried to the pond and dumped at long last into its muddy depths while his so-called friends danced triumphantly on the banks.

He evened the score, however, when he made them promise to wait for him to change before Matt told them what it was, and then kept them waiting for forty-five interminable minutes while he shaved, showered, washed and blow-dried his hair, and ironed a clean shirt. When he reappeared, sauntering casually toward them, it was touch and go for a moment whether he would find himself back in the pond, but curiosity proved a stronger emotion in everyone's breast at that moment than revenge.

"Come on, Matt," Lisa said, "Tell us what's in the box."

Exaggerating his original clumsy efforts, Matt began fumbling with it again, until Will said, "Just *tell* us, you jerk."

"All right," he said, as anxious to tell them as they were to hear. "It's a key."

"A key to what?"

"A three-year-old . . ." He gestured for applause, and they delivered it reluctantly. "Metallic-blue . . ." Their applause was less grudging this time. "V-Eight . . ." Oohs and ahs. "Mustang . . ." Loud cheers. "Convertible!" Screams of excitement from everyone, including Meg.

Way to go, Ryders! Meg was thinking as Matt went back inside to call his parents again. But she knew that if Matt decided to stay in Craigie, there wasn't a present in the world that could change his mind.

# 28

*If* Meg had only barely survived the week of switching jobs, Will and Lisa had thoroughly enjoyed it. Will was working hard on the A-frame, and Lisa had found time to help him almost every day—"not eating" her lunches with him or making herself useful during the trail rides when the ranch was emptied of guests. Will had managed one private talk with Gary about his views on life without further schooling and by Friday was ready to talk to someone about his own plans.

"Remember when we were talking about jobs and ways to spend our lives last week?" he asked Lisa suddenly.

"Mmm?" said Lisa. It was not one of her favorite subjects. Will knew this, but he had plans for her too. He would get to them in a minute.

"I've been thinking a lot since then. About my own plans, I mean. I don't think I'm going back to school in the fall. I'm going to work for Hank in L.A. instead."

"Quit school? But you've only got one more year to go."

"Yeah, but like Gary says, why waste the time and money when what I need to know is down the road at Hank's place?"

She was silent for a moment, considering all the angles, and he waited impatiently for her response. He knew he was going to face considerable opposition from a lot of people wanting to meddle in his life without an invitation, and he wondered whether her reaction was going to be typical of everyone else's. Knowing her situation as well as he did, he could have guessed what her first question would be.

"What about your father? What's he going to say?"

"That's a problem," Will admitted. "I don't know what he'll say. I'm not even sure I care. But he probably won't like it, and I guess I'll have to try to convince him it's a good idea. I mean, he *is* my father. I owe him that much."

"Can you go all the way to the top in the construction business without a high-school diploma?"

"I don't want to go to the top. I want to build things, work with my hands—not sit around in a fancy office wheeling and dealing."

"What about your brain? What's it going to be doing all your life while your hands are enjoying themselves?"

"You think it doesn't take brains to do a job like this?" Will said hotly.

"No, that's not what I mean." She wrinkled her forehead, flapped one hand vaguely, and finally shrugged. "I don't know what I mean. Something to do with being a thinker, I guess. Solving problems, saving the world—that kind of thing."

"I'm not the world-saver type," Will said curtly.

Yes, you are, she was thinking. She had learned a lot about him in the past few weeks. You care about a lot of things and, in spite of what you said last week, people especially. But he seemed touchy on the subject, so she let it go. "Well, lots of luck," she said. "I have a feeling you're going to need it."

He grinned and gestured for her to steady the other end of the panel he was nailing to the studs. "I have a feeling you're right." They worked in silence for a while, and then he said casually, "What would your father say if you told him you were going to college this year after all?"

"I'm not,"she said. It was her turn to sound prickly.

"I know. I'm just what-if-ing. What would he say?"

She had thought about this question herself. The last weeks of being accepted into the group, of being a part of everything for the first time in her life, had made the prospect of next fall's friendless, housebound existence almost unbearable. "I don't know. He'd probably yell a lot. Or he might go all glum and silent and make me feel like a rat."

"Why?"

"Why? What do you mean, why? Because he needs me. There isn't anyone else to run the house."

"He doesn't need you. He needs a housekeeper. The sooner he finds that out, the better for you and for him too, probably."

"Why should he pay someone when I'm perfectly capable of managing?"

"Meg used to say the same thing, but she learned. Why should you have to manage when he can easily afford to pay someone?"

"Will Schuyler," she said coldly. "Why don't you mind your own business?"

"That's what my little sister always says," Will told her smugly, "when she's losing an argument." Lisa hit him hard enough to send the box of paneling nails flying, and the next five minutes were spent at the exasperating job of picking the skinny, topless nails out of the cracks in the plywood floor.

They were unknowingly following the same crack when they bumped into each other hard and head-on. Sitting back on her heels, rubbing her head, Lisa surveyed Will critically. "When are you going to get your hair cut?"

Will grinned, recognizing the strategy—when you're losing an argument, quit defending yourself and attack from a new direction. "Tomorrow," he said calmly. "You know any good barbers in town?"

"Of course I do. Are you serious?"

"Of course I am. When am I ever not?"

"All right. Tomorrow. It'll have to be before the guests leave, because I have to clean cabins after they go. As soon as the breakfast dishes are done, you can drive us in and I'll introduce you to Sam."

"Don't tell anyone else," Will said as she was leaving to help with supper. "I don't want the rest of them hanging around offering idiot suggestions and snickering while I'm getting shorn."

"All right," she agreed. "But if you don't go through with it like you promised, I'm not going to be responsible for what happens when the rest of them *do* hear about it."

"Rat!" he yelled after her fleeing form. "Traitor!" But he had no intention of chickening out. Too much hair was a pain in the summer, hot and sweaty and needing washing every day. He would be glad to get rid of it.

He was having second thoughts the next morning when he and Lisa entered Sam's barbershop. Sam's first words, after he had Will pinned down and straightjacketed in his gleaming brass-and-black-vinyl chair, did nothing to reassure him.

"I think we should go with the curls," he said cheerfully, lifting a handful of the top straight-haired layer to reveal the curly mop that Will had been hiding underneath it all these years. Will gave Lisa a look in the mirror that was fraught with meaning. Lisa smiled blandly back.

Sam snipped off a little here and there, and Will began to relax, thinking that if that was all he was planning to do, it wouldn't be too bad. Suddenly Sam went after every hair on Will's head with his water spray bottle, then combed it all back into a ducktail. Will sent Lisa another look in the mirror and was not too happy about the horrified expression he saw reflected on her face.

But Sam had just begun. Singing along with his portable radio, oblivious to Will's mounting panic, he slashed and sliced away until Will could not bear to look in the mirror at all, and Lisa was perched on the edge of her chair, following every movement of Sam's skillful hands with mouth half-open, ready to scream "stop!" if he went too far.

Using his blow-dryer, Sam then brushed and dried Will's hair until it stood out all over his head like a blond Afro. Will took a swift glance at himself and mouthed a single desperate word at Lisa's reflection in the mirror. *Help!*

"You aren't going to leave it like that, are you, Sam?" Lisa asked nervously, wondering if she should get ready to run before Sam cut Will loose.

"No, no," Sam said reassuringly. "Just getting a little thickness into it first. Don't want it too flat, do we?"

Yes, we do, thought Will. The flatter, the better. But he was too demoralized to protest. Submitting numbly to the vigorous brushing that followed, he did not look in the mirror again until he heard Lisa's admiring "Well, hey! That's more like it!"

He did not immediately recognize himself. It was a new look, all right, and he wasn't sure it belonged to him.

"You remind me of someone," Lisa was saying as they escaped onto Craigie's sunlit main street. Will had just wished for a total and permanent eclipse of the sun. "Oh, I know!" she exclaimed, as if she thought this news was going to cheer him up. "The Sundance Kid!"

"Oh lord," Will groaned. "Don't say it. I'll never live this down. Why did I let you bully me into it?" But the reaction he got on his return was not what he expected.

"Will?" Meg said uncertainly, greeting him as he emerged from the car the way she had when he had first arrived from Los Angeles. Well, I wanted a new look, he thought gloomily. If my own sister doesn't recognize me . . .

She walked slowly around him, gazing at his hair until he felt like a fur-hatted guard at Buckingham Palace enduring the curious stares of a tourist. "I like it," she said finally. "Yes, I like it. I really do."

"Cooler, anyway," Matt said, not about to let him off so easily. He thumped Will consolingly on the back. "Cheer up, old buddy. Could be worse. You can always wear a hat until it grows back."

But Gary had the last word. Arriving just after lunch, he glanced at Will as if he were a strange visitor, did a double take, and flashed him an enormous grin. "Beauty, Newk!" he said enthusiastically, and since no one could think of a better way to describe it, silenced the rest of them on the subject forever.

He had brought Will a letter from Carey, which Will read aloud to bring everyone up to date on the continuing saga of Life with the Schuylers. It was a classic:

*Dear Will, Hi! Hope you're okay and having fun. We're okay and having fun here. Except for the housekeepers. The first one was so weird I never got to see her. She wasn't there anymore when I got home. Lew said she chain-smoked and called him sweetie pie. He was glad when she went. The new one calls both of us "You kids" and won't let us in the kitchen. Lew and I went to the shopping center yesterday on the bus and got ourselves some food before we starved to death. We keep it in a box in the garage. We're having a good time with Gwen. I told you it would be okay. She made Dad take her and Lew to another game last week, and she's going to go see Anne Frank with me this weekend. The only thing she's not too good with yet are the cats. This morning when I went up for breakfast, there were five cats and two kittens playing all over the family room and kitchen. She said she didn't know which*

*ones were ours, and every time she opened the door
for one, another one came along and wanted to be
let in too. Lew looks terrific in his glasses. Like a
real brain. He broke one pair already. They fell off
when he was skateboarding down Verde Canyon
Road, only he was almost to the bottom and he
didn't want to stop and get them, and when he went
back to look for them, they had been run over by
about ten cars. I think Gwen thought it was kind of
funny, but she was trying not to let Dad see her
laughing. She got Lew an elastic thing to go around
the back of his head and hold them on. Well, have a
great summer. We miss you (but not too much, ha-
ha) (That's a joke)*
    *Love, Carey.*

*P.S. Lew said to tell you he's going to soccer camp
next week. He wasn't going to go, but he changed his
mind. He says he thinks it's safe now, whatever that
means. Not too weird.*
*P.P.S. Only two of the cats were ours.*

"Sounds like they're doing okay without you," Matt
said, laughing.

"Yeah," said Will. "I wonder how long it's going to
last after we get back?"

"It had better last," Meg said. "Otherwise I'm moving out. Anyway, as long as Lew and Carey are happy. . . ."

Will had already had a bad experience with that ar-
rangement. It was not one he cared to repeat. "How
about letting me move out with you?" He was only half
joking. That was the part of his decision he had not
worked out yet—the part that included his family. He
had told Lisa he didn't care what his father thought of his
plans, but he knew that wasn't true. He did care.

He wanted his dad's understanding and support. What
he really wanted, he thought wryly, was for his dad to be

more like Hank. But if he couldn't get it—if he couldn't have both his place in the family and the future he wanted—which would he choose to give up? He wasn't sure, but he knew he would have to decide before he went home, and the moment of decision was coming up fast.

That night at the duck pond he told the rest of them about his plans to quit school, viewing it as a training exercise for the fight he would have on his hands when he told his father. He got all the flak he expected and then some, even from Gary, the traitor. When he was through defending himself and the smoke of battle had cleared, he was left with the impression that what bothered everyone most was not his working with his hands, or doing something he loved with his life, or even his not wanting to go to college. It was the idea that if he quit high school before graduating, he would be leaving one job for another before he finished the first. They had not persuaded him he was wrong, but it was something else he would have to find an answer to in the next three weeks.

# 29

During the seventh week the rains came. Meg and Marcie were hard-pressed to think up new games to keep the Under-Tens occupied, and with Matt spending a lot of time riding out with Art and some of the hardier guests, and Gary only coming over for supper and the night, they did not have much relief from the strain. Their tempers unraveled, and Friday night everything came to a head.

While they were doing supper cleanup Peggy asked if one of them would bathe Jason and put him to bed for her.

"I will," Meg and Marcie said simultaneously.

Laughing, Peggy left them to decide who would have the honors. They worked in silence for a while, Meg more preoccupied with Matt and the future than with Jase. Hanging the last gleaming pot on its hook, she held out her arms. "Bath time, Jase."

Jason grinned delightedly at her and was scrambling to his feet when Marcie stepped in front of her and scooped him up herself.

"Hey," Meg said.

"Don't you have enough," Marcie said bitterly, brushing past her on the way upstairs, "without taking Jase too?"

Meg stared after her. *Don't you have enough?* Enough of what? What did she have that Marcie could possibly want? Unless . . . Was Marcie going through the same agony she was? Over Matt? Oh lord, why did everything always have to be so complicated?

Later, when Marcie came down again, they exchanged rueful grins across the room but steered away from talking about feelings that, for both of them, were too private and painful to be shared.

When the sun emerged on Saturday, everyone was enormously relieved and threw themselves into the task of cleaning up with more enthusiasm than usual. Will accompanied Hank into Boise in the afternoon to take guests to the plane and to pick up some materials Hank had ordered for their work on the main house. On the return trip Will talked to him about the pros and cons of dropping out of school, about the kinds of jobs he would be able to do and the problems he would face later on.

"I'll get you started full-time in L.A., if that's what you want," Hank told him, "and if you decide to finish school first, I'll see you get all the work you can handle on the weekends. Think it over, Will. It's no either/or choice you've got here. You can have both things if you want—school and work.

"Right now you're high on the feeling of being able to do a hard job and do it well, but that feeling could wear off. You could decide you want to go into architecture— design houses and buildings yourself. Or city planning, or engineering. There's a lot more to this game than the carpentry. And if you decide someday that you want to play in the big leagues, you'll kick yourself for having thrown away that piece of paper that right now doesn't mean diddley to you. Think about it, Will, that's all I'm saying. Whatever you decide, you can count on me."

Will was thinking about it; it was all he had on his mind these days. Maybe that was why, when he got home after eleven that night and found Matt awake and wanting to talk to him, he wasn't much help.

Matt's hoarse whisper came out of the darkness as he tiptoed through the bunkhouse. "Hey, Will, I need to ask you something. What the devil is wrong with Meg?"

"Wrong with her?" Will had not seen much of Meg all week, but he dredged up a mental picture of her at breakfast that morning. "I don't know. Just tired, I guess. This has been a rotten week, for her and Marcie especially."

"She hasn't said anything to you about something being wrong?"

"No. Don't worry, she's tough. One week of sunshine and smiling guests, and she'll be her bossy, energetic self again."

Will might find it impossible to imagine a problem big enough to cause his sister the agonies and uncertainties he knew so well, but Matt was tuned in to Meg now in ways that even Will was not. Something was wrong, he was sure of it.

Ever since the week that Lisa had swapped jobs with Meg, he had been wondering what was going on. His birthday week had not been the great time he'd anticipated. Instead of arguing, teasing, bossing him around, and doing more than her share of the work—the way she did at the stables in L.A.—Meg had stood around waiting for him to tell her what to do. No matter what outrageous job he had given her, she had done it, silent and uncomplaining.

The last day of that week, after the guests had left, he had asked her to ride up with him to replace the salt licks in the high pasture. All afternoon he had joked and teased, told her stories about himself and his family, and tried to share his love for this place with her. All afternoon she had gotten quieter and further away from him until he could not stand it any longer.

"Meg," he'd said angrily, "what the hell is going on? What's wrong with you?"

For an instant she had frozen like a threatened animal, sending him a look that scared him—a look of real terror. Then she had straightened her shoulders, sent him a passable imitation of her mischievous grin, and demanded to know what made him ask such an idiotic question.

He'd told her what made him ask, and she'd told him "Bull!" He'd threatened her with the garden pond, and she'd stuck her tongue out at him and galloped away on Cricket, dodging and wheeling all over the pasture until he and the Black had managed to corner them against the fence. Hauling her off Cricket, he had wrestled her to the ground and tickled her mercilessly until she'd begged him to stop.

He had her pinned to the ground with his body, holding her wrists above her head with one hand and threatening with the other to start tickling her again. "Okay," he'd said ominously. "Tell me what's wrong, or you're going to have a long, lonely walk home."

Looking into her eyes, he had seen the pupils expand suddenly and then contract, leaving the iris as deep a blue as the sky over their heads but flecked with the gold that could so mysteriously turn them green. God, she was beautiful! A painful, urgent longing to kiss her had swept over him. He was leaning toward her when, unexpectedly, her eyes had filled with tears.

He had drawn back uncertainly. "Meg . . . ?"

She'd turned her face away from him. "Damn it, Matt!" she had said in a thin, high voice. "It's not important, I swear. Just something private and personal. Nothing you'd want to know about. Nothing to do with you."

Releasing her abruptly, he had sat up, swearing furiously at himself. What kind of sadistic creep are you, McKendrick? What gives you the right to bully her into telling you things she wants to keep to herself, just because you're stronger than she is? You think she's your private property or something? You think she's not entitled to her own life? You stupid jerk! Embarrassment had made his voice harsh and unsympathetic. "Okay, Meg. Sorry. Forget I asked."

"I'm sorry too," she had said miserably. It was the last time either of them had spoken on the way home.

They had seen little of each other during the week of rain, but today she had gone to town with Marcie all afternoon and then, when they went out for pizza and the movies without Will along to even things up, she had acted as if it were she and not Lisa who was the fifth wheel. She was obviously avoiding him, and he had to find out why. Her problem might be private and personal, but if it was affecting her this way, it was his problem too.

Week-Eight-with-Guests did nothing to improve the situation. It was bad enough having Gary monopolizing Meg's free time on the pretext of teaching her how to fix a car, but everyone in this group of visitors was over ten, and one of the guys had a definite preference for Meg's company. He passed up the Thursday-morning trail ride, and when Matt saw him heading for the main house as they started up the ridge trail, he could scarcely contain his helplessness and rage. Hustling everyone to the top of the ridge, he let them have a brief glimpse of Craigie, a fifteen-minute lunch, and was back in the corral at 12:30 sharp.

Meg and the guy, whose name was Rod, had spent the morning fooling around in the duck pond. In the afternoon the two of them organized a hike. Matt went with them, but Meg resisted his efforts to get her alone for a few minutes so they could have it out. When he discovered she was going to the square dance with Rod that night, Matt switched tactics and declared war himself.

He was certain she was playing games with him, teasing him to make him jealous. It wasn't like her, but she could be paying him back for getting along so well with Lisa. Maybe she was showing him that two could play at that game.

Well, you're right, he told her silently. I haven't been playing up to now, Ms. M. Schuyler, but since you've started it . . . He would not have to pretend to be enjoying Lisa's company at least. As soon as she had found a friend in Will, she had become much easier to get along with—less imperious and demanding, and surprisingly funny.

Fortunately for Matt's plan, Will was hard at work with Hank, replacing the old-style windows in the main house with storm-and-screen combinations, and did not want to go to the dance. Lisa was not thrilled about going anywhere without Will, but Matt finally persuaded her to come by pointing out that if she didn't go, then he couldn't either. Gary took Marcie, and the four of them ended up in a square together having a great time, while Meg and Rod were with a group of Klutzy tourists.

Matt ignored Meg all evening, so he could not tell what effect his strategy was having on her. The next morning when Meg saddled Cricket and joined them on the trail ride, he made it clear that as far as he was concerned she was one of the guests, and exchanged private jokes and small talk with Lisa all the way out and back. The one glimpse he had of Meg's face didn't make him feel too good about what he was doing, but she was the one who had started it. She was going to have to call it quits first.

At the barbecue supper at Chapman's Lake that evening, Meg seemed quiet and subdued. Matt saw with satisfaction that she and Rod were sitting about as far apart as they could get. They must have had a fight, and he could imagine what it was about. The guy had an arrogant attitude that Matt knew meant trouble where girls were concerned, and when everyone settled themselves around the campfire for the singing, Rod found himself a more willing female guest to curl up with.

They were well into Gary's repertoire before Matt, feeling more peaceful and mellow than he had for some time, decided it was up to him to make the first move after all. Looking for Meg, he discovered she wasn't there. Under cover of the next rollicking chorus, he asked Marcie where she had gone.

"Home," Marcie told him. "She said she didn't feel well. Matt, I think she could be sick—really sick, I mean. Have you noticed how quiet and unhappy she gets when no one is looking, as if she's hurting inside or—"

Matt did not wait for the rest of Marcie's question. He was already heading for the road to the ranch. Sick? Why hadn't he thought of that before? What if she were? What if she had an ulcer like Will's or something?

What if she had been sick all this time, and he had made it worse by pretending he didn't care? "Meg!" he yelled, no longer concerned about whether he had put enough distance between himself and the campfire. "Meg, wait up!"

There was no answer, but he heard the sudden clatter of stones on the trail ahead of him and quickened his own stride, too worried about Meg to let the hazardous footing slow him down. "Meg, wait!"

She was stumbling ahead of him. As he got closer he could hear her crying. Something must be wrong— something serious.

Catching up with her, he grabbed her arm, but she twisted out of his grasp. Reaching for her with both hands, he held her hard against him until she stopped trying to get away. "Meg," he said, loosening his grip and holding her away from him with a hand on each shoulder so he could see her face in the moonlight. "What's wrong with you? Something is, that's obvious."

She kept her head down so he could not see her eyes. "Don't ask me, Matt. I can't tell you."

"You've got to tell me. It's driving me crazy. Meg, are you sick? Really sick, I mean, like Will's ulcer or—" Lisa's description of her mother's illness came to him suddenly, but he could not bring himself to think of it where Meg was concerned, let alone say it.

She shook her head. "No, I'm okay. It's nothing like that."

"What is it, then?" he demanded, angry in the backlash of his overwhelming relief. "Meg, I won't let you off so easily this time. If you can't tell me, you'd better have a damned good reason."

"I do." He waited impatiently, and she finally mumbled, "It wouldn't be fair."

"Fair to who?"

"To either of us."

"Bull! Meg, listen . . . if I've learned one thing this summer, it's that even things you're sure you could never talk about in a million years, you can talk about. Usually you're glad you did. I thought you were having a great time."

"I was . . . I am."

"Until the last couple of weeks, right? Something's happened, and I want to know what. Please?" he added as an afterthought, and was surprised but encouraged when he heard a faint giggle.

"You sound like Lieutenant Ryder," she said.

"Don't change the subject. Come on, Meg."

She shrugged slightly, but he did not relax his grip on her. "Okay," she said finally. "I'll tell you, but I don't want to. I know it's wrong."

"My fault, then. I'll take the blame." When she did not go on, he shook her almost roughly. "Meg!"

"I will, I will. It's just . . . hard." Her voice was low, difficult to hear. "Matt, when the summer's over, are . . . are you staying here? For good?"

After the last anxious weeks, after his worrying and wondering and his desperate pursuit of her tonight imagining the worst, he was so unprepared for this question that he did not realize how long he had let the silence drag on until he heard her sobs. How could she have guessed? How could she have known about the impossible arguments he was having with himself over the future?

The trouble was, he couldn't answer her. He didn't know what he was going to do. And he couldn't tell her that and keep her dangling; it wasn't fair to her. "Meg, for crying out loud,'' he said roughly, hoping to head her off, ''where did you get such a crazy idea?''

''It isn't crazy,'' she cried. ''All summer I've been watching you, and listening. You belong here, Matt, you know you do. You said so yourself. You should stay if you want to; it would be a great choice for you. It's just . . . if you don't come back, it will be awful. For me . . . and everybody.''

He said nothing, slowly translating the message she was sending him.

''I didn't want to tell you,'' she sobbed. ''I didn't want you to know how I felt. It's so damned selfish of me, and I can't help it. But it doesn't matter. How I feel isn't important. Matt, please . . . I want you to do what you want. I really do. If you're happy, then everything will be okay, I swear.''

''Is that what's been bothering you all this time?'' he said finally. He wanted to be sure there was nothing else. ''Is that what it was—that day in the high pasture?''

Meeting his eyes at last, she nodded. Moonlight glittered in the tracks the tears had left on her skin. She loved him. The knowledge surged through him like the bubbling spring in the high pasture he had found and unblocked for Art. She loved him so much that she had tried to keep her own pain hidden to make sure he would be happy.

He loved her too—had loved her for a long time and in the same complicated, often painful way. Wanting her to be happy. Hiding his own hurt. He knew how it felt and wished he could reassure her by giving her the answer she wanted to hear. But he couldn't. He just didn't know.

Holding her face in his hands, he kissed her gently, trying to soften the impact his words were going to have. ''You're right, Meg. I have thought about staying here . . . thought about it a lot. Only I haven't figured out yet what to do.'' She turned her head away to hide her panic, but he could feel her trembling. ''Meg, don't! Don't cry. Even if I stayed here, it wouldn't be the end of everything, I swear. Every chance I got, I'd be down there ringing your doorbell, and vacations you could spend up here with us. It would work out. We could make it work if we wanted to enough.''

"Yes,'' she said hollowly, but she wouldn't look at him.

"Meg,'' he said desperately, "whatever I do, I don't want to lose you. I wouldn't make a choice that would mean I'd never see you again. I wish I could tell you right now that I know I'm coming back to L.A., but I can't. I'm sorry—''

"Don't be!'' she said fiercely. "I don't want you to be sorry, you idiot! Don't you understand?''

*I understand. . . . I love you too.* "Well, gee,'' he said plaintively, wanting to lighten their mood a little, "how can you expect an idiot to understand anything as important and complicated as that?''

She gave a shaky laugh. "Matt, you . . . !'' A second later her arms were around him, squeezing his ribs so desperately that it hurt him to breathe. They were still standing together when the lights of the pickup flickered through the trees above their heads.

"Come on!'' Matt said urgently.

Stumbling along with hysterical giggles, forcing each other on to greater efforts, and trying to save each other from repeated falls, they made their way along the treacherous road. They were not fast enough. Eventually the pickup and the noisy mob caught up with them, and like travelers caught in the path of a Big Creek flood, they were engulfed in the cheerful confusion and swept breathlessly away.

# 30

*Saturday* was a typical Craigie summer day—brilliant sky, hot sun, air so fresh and clear you could almost drink it—yet it had a gray, overcast feel to it. Part of that feeling came from the knowledge that the summer was nearly over—the Last-Week-with-Guests was beginning tomorrow—and part of it had deeper sources.

The calm straight stretch of the journey on which they'd embarked at the beginning of the summer was coming to an end as well. Choices had to be sorted out, decisions made, and like the sounds of white water coming up around the next bend, the knowledge put them all on edge.

For Lisa the bleak vision of empty, friendless days ahead did not bear thinking about. She threw herself so furiously into the job of cleaning tack that Matt was driven away from her sharp tongue and out to the corral, where he spent the rest of the morning going through the motions of grooming the horses. His mind was a long way from what he was doing as he wrestled with the momentous decision the summer had unexpectedly forced on him.

After last night's conversation Meg found her own mood swinging wildly from elation to despair. The summer had changed things for him too. He loved her. But she knew she had made the choice harder for him . . . and he still might decide to stay. Alternating between nonstop chatter and tense silence, she worked her way through the cabins with Marcie, neither of them really aware of the other.

Marcie had said little all morning. Leaving for home the instant the cabins were done, she met Gary as he was turning into the Pomeroys' gate on his trail bike. Stopping her car, she rolled the window down. "Hi," she said glumly.

"Hi, Marce. What's up?"

"Nothing." But they had known each other all their lives. She knew he'd had the same question on his mind all summer as she had—the same hope. "What do you think?" she said suddenly. "About—well, you know."

He knew. No point in playing games. "Can't tell yet. There's a chance, though—a good one."

"Let me know, will you, if he . . . ?"

"Yeah, Marce, sure. If he doesn't tell you himself."

"He won't."

"Hey, old buddy," Gary began an automatic protest at her tone. He stopped. What could he say? Matt and Meg—there was no denying the truth of it. It had been obvious to everyone right from the start. "Hey, old buddy," he said again, brushing his fist lightly across her chin. "You've still got me." She nodded, but as she drove off, face averted, Gary realized that the summer hadn't been all fun and games for her either.

Of the six of them, Will was finding himself in the worst straits. He had as much on his mind as everyone else, but little or nothing to do with his hands. All the major jobs were completed; nothing was left except minor repairs. Toolbox in hand, he wandered the ranch in search of missing nails, loose screws, drawers that wouldn't open, and doors that wouldn't close. Driven out of desperation to the stables, he was immediately put to work by Lisa shoring up the wobblier saddle racks and building five new ones—a job that took him most of the afternoon.

Lingering on longer than usual, Lisa found small tasks to keep herself occupied while she kept Will company.

To Will she seemed depressed and irritable, and he felt a surge of the anger he'd left behind in Los Angeles as he thought of her selfish, demanding father. From the daily timetable Lisa followed so rigidly and occasional remarks she had made, Will pictured her father as part grizzly and part Henry VIII—a bullying, blustering bear of a man. He had been putting off a confrontation with Mr. Lomax as long as possible. Okay, Schuyler, he told himself firmly. It's now or never.

His suggestion that they take in a movie by themselves that night was accepted with enthusiasm, but Lisa made him promise that under no circumstances would he pick her up before seven. His watch set half an hour ahead in case he needed an alibi, Will turned up at the Lomax front door at 6:30, knowing that Lisa would not be through with the supper cleanup and hoping for a chance to talk to her father. Ringing the doorbell, he fidgeted nervously while he waited for his first glimpse of the giant he had come to do battle with.

The door was opened by a thin, wiry man only slightly taller than Will. His tired face was lined with age and something else—something Will had seen in his own father's face not long ago—and his inquiring expression hardened suspiciously as he looked Will up and down. "Yes?" he said abruptly. "What do you want?"

"I . . . um, I'm here to get Lisa."

"She expecting you?"

"Yes, we're—"

"She's busy."

After a moment's silence Will said, "I'll wait." For an instant he thought Mr. Lomax was going to shut the door and leave him on the front porch. The man opened the door a shade wider and motioned Will inside. Well, Schuyler, Will told himself wryly, you're off to a great start.

Mr. Lomax led the way into the living room. From the kitchen Will could hear pots clattering and a radio keeping Lisa company. Her two brothers, ten and twelve years old, were lying on their stomachs in front of the TV and did not look up as they came in.

"Where are you from?" Mr. Lomax said without preamble. "You aren't one of the local boys."

"No, I'm working at the Pomeroys' this summer with Lisa. I'm—"

"What's your name?"

"Will Schuyler."

"You living at the Pomeroys' too?"

"Yes, we—"

"Where are you taking Lisa?"

"To the movies in town."

"That's all?"

"We might go for pizza afterward or something."

"No 'or something.' If you're taking my daughter anywhere, you're going to have my permission first."

Will had heard of fathers like this from disgruntled friends but had never met one before. He did not know whether to fall on one knee and swear to uphold Lisa's honor and safety at all costs or to tell Mr. Lomax to relax and trust Lisa to manage her own life. Even if he had possessed the nerve to do either one, he did not get the chance.

"You driving a car or a bike?"

"Car. Our station wa—"

"Tires and brakes okay?"

"Yes."

"You ever been arrested for speeding or drunk driving?"

"I don't drink."

"Not even beer?"

"No."

"Well, that's something anyway. Ever had an accident?"

Damn it, Will thought helplessly, half-amused and half-frustrated by this third degree. Abandoning hope of convincing Lisa's father to let her go to college, he was thinking he'd be lucky if he could get her to the local flicks. "No."

Mr. Lomax glanced at his watch. "I want Lisa back here at ten-thirty. Not ten-forty or ten-thirty-five, but ten-thirty."

"Yes, sir," Will said.

"He means it." One of the boys rolled over to stare at Will. "You should have seen what happened to Chris Johnson once when he brought Lisa home late after a dance."

Will was wondering whether he was going to get the gory details of what had happened to Chris Johnson and was pretty sure he didn't want them, when Lisa suddenly appeared in the doorway.

"You're early," she said accusingly. "I'm not ready."

"You look terrific," Will told her fervently. Thinking her father might misinterpret that remark, he added, "Just like you always do." Worse and worse, he told himself. Shut your big mouth, Schuyler, and get out of here before you get a fist in it. He hustled Lisa toward the door. "Come on. We're late."

"We aren't late," she protested.

The laughing note in her voice told him she knew what had happened. Her knight in shining armor had ridden boldly up to the ranch to do battle with the resident dragon, and had been sent ignominiously away, singed and scorched.

"I left my wallet back at the ranch," he lied for her father's benefit, making a hideous face at her.

"Ten-thirty, Lisa," her dad called after them. His voice was so gentle and affectionate that Will thought he was hearing things. "Have fun, sweetheart."

"Thanks, Dad, I will. Serves you right," she added as the door closed behind them. "I warned you not to come until seven. Did you really forget your wallet?"

"No. Just saving my cowardly hide. What happened to Chris Johnson, anyway?"

"Nothing. Those brats always say that." She smiled reminiscently. "Dad did knock Matt out once, though."

"I'm glad I didn't know that before now. I would have let you pick *me* up. How come?" From what he had gathered, Matt and Lisa were never on dating terms.

"It's funny now, but it was awful then. Matt brought me home from a trail ride. He was right to do it. I was pushing my horse too hard—trying to keep up with him, believe it or not. I did a lot of stupid things in those days, trying to get him to notice me. Anyway, he tied a rope around me and made me walk all the way home behind my horse. When we got into the yard, my dad took one look and flattened him before either of us could explain. I was furious with Matt, but I didn't want him killed. I had to tell Dad it was my fault. It's the only time I ever heard Dad apologize to anyone outside the family. Will . . ." She hesitated. "Thanks for . . . for what you wanted to do tonight."

"Don't mention it," he said lightly, embarrassed at having been caught meddling so ineffectually in her personal affairs.

"You see how it is, though? It isn't what you thought."

It wasn't. Love was always harder to defy than bullying demands and selfish threats.

"I'll go, Will—to college. I promise. Maybe before this summer I wouldn't have. I think I was using Dad as an excuse. I was really afraid to go."

"Afraid?" It was the last word he would have used in connection with Lisa.

"That I wouldn't . . . I don't know. Belong, I guess. This summer—it's the first time I ever felt as if someone besides Dad wanted me around. Really enjoyed me. Not as a decoration, but for myself. I'll go, Will—maybe winter quarter. Next year for sure. I promise."

This was how he should have felt at the beginning of the summer when he was set free himself—dancing in the streets, the rockets' red glare, the works! "Fantastic!'' he crowed, feeling like hitting Mach 5 and heading for the moon as he drove decorously down the Lomax's drive. ''Let's get this celebration on the road! We've got only—'' he checked his watch—''three hours left.''

''Your watch must be fast,'' said Lisa innocently. ''Mine says we have three and a half.''

They were almost to Craigie before Will could stop whooping and hollering long enough to share with Lisa the hilarious image of himself as the young knight riding up to her father's castle, supremely confident of his ability to rescue her, and being unhorsed in the first round.

''It's your own fault,'' Lisa said mischievously. ''High time you learned to ride.''

On a night like this anything seemed possible. ''Okay. I'll learn,'' he promised recklessly, ''if you'll teach me.''

''Tomorrow,'' she said instantly.

Will knew he had been outmaneuvered by an expert. ''Tomorrow,'' he agreed with a laugh. ''Which I guess makes this the last night of my life. Watch out Craigie— here we come!''

## 31

*Everyone* except Will and Lisa, who were hatching some secret plot of their own in the lower corral all morning, found Sunday twice as long as usual. By the time they were all assembled in the yard to welcome the last group of guests, they were desperate for some distraction and greeted the dust cloud rising through the trees at the Gap with shouts of relief.

An old hand by this time, Meg automatically began sizing up the group as it emerged from the van and the Pomeroys' wagon. An elderly couple, white-haired and frail. Happy to potter around the ranch on their own, probably. No problems there. Two small black boys about eight and eleven wearing Batman T-shirts and eager smiles. One of them was carrying a copy of *The Hobbit*. Not TV addicts, thank heavens. They were followed by their father—in his middle thirties and fit enough to be another runner, Meg thought with a sigh— and their mother. It was easy to see where the boys' smiles came from. She was carrying a baby who looked around him as eagerly as his big brothers. Catching sight of Meg, he considered her solemnly for several seconds and then gave her a superb, crinkly-eyed grin that outdid everyone in his family. So far it looked like a great group.

Next to appear was an elegant, fashionably dressed blond woman, whose spike-heeled shoes were sinking rapidly into the soft earth underneath them. Hmm, Meg thought. What's she doing in an uncivilized place like this? Must have gotten into the car by mistake.

A boy about ten or eleven emerged from the van—his gold-rimmed glasses giving him a studious look. He turned to say something to the girl who followed him out. A little older than he was, with short curly hair, she glanced over at the lineup of ranch hands and sent them all an uncertain smile. Behind her was another smaller boy and his even smaller sister. She burst out of the van with a glad shout, as if she were coming home after a long absence instead of arriving in this place for the first time in her life, and came toward them at a run.

"Doesn't that older girl look a lot like—" Will began.

"That's funny. The biggest boy reminds me of—" Meg was saying.

"Isn't that— No!" Matt exclaimed. "It can't be! I don't believe it!"

It could be and it was. Lew and Carey, Michael and Jenny, and last out of the van, Ryder and Sally.

Jenny got to Matt first and flung her arms around his legs.

"We're here! We're here!" she shouted. "Aren't you glad?"

If Beth had not already been in possession of his shoulders—her favorite vantage point from which to take stock of arriving guests—Matt would have scooped his small sister up and tossed her over his shoulder to show her how glad he was. He rumpled her hair instead until she grabbed his hand and swung back and forth on it, still shouting. With Michael in firm possession of his other hand, Matt was immobilized.

"I'm glad, I'm glad," he told them, laughing. "Why didn't you— How long have you been— What *is* this?" he said helplessly and happily to Sally and Ryder, who had finally arrived to free him and claim their share of the welcome.

"We haven't had a vacation in six years," Ryder said. "Not fair for you to have all the fun."

"We weren't sure there would be room for us until the last minute," Sally explained. "Didn't see any point in getting everyone's hopes up too soon, and by the time we knew—well, it seemed too bad to spoil the surprise. You don't mind?" she added, half-serious.

"You can't tell by my face?" Matt teased. "You must be losing your touch. No one to practice on all summer without me around. Oh, I get it," he added, catching sight of the camera in Sally's hand. "You didn't trust me to take any decent pictures."

"Well, have you?" she asked, and nodded at his guilty expression. "What did I tell you?" she said to the laughing Ryder. "Lost my touch? Never!"

Lew and Carey were more offhand about the whole thing.

"Howdy, podner," Lew said to Meg. "Bet you're surprised, huh?"

"I'm surprised, I'm surprised," Meg told him. "My, how you've grown!" He had—two inches at least. At this rate he'd be as tall as she was in another year.

"Not me," he said. "I'm the same as always. You look like you've shrunk."

"Watch it, buster," Meg said, doubling her fists and raining blows on him. "I learned how to fistfight this summer."

"You did?" Lew hooted, fending her off with one hand. "Who taught you—Muhammad Ali's grandmother?"

"Hi," Carey was saying to Will. "I like your haircut, I think."

"Thanks," Will said. "I like your haircut, I know." He looked around, but the van and the station wagon were emptied of passengers. The other guests were watching their noisy reunion with interest and amusement. "What about Dad and Gwen? Didn't they want to come?"

"They do, but they couldn't leave on such short notice. They're coming Wednesday."

Wednesday, Will thought. Armageddon. D-Day. The Day I Talk to Dad. How come I never seem to be able to choose the time and place for life's major moments?

Peggy joined them a moment later. "Introduce me," she said with a twinkle that made it obvious she had been in on the surprise, "and then come and meet the other guests."

The other guests were Elsie and Joseph Cumberland, both in their seventies, and the Fieldings—Greg and Diane, Julian, Chris, and the infant Sam who, having bestowed his thoughtful smile on everyone from Jase to Lieutenant Ryder, was christened Samwise the Beautiful on the spot. The elegant, out-of-place blonde turned out to be Hank's wife, Cleo. It was the second surprise in a week that managed to produce quite a few of them.

The rest of the afternoon went by in typical Sunday fashion—guests escorted on foot to their cabins while Will delivered their bags and belongings in the van, everyone meeting back at the main house for early supper and a chance to get acquainted.

Supper was followed by a leisurely tour of the ranch. It usually took until Monday night or Tuesday before strangers had spent enough time together to relax and become acquaintances and sometimes friends, but Meg noticed this group was already beginning to mingle. Cleo had stayed behind with Peggy, Jase, and the sleeping Samwise, but the rest of them were strolling along the road in little groups.

Sally, Elsie Cumberland, and Diane Fielding were admiring the landscape from the perspectives of photographer, artist, and gardener, with Marcie naming the birds and wildflowers and promising to show them her favorite places in the morning. Greg Fielding was bombarding Art with questions about ranching, and Lieutenant Ryder, Hank, and Joseph Cumberland were debating Los Angeles politics. Lew, Michael, Julian, and Chris were out in front, racing each other and Jenny to the gate, while Beth hung back shyly with Matt and Will.

Only Carey hadn't found a partner, and she fell in beside Meg, looking decidedly unhappy.

"What's up?" Meg said, hoping this wasn't going to be a moody week for her sensitive sister.

"I'm outnumbered," Carey said grumpily. "All those boys—*little* boys, for crying out loud—" and Meg suddenly was aware of her sister moving on, growing out of childhood and into a time in her life when boys—big boys—would become important. "And Jenny." They both laughed at the idea of spending a week in Jenny's unpredictable company. "And all you grown-ups—"

"What do you mean—all us grown-ups?" Meg said, startled by the thought.

"Just what I said—all you grown-ups. You aren't kids anymore, are you?" Not waiting for Meg to answer, she blurted out a sudden request. "Meg, would you mind— if it wouldn't spoil anything, I mean—could I sleep in the bunkhouse with you and Marcie?"

"How could it spoil anything, Care? I think it's a great idea. And I've got one to go along with it—Gary's sister, Susan. As soon as we get back to the house I'll call the Maitlands and see if she can spend the week. Gary can bring her with him when he comes back tonight."

"Hey, great! Thanks, Meg." Carey brought out a small gaily wrapped package she had been hiding behind her and thrust it into Meg's hands. "Happy birthday . . . a little late. I hope you like it," she added as Meg fumbled with the ribbon and paper. "I made it at camp. Everyone said it wouldn't work, but I did it anyway." It was a ceramic picture frame, a little rough around the edges and not quite rectangular, but the glaze Carey had chosen for it was the breathtaking blue of a Craigie summer sky.

"Care, I love it!" Meg exclaimed. "And I've got the perfect picture to put in it. Another birthday present. Remind me to show it to you later."

"Okay. Thanks, Meg!"

"Thanks yourself," Meg was saying, but Carey—not

quite ready to abandon childhood altogether—was dashing down the road after the boys, whacking Will on the rump as she sprinted past.

Meg was wondering whether to join the women or catch up with Matt and Will when Sally glanced back, saw she was alone, and came to join her. "I've been looking for a chance to talk to you all evening," she said with a smile. "Can you spare a minute?"

Meg laughed. "The first day is always wild," she said, "but once the guests learn their way around and get to know each other, it settles down."

"I'd ask you how the summer has gone, but I can tell the answer by looking at all of you. No regrets?"

"No regrets." Not yet, anyway. If Matt would just hurry it up—

"Meg, you're the only one I can ask this question. I hope you won't mind."

"Of course not," Meg said, startled by the sudden seriousness of Sally's expression.

"You might. It's a tough one." Sally hesitated, then plunged in. "Meg, has Matt made up his mind what he's going to do?"

"Going to do?" Meg repeated blankly, wondering if Sally was thinking the same thing she was, and knowing it wasn't possible. Matt hadn't told anyone else, she was sure of it.

"Is he going to stay in Craigie?"

"I . . . he . . . How did you . . . ?"

Sally smiled slightly at Meg's bewilderment. "I've known he'd have the choice to make ever since he told us about Gary's phone call. It's been on my mind all summer, and when Hank invited us up here, I leaped at the chance. Waiting wears me down."

"I know what you mean," Meg said. But neither she nor Matt had been forced to worry about it all summer. They hadn't been able to see that far ahead. Matt often kidded Sally about being a witch, a nice one, able to read people's minds. Was that how she knew things like this?

Or was she just older and wiser? Did the two always go together? Not always, Meg decided, thinking of her father.

Will had a metaphor for growing up that he'd shared with them one Saturday at the duck pond. It was like one of those glass elevators on the outside of skyscrapers, he said. You start off as a little kid on the ground, closed in and looking at your own reflection. Then you start going up and the view gradually expands until you can see over rooftops and out in most directions to the horizon. Only some people, they agreed, get stuck partway up, and others never seem to get off the ground.

"Meg, love . . . ," Sally said again.

"I'm sorry. I didn't mean to keep you hanging, but I don't know the answer either. He said he'd tell me when he makes up his mind, but he hasn't said anything yet." It was Meg's turn to hesitate. "Sally," she said slowly. "If you knew at the beginning of the summer that he might not come back, how could you let him go?"

"How could we not? Even if it had been our decision—which it wasn't—we would have said yes. He had to come, Meg. It was his only chance to heal the hurt . . . to make himself whole again."

"I know," Meg said. "I'm glad it worked." They looked at Matt striding down the road ahead of them, laughing at something Will was saying. Beth was jumping and swinging from their hands. "I wish he'd hurry up and decide," she added. It was almost as hard to deal with as her own struggle a few months ago had been. Given the choice of leaving home and hassles behind to go to college or staying in L.A. and sharing both the hassles and the high points—she had finally decided to stay. "It's driving me crazy."

"Me too." After a moment Sally added, "And if it's this bad for us, think what it must be like for him."

Lousy was the word Matt would have used to describe his own condition. It felt as if his head were inhabited by a swarm of bees, and his stomach by an ulcer in the making. Every waking moment the debate raged within him. Should he stay in Craigie where he belonged, where he was welcomed again, where there was a place for him with people he loved and people who loved him? After the last two years in L.A.—constantly on guard against accusations and attacks by strangers—it would be a relief to feel safe again and protected in this tiny community where there were no strangers. He could get on with the life he had been planning before everything fell apart—the University of Idaho and a degree in animal science and agribusiness; working for Uncle Frank instead of his dad; and someday a ranch of his own.

But what if staying here meant losing the people he loved in L.A.? Meg and Will, Ryder and Sally, Tony and Don, the younger Ryders and Schuylers—they meant too much to him. Cutting them out of his life completely would be as impossible as amputating his own legs. Would they believe him? Could he explain without hurting their feelings and making them hate him? Michael would never trust him again. And Sally and Ryder? "We won't yell about promises," Ryder had said, but how would they feel?

Was there anything else for him in L.A. besides the people? Not safety. Even with Katie's murder solved, there would always be people who hadn't heard about the old bum's confession or who would choose not to believe it. No certainty about the future either. A liberal-arts degree and a career in teaching, which he might not be any good at. Running and maybe, if he was good enough, a shot at the Olympics.

So what made the decision so hard to make? He didn't know. Just that every time he thought he was sure, he'd begin thinking about what he would lose if he didn't go the other way. Right now Craigie had a stronger pull on him than L.A., but that was partly because he was here and having such a great summer.

He was glad the Ryders had come for the last week.

Having them around would remind him of the good times in L.A., balance his feelings about the two places a little. All he needed was for something cataclysmic to happen in the next eight days that would make the choice clear to him. And if it didn't? Oh lord . . . No matter what he did, he was going to hurt someone he loved.

# 32

As Meg had predicted, Monday morning the guests began to settle into the routines, although Jenny caused an uproar when she discovered Carey had abandoned her for Susan and a bed in the bunkhouse. She insisted on moving to the bunkhouse too, but the only free bed was on the boys' side, and they flatly rejected the idea. When Jenny retaliated by sticking her tongue out at Matt and calling him an old poop, they laughed about it for hours and spent the rest of the day looking for opportunities to call each other old poops.

Lisa took the experienced riders on the morning trail ride. To everyone's surprise these included Will, who calmly mounted the roan as if he'd been doing it all summer and accepted their cheers and congratulations with a regal wave, and the Cumberlands, who had ridden elephants in India, camels in Australia, and taken annual trips on horseback in the Rockies. So much for appearances, Meg told Marcie, laughing over the way she had stereotyped them on Sunday.

She and Matt signed up the beginners who were left—

everyone under thirteen and Lieutenant Ryder—for morning and afternoon instruction in the corral. Ryder good-naturedly endured Matt's kidding about his flapping elbows and uncontrolled bouncing and seemed to be enjoying the switch in their usual roles as much as Matt, but he did not turn up for the afternoon session. Driving past the corral as everyone was saddling up, he leaned out the car window to tell Matt he'd accepted a better offer. He was heading to the public courts for a civilized afternoon of tennis with Will, Joseph Cumberland, and Greg Fielding.

"I'll give you a private lesson when you get back," Matt promised. "Otherwise you'll miss the breakfast ride."

"I should be so lucky," Ryder said with a grin as the car pulled away.

They did not get back until just before supper. Matt was in the bunkhouse getting cleaned up when Will came in and dropped, happy and exhausted, on his bunk.

"How was the tennis?" Matt said.

"High-powered. Joseph's given me a whole new perspective on seventy-year-olds. How come you never told me Lieutenant Ryder was a pro?"

"A pro?" Matt echoed in astonishment. "You mean a professional tennis player?"

"Yeah. Ranked in the top sixty before he quit. He must have been really something," Will said ruefully, flexing muscles that had been on vacation for several months. "He's still good, and he hasn't played regularly for years."

"A tennis pro!" Matt said again, intrigued by this glimpse of a Ryder he hadn't known existed. For the first time it occurred to him to wonder about all the years Ryder had lived before he knew him—about his childhood, and about the kinds of choices he had faced at eighteen. He could hardly wait to find out more.

The opportunity to have a private conversation with Ryder presented itself after supper when Matt left early to get the horses and wagon ready for the hayride and asked the lieutenant to give him a hand. He did not get the conversation going until he had cut the two horses out of the mob in the corral and they were heading down the road to the equipment shed, the horses plodding unenthusiastically along behind them.

"How come you never told me you were a tennis pro?" he said.

Ryder thought about it. "Maybe because you never asked."

"Will says you're still good. What made you decide to become a homicide detective instead?"

Ryder didn't answer immediately, and Matt had a sudden feeling that he might be trespassing where he didn't belong. He started to apologize and change the subject, but Ryder interrupted.

"No, that's all right. I was just thinking—do you remember the night I promised I'd tell you about myself someday, about why I'm such a cold and undemonstrative SOB?"

Remember the night? Matt would never forget it. The incredible night in the Ryders' library when the lieutenant had apologized for not making it clear to Matt how much he loved him and had asked him to stay and become a permanent member of their family. Matt waited, wanting and not wanting to know.

"I quit tennis because of my father," Ryder said slowly. "Quit tennis and went to law school because I thought he might respect me if I became a lawyer and made a six-figure income like he did. I'd spent my life up to that point doing things I hated in the hope of getting my father to look at me with something other than cold dislike—and nothing I ever did succeeded in changing that."

"Not even law school?"

"Especially not law school. When I graduated fourth in the class, and he was vacationing in the Bahamas—didn't even bother to send a telegram—I swore I'd never do anything just to please him again.'' Ryder snorted. ''An equally stupid motive for making choices for yourself.''

''So you went into the police force.'

''Eventually, yes. Bummed around first; traveled all over the world, mostly on foot—that's when I picked up that puzzle box I gave you; did a hitch in the Army. Came back to L.A. finally, my emotions hidden under skin so thick it took Sally a year to decide there was someone inside worth the effort of getting to know.''

They reached the shed and Matt began getting the harnesses off their racks and onto the horses, making conversation unnecessary for a while. He was seeing Ryder in a totally new way—as a lonely boy desperate to earn his father's approval; as a bitter young man cutting loose and rejecting everything his father represented; as someone who had struggled to live with pain, the way he had. What kind of father would do that to his own son?

Nature makes it too damn easy to have children, Matt thought suddenly. There ought to be some kind of test you have to pass first, to prove you can handle the job. Too many people are out there screwing up their kids. Too many kids are out there thinking it's their faults— that *they're* the ones who screwed up.

''Bastard!'' Matt said suddenly and vehemently, to his own embarrassed surprise.

Ryder laughed. ''My feelings exactly. He was wrong, Matt, but he did have a reason. My mother died giving birth to me. He wanted the doctors to save her and let me die, but they had no choice. There was no way I could take her place, and he could never forgive me for being the one who survived. It was years before I understood that. Even longer before I forgave myself.'' He paused. ''When I think how close I came to making you feel the same way about me that I felt about him. . . .''

For a long time neither of them said anything. Ryder finally broke the silence. ''It's like they say, Matt—you lose some and you win some. I've been lucky. With

Sally and Tony, and the kids and you—I've won all the ones that mattered.''

Matt sent him a quick grin, not sure he could manage anything else, and busied himself checking the buckles on the harnesses. The morning in the corral with Matt as teacher and Ryder as novice and the glimpse of himself as a vulnerable human being that Ryder had shared tonight had changed their relationship subtly, moved them away from being parent and child and closer toward being friends and equals. Matt was glad they'd had this moment alone, but he was going to need some time to get used to the idea.

Tuesday began much the same way as Monday, with Jenny creating a scene over the pairing of horses and riders for the breakfast ride. Matt and Lisa had done all the matching the night before, and Matt planned to let Jenny ride behind him on the Black, but Jenny wanted to ride by herself on the pinto. In addition to being the most reliable horse in the string for children to take their first rides on, however, the pinto had earned himself the right to be Beth's personal mount when she wanted to ride. The answer to Jenny's pleas was a firm no.

When Jenny refused to accompany Matt on the Black, stamping her feet and screaming "It's not fair!", he told her that horses didn't like people who screamed and kicked, and she would have to ride in the pickup with Peggy and Marcie and the babies. She was still not speaking to him when breakfast was over.

"Makes me appreciate Beth even more," Marcie said with a laugh as she and Matt were repacking the breakfast gear in the pickup. "Doesn't she wear you out?"

"She's not usually this bad," Matt said ruefully. "Most of the time she's a lot of fun—tough and invincible, and raring to go. I don't know what her problem is."

The afternoon's expedition to the big lake took some organizing, but eventually everyone was ready to go except for Greg Fielding, who had volunteered to ride fences with Art so he could continue their discussion about ranching. Greg was on a fast track in the computer world and making good money, but Diane and the three boys were the heart of his life. He was looking for a way to get them all out of the city, and farming or ranching had definite appeal. Watching him playing soccer with the little boys and girls, rocking gently in the hammock with Samwise or Jase, or smiling across a noisy room at Diane, Meg felt he was on a better track than computers and hoped he could find a way to make his dream a reality.

Cleo, who was in the travel business and always on the lookout for intriguing places to send her clients, had already gone off somewhere with Hank for the day, and Diane and Peggy, enjoying each other's company, chose to stay at the ranch with the little ones, freeing Marcie and Meg to go with the others.

Once at the lake Joseph rented a small boat with an outboard motor and took Michael, Jenny, Chris, and Julian on a voyage of exploration. Lew was invited, but decided to stay behind with the older ones. Elsie set up her little camp stool, which she was never without, and settled herself for an afternoon of sketching and painting while Sally faded into the background with her camera and telephoto lens. At breakfast on Monday she had asked permission from every member of the group to take candid photos for a photographic essay and a book she was planning, and although on the first day they had all felt self-conscious about the whirring and clicks and the black reflective eye staring at them, they were so used to it now that they no longer noticed her.

Ryder rented a Windsurfer, and for the first hour everyone took turns giving it a try. Only Gary felt there was any likelihood that he would ever want to get on one again. They were sprawled on the beach, watching Ryder struggling back on the board for the twentieth time and talking about impossible things and why people want to do them, when someone asked what was the most impossible thing anyone had ever tried. Gary and Matt spoke simultaneously.

"The cliff jump."

"What's the cliff jump?" Lew asked.

"It's a place on the east side of the lake, a couple of miles up," Matt said, gesturing vaguely. "A rock wall that comes out of the water, straight up for maybe fifty feet."

"Exactly fifty feet," Gary said. "We measured it, remember?"

"And you jumped off?" Meg asked. "Why?"

"Someone said we couldn't." Matt grinned at her. "Why else?"

"Sounds dumb," Meg said. "Fifty feet is a four-story building. I bet it hurt."

"It did. You have to hold on to your nose so it doesn't get ripped off your face, and your head feels like it's been jerked right off your shoulders."

"The worst is the feet, though," Gary said. "Definitely the feet. Even when you wear sneakers, they hurt like—" noticing Elsie's back a few feet away, he modified his description—"a lot!" Meg heard Elsie's low chuckle and grinned herself.

"It's a rite of passage for Craigie's youth," Gary said. "We all have to make the cliff jump to prove we aren't little kids anymore."

"Are you going to do it?" Carey asked Susan.

"No way," Susan said. "People have really hurt themselves doing the cliff jump. I can think of better ways to prove I'm not a little kid than spending my life in a wheelchair."

"What?" Gary hooted. "After all those years of tagging along in our footsteps, trying to follow our shining example and do everything we did—you're finally admitting defeat?"

"I've already done all the dumb things you did," Susan said.

"Not everything," Matt put in. "You never made it across the rope bridge without falling in, did you?"

"Neither did you," Susan said hotly.

"How old were you guys when you did the cliff jump?" Lew asked Gary.

"Thirteen. That's when most people do it for the first time."

"I know of one guy who did it when he was twelve," Matt said.

"A girl in my class did it this year," Susan said. "She was twelve too."

"I want to see this place," Lew said skeptically. "I don't believe you jumped off something four stories high."

"Wait until they get back with the boat," Matt said, accepting the challenge. "We'll take you up there. Can't have the younger generation doubting their elders and betters."

# 33

*When* the boat returned, everyone went to see the famous cliff except Will, who had too much on his mind. He understood why Meg thought that jumping from something as high as the roof of a four-story building sounded dumb, but he was beginning to see why people did impossible things like that—especially kids. It was a way of getting control, of making the rules, of testing your limits and defining who you were on your own terms instead of other people's. People like Meg and Matt who had challenges thrown at them by life—who were constantly being tested and had to grow up fast— didn't have to go around inventing tests and challenges for themselves.

Right now he would gladly have jumped off a hundred-foot cliff instead of facing his own Most Impossible Thing, which life had arranged that he deal with tomorrow. Although Art had volunteered to pick up his father and Gwen, and Carey had asked if he wanted her to come, he knew he had to go alone to the airport. It might be his only chance to speak to his father about his decision without a large audience around to observe the response.

He was hoping that what happened in the morning was going to prove that he wasn't a little kid, but he wasn't sure how he was going to handle it if his father said no. Give in? Fight? Run away? Did he have any other choices? Did he have *any* choices? In exactly eighteen hours and thirty-seven minutes, ready or not, he was going to find out. . . .

Getting a late start Wednesday morning, Will made it to the airport in record time. The plane had already landed by the time he checked in at the counter. Heading for the baggage-claim area, he searched the crowd of unfamiliar faces anxiously, but his father wasn't there. Take it easy, Will told his agitated stomach. If he had changed his mind about coming, he would have called. Maybe he's in the men's room or something.

"Will?"

At the sound of Gwen's voice he swung around. His stepmother was gazing at him uncertainly, her laser look no longer in evidence. That's over, he told himself firmly, reminded of Carey's insistence that things were different now and his promise to give Gwen a chance.

But how, he wondered, do you tell someone twenty-five years older than you are that you're sorry about the stupid things you said and you want to begin again?

"It's me," he said with a tentative grin. "I got a haircut, that's all." He had no way of knowing that the physically demanding and emotionally satisfying summer had changed him in more subtle ways—filling him out across the chest and restoring to his angular face the look of quiet confidence and good humor that Gwen had never seen.

Smiling suddenly herself, Gwen held out her hand. "Hi," she said. "I'm Gwen Schuyler. You must be Will. Carey's Will," she added. "The one she's told me so much about. I don't think we've met before."

Haven't met before? It took him a moment before he understood what she was offering—a second chance for both of them. "Glad to meet you," he said, accepting her outstretched hand with a rush of relief.

"You and I got off to a bad start, Will," she continued as they made their way through the crowd to the moving baggage carousel, "and it was mostly my fault. I've learned a lot this summer, though, and I'd like to forget all that and start again, if you think we can."

"I'd like to too," he said. "It wasn't your fault we weren't getting along. Carey tried to set me straight a few times."

"Thank God for Carey," Gwen was saying emphatically when they were interrupted by the arrival of Jim Schuyler.

"It's all set," he said to Gwen without a glance in Will's direction. "Woody will file the papers this afternoon."

"Jim . . ." she said, looking at Will.

"Hello, Dad," Will said.

"Will?" His father stared at him, amazed. "Good God, I didn't recognize you! My own son . . ." He shook his head, grinning ruefully. "How've you been? More than all right, from the look of you. Let's get the bags and get out of this mob before we start catching up on your news.''

Gwen had already snagged one bag off the carousel while his father was talking, and the other one appeared a moment later. His father, Will saw with a flicker of irritation, was carrying a bulging briefcase. It was not, he thought, a good omen, and he was even more discouraged when, as soon as they were settled in the station wagon with Gwen in front and his father in back, his dad opened his briefcase and began shuffling through the papers, looking for something.

Gwen had a lot of catching up to do, and for most of the drive north she and Will exchanged details about the summer, sending and getting messages from each other that were long overdue. Feeling good about this budding friendship with his stepmother, Will had mentally resigned himself to putting off the conversation with his father until another better time when he heard the heavy case shut with a thump and a couple of clicks and his father heave a satisfied sigh. Before he knew it, the moment he had been dreading for weeks was on him.

''You look as though the summer has agreed with you, Will. Done you a world of good, in fact.''

''It has.''

''Well, good. That should see you through your last year at Lowell at least, and then it's on to college. Have you thought about where you want to go?''

''Well, yeah,'' Will said, stalling a little. He wanted to slow this moment down, take it one step at a time. Everything calm and rational. ''As a matter of fact, I wanted to talk to you about that, Dad.''

''You know I went to Stanford, Will. The fees are pretty steep, but we'll try to swing it for you if that's your first choice. You can work during the summers to help out with your living expenses, but I wouldn't recommend working during the school year, at least not for the first couple of years. It's tough trying to handle everything at once.''

"Sounds good, Dad, but—"

"And while we're on the subject, what about after college? Any ideas yet about what you want to do with yourself? Teaching . . . business . . . law?"

The last was a loaded question. *Do you want to follow my example?* is what it meant. *Do you want to be like me?* But the way his father kept interrupting—asking questions but not waiting for the answers, as if Will's answers weren't important—brought back to Will the years of benign neglect and disinterest. Burning contempt for his father's inability to understand him engulfed Will once again, and when he spoke, it was with his old sarcasm. Gwen, who had been basking in the good-humored warmth of their new relationship, tensed at his tone.

"That's a great scenario, Dad, but you'll have to wait a few years until your leading man is old enough."

"What?"

"I mean you've got the wrong person in mind. That's Lew's future, not mine. We're almost there," he added as he took a left on Little Creek Road.

Jim was silent for a moment. "Explain," he said.

"I'm through with school. College isn't important to me now. I know what I want to do."

"What do you want to do?" Jim's voice was dangerously soft. Gwen recognized the tone, but Will had never heard it.

"Build things."

"Build things? What things? Are you telling me you want to quit school and try to scrabble through your life with no education, no marketable skills, no intellectual investments to fall back on—so you can build things?"

"Dad—"

*Listen to him, Jim,* Gwen begged silently. *For God's sake, listen to him.*

"No, Will. You may not see it that way now, but you'll have to accept my judgment on this—"

*"Dad!"* Will was through waiting for his turn, through

being a child. He gave his father sixteen years' worth of longings, disappointments, and needs never met in one gigantic broadside. ''I don't have to accept anything from you! For sixteen years you haven't known or cared a damn thing about me, and how you want to put in your two cents' worth and expect me to step right into line.

''Forget it, Dad. It's too late. If I thought you knew me—if I thought you were tuned in to me and thinking about who I am and where I'm going, I'd listen to you, sure. I'd even trust your advice because I'd know you were thinking about *me*. But you don't know me from the kid next door. You don't know what I want, or who I am, or how I feel about anything and everything. You're thinking about what *you* want—just like you've been doing all your life—and your so-called advice doesn't have a damned thing to do with me. That's why I'm not taking it.''

A long silence followed Will's angry outburst, a silence vibrating with unanswered questions, with words almost spoken and thought better of. The thunderous rumble of the tires on the cattle guard finally brought the silence to an end.

''I'm sorry, Dad,'' Will said as they started up the road toward the ranch. ''I wasn't planning on giving it to you all at once like that. I wanted to talk about it—make sure you understood.'' Another pause. ''I still do, if you're interested. This is the cabin you're sharing with the Ryders,'' he added, pulling up at the path that led through the pasture to the A-frame. ''It's not locked. Nothing is around here. Once you've unpacked, keep following the road up to the main house. Almost everyone went rafting on the Salmon River today, but they should be back soon. Anyway, someone will be at the house to show you around. I'll see you later.''

He did not offer to take their bags in but drove off as if he had some important errand to do, leaving them staring after the cloud of dust. In fact, he had nothing at all planned for the rest of the day beyond that rational, intelligent conversation with his rational, intelligent father that he had replayed so many times in his imagination this past week.

He did not know whether he had permanently destroyed his chances of getting through or whether he had made a breach in the fortress walls and made his father look out and see him for once. The next move was up to his dad. Leaving the station wagon at the equipment shed, he took the pickup to Chapman's Lake, looking for wood for the last two campfires and a chance to think things out.

It looked like a long fight ahead, but now he had taken the impossible jump, he knew he could handle it. His nose was a little bent, and his feet hurt like hell, but he had survived. He wasn't a little kid anymore, needing his father to make decisions for him. He could make his own choices and live with the results.

With or without his father's approval, he was going to become a carpenter and builder. By himself he might not be able to convince his father that he was doing the right thing, but with Gwen's help . . . Will grinned suddenly. Talk about impossible things! People *can* change, he thought—with a little help from their friends and relations.

Now if his dad could do the impossible too—put himself in his son's place and try to understand him—they might have a chance to get acquainted . . . maybe even become important to each other. Come on, Dad, he said silently as he maneuvered the pickup expertly along the bumpy trail. Go for it! If Gwen and I could do it, you can too.

# 34

$B$*ecause* of the holiday weekend, the guests would not be leaving until Monday morning. The normal schedule had been abandoned, the final campfire planned for Saturday night, and the mid-week arrival of Gwen and Jim Schuyler caused only a minor ripple in the smoothly running operation of the ranch. Introduced around by Sally, Gwen quickly discovered interests in common with Cleo and Elsie, but Jim Schuyler had trouble detaching himself from his work and remained the odd man out. On Thursday, when everyone else went to the big lake again for the day, he stayed behind to make phone calls and finish up some paperwork.

Friday morning Jim declined Gwen's invitation to accompany her and Sally on the morning trail ride. He and Will had not been able to talk privately since their arrival and he had no intention of letting the matter drop. This was no summer job his son was talking about; it was a decision that was going to affect the rest of his life. No matter how Will or Gwen felt about the idea, Jim could not let him make such a devastating choice.

Looking for someone who could tell him where Will was, Jim headed for the main house. He found Hank Pomeroy on the patio, reinforcing the legs on one of the picnic tables. In his overalls and tool belt Hank looked like the glorified handyman he was, Jim thought irritably. Knowing the man was responsible for Will thinking he could spend the rest of his life "building things" did not make it easy to be civil to him.

"Hey there, Jim," Hank said. "Trail riders back already?"

"No, I didn't go on the ride. I'm looking for Will. Any idea where I can find him?"

"He and Ryder went to the public courts to play some serious tennis."

Jim studied Hank for a moment, wondering whether there was any point in trying to persuade him to undo the damage and change Will's mind. With so much at stake, it was worth a try.

"I'd like to talk to you before Will gets back," he said abruptly.

"What's on your mind?"

"Will," Jim said curtly. "He's talking about quitting school so he can build things. Build things, for the love of—"

"What's wrong with that?"

"Because he could do better for himself—a lot better. I don't want him scraping through life, living from job to job—"

"What about what he wants?"

"He doesn't know what he wants. He's a sixteen-year-old boy."

"*Your* son," Hank said, and Jim missed the heavy emphasis on the first word.

"Yes, my son. I don't know what you've told him this summer, but he deserves better than—"

Hank interrupted with an angry expletive. "Will doesn't deserve a damn thing, and lucky for him he knows that. What he gets, he'll earn, like the rest of us. This summer is probably the best thing that could have happened to him." He cut Jim's intended reply short. "Don't say anything. We both might regret it."

They measured each other for a moment.

"Listen, Jim," Hank said more calmly. "If you think I've been working on Will all summer, trying to get him to quit school and come work for me, then you don't know me or Will. Do yourself and him a favor. Get acquainted. You can start by cutting the 'my son' crap. Call him Will—makes it easier to see him as someone separate from you. Ask him to show you what he's already built. Find out why he loves the work. It's the least you can do.''

Hank headed inside, and Jim strode off, looking for a private place to simmer down and think. By the time Will and Ryder returned from their tennis match, he was ready to deal with the immediate issue—that of Will's finishing out his last year of high school. The question of college could wait until they were back in Los Angeles and memories of the summer began to fade. In the meantime he would do what Gwen and Hank, and Will himself, had suggested—get acquainted with his son. Thinking it over, he had realized that Will *was* a stranger. He had no idea what kinds of music Will liked, what books he was reading, what he did in his spare time, or even what he thought about the major and minor problems facing the world today.

As Jim went to greet Will he was thinking that in all his years as a defense lawyer he had never been so poorly prepared to defend his point of view—and had never felt as strongly about the outcome of a case as he felt about ensuring his son a chance at a decent future.

# 35

*The* trail riders returned in the early afternoon. Leaving the little ones with Marcie, Peggy came down to the corral to report to Meg that she was worried about Lew. He had borrowed her bike right after the group had left on the ride and had not returned for lunch.

Under Will's tutelage the four little boys had been working on the tree house. This morning everyone assumed Lew had skipped the trail ride so he could finish it up, but neither Chris nor Julian had seen him since breakfast. When Michael said Lew had told him that he was going to do something no one else had ever done, it meant nothing to Meg, but Matt's face went white. Telling her to wait for him, he took off for the main house at a run.

Back with the Schuyler station wagon a moment later, he yelled at her to get in and was driving away in an explosion of dust before she had time to close the door.

"Matt, for heaven's sake!' she said, frightened and angry. "What is going on?"

"The cliff jump," Matt said tightly. "What else could it be?"

"The cliff jump? Why would he want to do such a stupid thing?"

"Don't ask me," Matt said. "Get the gate open."

They roared along Little Creek Road, Meg clutching the armrest to hold herself in the seat. "Slow down," she said once. "Matt, you're going too fast." He slowed briefly through Craigie, but as they made the turn and headed up the east side of the lake he speeded up again.

"Matt, will you please slow down?" Meg said angrily. She was mad at Lew for pulling such a stupid trick, and mad at Matt for scaring her so badly.

"I can't. Meg, listen. There's a rock . . . under the water. You have to know it's there and jump to the left. Otherwise . . ." He swallowed. "A guy hit it—about ten years ago. Broke his back. Been in a wheelchair ever since."

Lew was alone. If he hit the rock, nobody would be there to drag him out so he could spend his life in a wheelchair. He would drown. A small sound burst out of Meg's throat—half protest, half prayer—but it was lost in the roar of the engine and Matt's agonized words.

"I can't remember if I told him . . . on Tuesday when we went up there in the boat. He asked me a lot of questions, but I never thought he might be thinking about making the jump. Oh God. . . ."

They swung abruptly into a small dirt parking area and skidded to a stop. There were a couple of picnic tables under the trees, but no one was using them. There was no bike either. "He wouldn't have left it where someone might take it," Matt said. "Come on!" He did not wait for Meg but took off through the woods, scrambling up rocks that rose higher and higher as they neared the lake.

The bike was there, partly hidden under an overhanging boulder. Using hands and feet, Matt went up the last twenty feet in a frantic burst of energy and disappeared from view. Head pounding, sweat running off her forehead and into her eyes, Meg scrambled after him.

The first thing she saw when she reached the top a minute later was Matt, crouching about fifteen feet away and looking down. What was he looking at? What did he see? She had a sudden vision of the fifty-foot drop into the water, the rock, hidden and waiting. And Lew . . .

Matt's lips were moving. Was he talking to someone or praying? As she staggered up, panting hoarsely, she saw the top of Lew's head. Oh God, he was safe. He hadn't made the jump.

"Lew Schuyler—" she began, but Matt gestured sharply with one hand to shut her up. With her frantic heartbeat filling her ears, she dropped down beside him and looked over the edge. The shock was so bad that a moment later she was heaving everything in her stomach into the bushes on the opposite side.

When she stopped coughing and shuddering, she moved a little closer to Matt and the silent Lew, who had climbed back up to sit beside Matt on top of the cliff. She was glad she did not have to lean over the edge to talk to him.

"Lew Schuyler," she said again, and found her throat too sore and her voice too unsteady to continue. The glimpse she'd had of the long drop—the way the rocks angled out so the jumper had to run as fast as possible and leap far out to clear them, and the waves sucking hungrily at the base of the cliff—had so unnerved her that she could not face the thought of her brother's body falling through the air and disappearing into the dark water. Someone else she loved had died that way. She had seen it happen. The image was burned into her brain.

"Sorry," Lew said gruffly, and looked away from them, out across the water.

"Lew," she said, fighting to stay calm. "Lew, damn it!" And to her own astonishment and theirs, she burst into sobs—terrible, wrenching sobs worse than the spasms that had forced her lunch out of her a moment before.

"Hey . . . hey." Kneeling beside her, Matt hugged her hard. "Hey, Meg, take it easy. He's okay."

"I know he's okay," she cried. "But he might not have been. If we hadn't gotten here in time . . ."

"We didn't get here in time to stop him from jumping, if that's what you mean."

Meg looked at Lew, taking in the significance of his

damp, rumpled hair, the soggy sneakers with one lace untied, and the new raw scrapes on his hands and knees. Gulping and swallowing, she fought for control. "You jumped?"

"Yeah," he said. A tiny satisfied smile lifted the corner of his mouth. It was the last straw.

"Don't you ever do such a goddamn stupid thing again!" she screamed. "Never, do you hear me? Isn't one in the family enough?"

Lew stared at her. He had been there that day too. She could see him remembering—their whole family sitting together on the flat rock above the wild river eating a picnic lunch; hearing their mother say, "Oh my God!"; seeing her in the air, arms and legs stiffened and ready for the landing in the water roaring and foaming over the rocks below, the boy she was trying to save already yards away. It was the last time they saw her alive.

Lew was crying now too. Matt looked from one to the other. "Hey, guys . . ." he said helplessly.

Finding the strength from somewhere, Meg crawled over to Lew and hugged him until her own desperate longing for their lost mother came through to him and he hugged her back. When they were able to stop sobbing and begin swiping futilely at the tears, Matt stripped off his sweaty T-shirt and let them use it for a towel.

Because the doctor had warned him to keep the sun off his healing back, it was the first time all summer Meg had seen Matt without a shirt. "Your back looks better than when I saw it last,"she said, grateful to have something else to concentrate on. The last time she had seen it was in the hospital in April, right after the beating by friends of his fiercest rival that had almost taken Matt out of the competition for Runner of the Year.

He looked at her, surprised by the change of subject, then grinned in relief. "Yeah, well—lifetime scars or not, one summer in the dark is all it gets. I can't stand the delicate, consumptive look."

"You do look pretty pale and weak," she said, glad to

be able to talk nonsense for a while. "I'm surprised they let you out of the sanitarium."

"What are you guys talking about?" Lew said, and looked annoyed when they both laughed.

"Shall we get going?" Matt said. He looked at Lew. "How are the feet? You want me to carry you?"

"No!" Lew said, but he slid most of the way down the rocks on the seat of his pants.

Matt stuffed the bicycle into the back of the station wagon, and the three of them rode together in the front. They drove sedately through Craigie and were heading down Little Creek Road when Matt asked Lew what he wanted people to know about this afternoon.

"Everyone will be wondering where you went and why we took off after you at a hundred miles an hour. How do you want to handle it?"

"Just tell them I'm not a little kid anymore," Lew said. After a long pause he went on. "You guys don't know what it's like being the youngest. No matter what I do, somebody else in the family has already done it, and everybody can always do everything better than I can. This is the only thing I've ever done that nobody else can do."

"But, Lew," Meg protested, "a lot of people have jumped off that cliff."

"No one ever did it at the age of ten," Matt said. "Somehow I think the record is safe with Lew."

"No one else is crazy enough," Lew said, grinning.

"Or brave enough," Matt said, ignoring Meg's look of exasperation.

"Well, okay," Meg said. "We'll keep it casual and low key." She stopped as a thought struck her. "Lew," she said slowly, "I don't think you want Dad to know about it."

It took Lew a fraction of a second to come to the same conclusion. "Yeah, you're right. Maybe when I'm an old man, I can tell him."

Meg opened her mouth to say "If you live long

enough," and shut it again. Right now she didn't feel there was anything funny about Lew not living to a ripe old age. "Promise me something?" she said instead.

"What?" Lew said warily.

"That you *will* be an old man."

"I'm planning on it," Lew said. "Joseph says it's the best time of your life. You can go where you want and do what you like, and nobody tells you what to do. I can't wait!"

"Sounds good," Matt said. "Guess I'll be an old man too."

"Guess I'll have to be an old woman then," Meg said, and they arrived at the main house laughing wildly at the thought of themselves, white-haired and tottering, still galloping bareback, sliding into home plate, and climbing trees.

"Why not?" Lew said. "Joseph does." And as soon as he was out of the car he headed for the patio, where, as if to prove his point, Joseph, Michael, and Julian were playing a fast and furious game of table tennis. As they welcomed Lew into the game Meg let out a long sigh.

"Thanks, friend," she said. When Matt didn't answer, she glanced at his face and realized she hadn't seen that tense, closed-in look since the beginning of the summer. "Matt?" she said hesitantly.

"Ride with me somewhere?" he said abruptly. "Anywhere—where we can be alone."

Meg felt herself grow cold. Not now, of all times. She was too wrung out to deal with it. There was only one reason for him to look like that. He had made up his mind he was going to stay in Craigie, and he wanted to tell her privately, in case she yelled at him or cried.

"If Peggy doesn't need me for anything," she said, praying that Peggy would, "I'll meet you at the corral."

# 36

**P**eggy didn't need her until 4:30, and the other guests were all happily occupied. Meg met Matt coming up the road, riding the Black bareback and leading Cricket. Heading for the high pasture, a place where no one else was likely to come on foot, they turned the horses loose and settled themselves under a tree. Matt settled himself, anyway. Putting his arm around her and pulling her tightly against him, he closed his eyes.

Meg was too nervous to wait while he psyched himself up to tell her. Desperate to get the conversation going and over with, she asked him rudely if he was asleep.

"What? No."

"Talk to me," she said.

"I don't want to talk. I just want to sit here with you for a while."

"You didn't bring me up here to tell me what you're going to do?"

"I . . . no. Meg, is that what you thought? I'm sorry. I didn't—"

"Damn it, Matt!"

"Don't yell at me, Meg," he said miserably. "It's just . . . today. With Lew. I was really scared. I thought I'd done it again."

"Done what? Matt, it wasn't your fault—"

"It was, Meg. I told him about it. Made a big deal out of it. Showing off like a stupid jerk. What if he'd . . . ?"

His voice shook. Meg put her hand on his lips. "Shh,"

she told him. "Shh. It's okay. He's all right. Nothing happened." Unable to stand the pain in his voice, she pulled him down in the grass so they could lie close and put their arms around each other.

She kissed his eyebrow first to comfort him, and then his closed eye. Drawing back, she surveyed his entire face before kissing his nose, his bony cheek, and the upturned corner of his mouth. When she drew back the second time he was looking at her, his dark eyes full of laughter. I love your eyes, she told him silently. I love you.

He gazed at her for a long time, examining her face as if he were memorizing his favorite features. Then he pulled her against him, kissing her the same way she had kissed him, telling her he loved her too.

Both of them had thought about being in love a lot, had seen it in movies, read about it in books, talked about it with friends. But they had never *felt* love, not like this—wanting to get closer and closer, wanting to wrap themselves around each other, hugging each other so hard their bodies ached with the urgency of their need to make up for all the pain, to make each other happy, to love and be loved. . . .

Neither of them was prepared for what happened next. One moment they were comforting each other; the next they were caught in a rush of emotions too powerful and exhilarating to be held back or denied. They had no sense of how long the storm lasted; it swirled through them, buffeting them unbearably, and subsided as swiftly as it had come. The tension left Matt's body suddenly and he buried his face in Meg's neck.

Gradually Meg became aware of his rapid breathing and racing pulse, his birthday belt buckle digging into her hipbone, and the weight of him pressing her against the uneven ground. An insect whirred past her on some important business while a few feet away the Black and Cricket were calmly tearing up grass clumps and munching noisily—just as if the entire universe had not been in turmoil and chaos a few seconds before.

"Wow," she said softly, wondering whether Matt was feeling as confused and excited and frightened as she was. When he did not respond, she added uncertainly, "You okay?"

"I will be," he mumbled without lifting his head. "Give me a minute. Are you?"

She thought about it. Okay seemed a pretty tame way to express the way she felt. "I'm not sure. Give me the rest of my life. I'll let you know."

Laughing weakly, he rolled on his back. Wanting to hold on to the feeling of closeness, she curled up beside him, head on his shoulder, arm across his heaving chest.

After a while she said "Wow!" again. Somehow it was the only word that described whatever had just roared through them. The only time she had ever experienced feelings even remotely similar was on a roller coaster going sixty miles an hour while doing 360-degree loops.

"I know," he said in something closer to his normal voice. They were moving away from the experience and back toward safer, more solid ground. "Is that what it's all about?"

"I don't know," she said. "Maybe."

Matt was running his finger lightly along the line of her jaw, down her neck, and along her collarbone. She felt herself responding to his touch. "Matt," she said quickly.

"Yeah?"

She felt awkward about saying it, wondering if his thoughts were as confused and anxious as hers, and if he would understand without her having to explain. "I don't want to get pregnant."

He stopped playing with her neck. "I know," he said. "I don't want you to get pregnant either."

"How can we stop? If it's going to be like it was

today, I mean? I didn't want to stop. I didn't even think about what might happen until afterward.'' She paused. "It's scary.''

"Yeah, it is.'' His voice reflecting his own uncertainty about how she was going to react and what she wanted him to say, he went on slowly. "There are ways . . . things we can do. Like condoms. Or the pill.''

Meg was quiet for a long time. She wanted to talk about what had just happened and what was going to happen in the future—they had to talk about it, obviously. But not yet. She felt too exposed, too confused and nervous to be able to deal with the subject right now.

It was one thing to discuss sex and love in a family-life class, or with her mother. When she had never met anyone she wanted to have sex with, it was easy to decide how she'd handle it when she did, easy to explain to an imaginary guy why she was going to wait until she was through college and preferably married—no matter how much they loved each other.

Now that she knew who the guy was, and how it felt to love him, she wasn't at all sure she could handle it. What should she say first? What if he didn't feel the same way? What if he thought sex was okay if you protected yourselves, and she had to convince him there was more to it than that? Was it going to spoil everything or make it better? Oh lord . . .

Her breath came out of her in a long sigh. "Maybe someday. I don't think I'm ready for that yet.'' She laughed shakily. "I don't think I'm ready for any of this.''

"I know what you mean.'' Matt was silent for a while too, trying to figure out what she was really telling him. "Okay,'' he said finally. "What if we make each other a promise? No matter what, we don't go all the way until we've talked it over beforehand, calmly and rationally, and both of us agree?''

It was a start. They were together on this; they would

deal with it somehow. She felt her mood lifting. "Calmly and rationally, huh? Do you think it will work?"

"How do I know? Probably not. We could wear suits of armor, just in case."

Suddenly they realized what time it was. Still laughing at the idea of armor—"Pretty noisy," Matt had said— they rounded up the horses and headed for home in a hurry.

Meg was late. She raced off to shower and get started on supper preparations, leaving Matt to feed and water the horses and try to sort out the afternoon's events on his own. They had been cataclysmic, all right, but not the kind he was thinking of when he'd hoped something would happen this week to help him make a decision. The experience in the high pasture had only added to his confusion.

This summer had changed so many things, complicated his life to an unbearable degree. The last thing he needed right now was having to deal with any more of life's major questions like having sex. With Meg it would be making love, but the risks and the consequences were the same—and Meg would be the one who had to face them. He had made too many decisions already in his life that had rotten consequences for someone else. He was not going to take a chance on messing up Meg's future too.

What if she got pregnant and had to choose between abortion, adoption, or taking care of it herself? Abortion sounded bad enough, but worrying all the rest of their lives that their own kid was out there somewhere being hit or yelled at, feeling lonely and scared—he couldn't stand that either. When he decided to have a kid, he— and nobody else—was going to be its father.

Was it possible to love someone so much that you ached to make love to them—and because you loved them that much, tell yourself no and stick to it? He knew what his parents would have said. Being big for his age meant he'd had to deal with a lot of things before he was ready, and even his own family forgot sometimes how old he really was. They'd started telling him about the responsibilities and the consequences of sex while he was still trying to get up the nerve to hold a girl's hand. Six years ago the whole idea had seemed weird and impossible, but now . . .

Out of the corner of his eye he saw a small figure tearing past on the road. "Hey, Jen!" he called, but she did not acknowledge his shout. Leaning on the fence, he watched her heading for the gate. He was about to go after her when she veered off the road and across the pasture, scrambling up on the old stump and disappearing into its hollow interior. When she did not reappear, he nodded to himself, figuring she was as safe there as anywhere, and headed for the bunkhouse in search of a restorative shower and some casual conversation to distract him from his thoughts.

When the supper bell rang, Jenny was not among the crowd gathering on the patio. Telling Sally he knew where she was, Matt set off at a slow jog, savoring the summer smells and memories of the summer itself, especially today—the high-pasture part anyway. Talk about ups and downs, he thought with a grin. As he vaulted the fence and headed for the hollow tree he had the feeling of having been on this same mission many times. Only this time it was his other small sister who was curled in the crumbling lap of the old tree.

Leaning on the edge of the stump, he peered down at her. "Hi, Jen. Supper's ready. Didn't you hear the bell?"

She scowled up at him. "Go away!"

"What are you so mad about?" he said, surprised by her vehemence. He was even more surprised by her next outburst.

"I hate you too!"

He was about to ask why when the "too" hit him. "What makes you think I hate you, Jen?"

"You like her better than me."

"Like who better?" he said, stalling. He was thinking of Meg and wondering how to explain something like this afternoon to a just-turned-six-year-old.

"That stupid Beth. I hate her!"

"Beth . . . ?" Oh lord, of course. His mind flashed back to last Sunday—Beth on his shoulders, Jenny looking up at them from the ground; the fracas over the pinto; the scuffles over his hand or for a place on his lap.

"You're my brother!" Jenny shouted. "She can't have you, you're *mine*!"

He held out his hand. "Come out here, Jen, where we can see each other."

"You come in here."

"I can't. I'm too big. That's your place now." As it had once been his and Katie's. And someday, maybe . . . Matt had a startling glimpse of a grown-up Jenny, leaning over the edge of this same stump and talking to *her* small angry child.

It took him a while to persuade Jenny to exchange the comforting hollow of the tree for his own lap, and even longer to convince her that whatever happened she would always be his sister, something no one else in the world could ever be. Their grumbling stomachs finally got them up and moving toward the house—Jenny galloping ahead, shouting, "Giddyup, Black!"; Matt jogging in her wake and wondering how old you had to be before you stopped thinking *mine* about other people and began to think of them as important for their own sakes.

Was that how you knew you weren't a kid anymore? He was beginning to think there was no way to figure that out. Or was it when you stopped letting other people make decisions for you and started making them for yourself? Several times in the last week he had caught himself wishing that Ryder and Sally or Aunt Belle and Uncle Frank would end his agony and tell him to stay or go, but the time when he could expect that to happen was over. No one was going to make this one for him.

Sally confirmed that after supper when she asked him to walk back with her to the A-frame so she could get a different film for her camera. They strolled along, Sally chatting about the week and how much fun they'd had, the evening light and how beautiful it was, life and how impossible it was. . . .

She's dancing all around the subject, Matt thought. She wants to ask me if I'm going to stay, and she doesn't know how. I love you too, he told her silently. Sally, please . . . tell me what you want me to do, and I'll do it.

"This is ridiculous!" she exclaimed suddenly. "Matt, love, I want to say something important, and every time I open my mouth, something else comes out." She laughed, nervously he thought.

"I've been elected message bearer," she went on, "and this is the message. Les and Belle and Frank and I—we know what you're going through. And all we can do to help is tell you that where you are is not what matters to us. We all love you, and we'll care about you and enjoy you, and back you up for the rest of our lives. None of that is going to change, whether you're down the hall or hundreds of miles away. Leaving home doesn't mean losing everything, or leaving all the important things behind, Matt—not this time."

He stared at her for a minute, absorbing what she'd said. *Not this time.* As if he had suddenly found the right strand to pull in a knotted ball of string, the massive confusion he'd been living with for weeks untangled itself. No wonder he couldn't make a choice. The last time he left home, he *had* lost everything. He'd been so hung up on what he would lose this time that he couldn't see any way out. But if he wasn't going to lose the important things . . .

Stripped of their emotional baggage, his options suddenly became clear. Choosing between them seemed almost simple. Impatient to get moving, to get the decision made, he began jogging in place.

"You look like you could use some time alone," Sally said, recognizing the signs. "Go for it, love. And good luck."

"Thanks," he said fervently. "Sally, tell them . . . tell them . . ."

"I will," she said.

Laughing, they hugged each other hard before he took off, his feet taking him instinctively through the darkness from one familiar place to another while he wrestled with his future. He did not have to choose between two sets of people. He understood that now. No matter where he went to college, or went afterward, all his life he would belong to the people he loved. And Meg? Well, they could work it out if they had to. Four years wasn't forever.

There was no point trying to chose between places either. Craigie won hands down over L.A. as a place to belong to, a place to call home, but Los Angeles offered variety and opportunities that Craigie couldn't match. Whichever he chose, he would wish sometimes that he had chosen the other. No . . . what he had to decide was the kind of future he wanted. One was known and therefore safe; the other uncertain, challenging. The trouble was, he wanted both.

He had been born to the tough, physical life of a rancher—had grown up with it, planning someday to pool his own dreams and experience with his father's. Like Art, he loved it, and he felt he owed it to his dad to continue the tradition. But the idea of teaching appealed to him. And he had been born to run as well. He had been dreaming about the Olympics since he was twelve—not just dreaming but training hard, pushing himself beyond his limits, working toward the moment when he could measure himself against the best long-distance runners in the world. He wasn't ready to cut that part of himself off and forget about it.

So that's what his choice had come down to—or what it had been all along—ranching, or teaching and running.

Did he have to choose? Maybe not. Maybe he could have both. He could always come back to ranching, couldn't he, if teaching didn't work out? Aunt Belle and Uncle Frank had given him the sign as a reminder that somewhere in this world he could carve out a place of his own to hang it. And he could become a teacher later on too, if he started off in ranching and changed his mind. People began new careers in their thirties and forties all the time.

Not true with running, though. If he wanted to go as far as he could with his running, the time was now. Running was the only one of the three choices that couldn't be postponed.

Finding himself on Craigie's main street, Matt wandered up one side and down the other, looking into the dimly lit shop windows. Several blocks away the Trueloves' spaniel was yapping—probably at a prowling cat—but the only other sign of life was a lone car passing through on its way south toward Boise. When his feet finally began taking him homeward at a steady jog, he had made up his mind. Now all that was left was the hard part—telling everyone.

# 37

**B**ecause he thought they'd be the hardest to tell, Aunt Belle and Uncle Frank were the first on his list the next morning. Leaving his running companions at the gate, he headed up the Maitlands' drive, rehearsing what he was going to say to be sure he got it right.

He had talked with them so often during the summer about his parents' death and all that happened afterward that he knew Aunt Belle and Uncle Frank were carrying a burden of remorse and guilt as heavy as his, blaming themselves for not listening to him and Katie, for forcing them to run away. He had to be absolutely sure they understood that his choice had nothing to do with that—that he didn't hate them. He'd read enough since then, talked to enough people, to know that Katie would have done fine at the deaf school. It would have been a great opportunity, not the exile he'd been so afraid of. Running away had been his choice and his mistake, not theirs.

Aunt Belle let him stammer his way through a couple of sentences before wrapping her arms around him and taking over the conversation. "We've known all summer you'd have to choose, Matt. I figured you wouldn't be able to turn your back on the opportunities and the challenge L.A. has to offer."

"Our offer's always open, though," Uncle Frank added. "Anytime you want to come back and for as long as you want to stay, you know you're welcome."

"Maybe between semesters . . . next summer for sure," he told them, glad to be able to promise this much. "Hank's already signed us all up."

Gary was next on his list to tell, and a lot harder than he'd expected. He asked his good buddy to meet him at the equipment shed after breakfast, and Gary made him wait for twenty minutes before he came sauntering in.

"Gare . . . ?"

"You don't have to say it. I already know."

"How could you? I didn't know myself until one-thirty this morning."

"If you were going to stay, you wouldn't look so unhappy about telling me."

"Look, Gare, it's nothing personal, man."

"Forget it. I know."

"Gare, we aren't leaving here until you—"

"Quit worrying about me, will you? It's none of my business what you do. It doesn't matter." Silence. "Like hell it doesn't," he said suddenly. "But I know why. You've got to try it out, right? See if you can handle it?"

"Yeah. If I didn't, if I passed up the chance, I'd always—"

"Wonder what you missed. Yeah, I know."

"There's something else too. It would be like climbing all the way to the top of the cliff and not jumping."

"You'd never know whether you were too smart to try—or too scared."

"Yeah." They were silent for a moment. "Even if I stayed, Gare, I'd be at college most of the time."

"Moscow, Idaho's a lot closer than Los Angeles."

"It's nest-leaving time, man. You're flying too."

"Just down the road."

"You never know. Roads can lead anywhere."

"Like Rome?"

"Yeah . . . or Oz."

"Or hell." Silence. "I'll get used to the idea, old buddy. Just give me a little time."

It took Matt until lunch to manage private conversations with all the people he had to tell, but by the time he had been through his reasons for the eighth time, his spirits were soaring. He had saved Meg for last so they could be alone, but she took one look at him in the lunch line and let out a joyful whoop.

"Sorry," she said, her mischievous grin at full strength for the first time in weeks. Looking at her, he suddenly understood why people could read his own thoughts so easily. Everything about her, from the way she was moving to the lilt in her voice spelled happiness. Flying as high as he was—if there hadn't been a table full of food between them and thirty people milling around, he would have kissed her.

Lisa put the crowning touch on this fantastic day by agreeing to sell him the Black. They had a real battle about it—she wanted to make him a present of a horse she had never thought of as hers anyway, and he insisted that he pay her whatever she had paid at the auction. With the other four shouting "Compromise, you jerks!" they finally agreed on half of what she'd paid, since as Lisa pointed out, the Black had had two more years of wear and tear.

She had probably lied to him about the auction price, since she was the only one who knew what it was, but he could not have paid any more than the compromise amount anyway. Almost half of what he earned this summer had to go to pay the insurance on his 'Stang. When Ryder told him what car insurance cost for an eighteen-year-old male in L.A., he nearly choked. Between the Black and the Mustang—his string, as Gary had christened them—all he'd have left from his summer's earnings would be enough for a few month's feed and board at the stable and a couple of tanks of gas.

With all that decided, he was ready to settle down and enjoy their last week here. Because he and Meg weren't expected at UCLA until the third week of September, they were staying on to help clean and close up the unoccupied cabins in preparation for winter. Will had decided to go back on Monday with his family and get started at Lowell.

"I let Dad think he'd talked me into it," Will told Matt after he had shared his own news, "but I was pretty sure I'd end up finishing Lowell all along. It's like Hank said—it's no either/or choice. Not like yours was. If I can work for Hank and still get the diploma, it would be stupid not to."

He laughed. "The last few days have been a little rough, but it's going to be okay. Poor Dad. He thinks when we get home, he'll be able to work on me in private . . . wear me down. But he's all alone on this one; I've got the big guns on my side . . . Hank and Gwen and you guys—and me," he added, a note of pleased surprise creeping into his voice at the realization of his own strength. "I'm kind of looking forward to proving to him that my being a builder is a great idea." He paused. "Matt . . . ?"

"Yeah?"

"Thanks for the summer. I can't believe what a great time we've had . . . in spite of the horses."

Laughing, Matt agreed. It *had* been a great summer. Not the gloriously irresponsible summer in L.A. he'd been planning in June, but better. Much better. When he thought about how close he had come to chickening out before it began . . .

That night at the final campfire, gazing around the circle of loved and familiar faces, Matt found himself wishing that three more were there and realized that the wall—the stark, unbearable fact that his parents and Katie were dead—had come down for good. When he thought about his family now, it was with a sense of exhilaration, the joy of being alive, and all the living and the loving they'd shared. Wasn't there a song about that? Gary had sung it at the beginning of the summer— something about love being a way to live and die.

"Hey, Gare," he said into a pause between two songs. "How about giving us that song with the great chorus? You know—the one about John Denver's uncle?"

When the song came to an end, Meg shifted inside the circle of his arm. Raising both fists, thumbs up, she grinned at someone across the circle. Following her gaze, Matt saw Gary returning the gesture and the grin.

"What's that all about?" he said.

"Nothing, nothing," Meg said airily, her delighted laughter mingling with the opening chords of Gary's next song. "Just something private and personal. Nothing to do with you."

Which meant it had everything to do with him. One way or another he planned to find out what it was.

# 38

*The* six of them met at the duck pond late Sunday night for a private celebration. They had their swim first and were drying off on the grass when somebody exclaimed for the hundredth time, "What a great summer! I can't wait to see Sally's photographs. I bet she got some beauties."

"I know some beauties she got," Marcie said. "She was clicking away yesterday when we were falling off Susan's and Carey's rope bridge into Little Creek."

"I hope she captured Matt's and Gary's expressions when they saw Carey and Susan waltzing across it as if they'd been tightrope walking all their lives," Meg added. "Now I know why the clothesline has been crammed with their wet shorts and T-shirts all week."

"She came with us this morning too," Marcie went on. "When I took the group to Little Creek."

"How did Jenny do?" Matt asked. Marcie had planned to take the quiet ones—Michael, Chris, Beth, and Elsie—on a predawn expedition to watch for deer coming to drink at the creek. They couldn't keep it secret, of course, and once Jenny found out, it would have been cruel not to include her.

"She was amazing," Marcie admitted. "She promised to sit quietly, and she did."

"I saw Sally taking shots of Cleo showing Carey and Susan how to use makeup," Lisa put in, "and Chris, sitting on a rock next to Elsie, experimenting with some watercolors she'd given him."

"And Ryder and me killing each other on the courts," Will put in.

"What was the final score in sets?" Matt asked.

"Six to two—Ryder," Will said. "But three of them went to tiebreakers, and he's promised to give me a chance to even things up when we get back."

"I wish she'd been here the day Will had his hair cut," Lisa said.

"And the night Will and Matt had their fight," Meg said.

"And the week the Under-Tens took over," Gary said.

"And that famous moment when you finally went into the garden pond," Matt added. Everyone laughed at the memory, even Gary, who was remembering with satisfaction the way he had had the last laugh.

Everyone had memories of the summer that couldn't have been captured by Sally's camera. Pairing up and sharing towels, they lay on their backs, watching for meteor showers in the night sky and savoring their favorite moments in private.

Meg finally broke the silence. "I thought I was going

to hate having the summer end," she said, "but I'm really looking forward to this fall."

Everyone agreed except Lisa. "I'm not," she said.

"Why?" Will said, instantly alert. "I thought you were going to register for the winter term."

"Up until this morning I was," she said. "I had a nice, uncomplicated choice—stay home with Dad and the boys and wait for Prince Charming to come along and rescue me by giving me my own house and family to take care of—or go to college."

"And?"

"And now I've got another one. Cleo thinks I could make it in modeling. If I want to give it a try, she'll introduce me to a friend of hers in Los Angeles who runs an agency."

"In L.A.?"

"Modeling?"

"Hey, wow!" Marcie said enthusiastically. "She's right. I can see you on the cover of about six different magazines already!"

"Thanks," Lisa said. "The thing is—I don't know what to do. Can anybody give me any ideas on how to make the right choice?"

The silence that followed this request was eloquent.

"Nothing to it," Gary said finally. "All you need is a little luck."

"Luck and courage," Will said, thinking about cliff jumps and other impossible things.

"And intelligence," Meg added, thinking along the same lines.

Matt laughed suddenly. Replaying the summer in his mind, he had finally figured out why Gary and Meg had been congratulating themselves at tonight's campfire. He didn't mind admitting that he owed them both for this summer, owed them a lot. If it hadn't been for the two of them, he would never have come or stayed long enough to feel the way he did now. "Make that luck, courage, intelligence, and . . ."

They waited. "And?"

He made them wait a fraction of a second too long. "And a little help from your friends!" he yelled as he found himself airborne and on his way into the duck pond. Making a mighty effort, he managed to take everyone else in with him.

Everyone, that is, except for Gary. . . .

# ABOUT THE AUTHOR

Frances Miller was born in the Northeast and grew up in a sprawling, affectionate, book-loving family. After graduating from Wellesley College in 1959, she moved gradually westward and settled eventually in California. There she raised a large, affectionate, book-loving family of her own before moving temporarily to Australia. During this time she worked in school and public libraries, and as a camp counselor, Book Fair lady, math and reading tutor, and English and reading teacher. She also began writing books herself.

Her writing is a product of two loves—children and books—and reflects her admiration and respect for the human spirit, which survives and flourishes against all odds. This is her fourth novel about Matt McKendrick; the first three were *The Truth Trap*, for which she won the 1985 California Young Reader Medal; *Aren't You The One Who . . . ?;* and *Losers and Winners*.